Along the Trail

by

Kaci Curtis

Along the Trail

Cover Art by *Teddi Black*

The Wild Rose Press, Inc.
PO Box 708
Adams Basin, NY 14410-0708
Visit us at www.thewildrosepress.com

Publishing History
First Edition, 2025
Trade Paperback ISBN 978-1-5092-6316-5
Digital ISBN 978-1-5092-6317-2

Published in the United States of America

Dedication

For my parents, who let me read under the covers with a flashlight.

For my fellow military spouses, who support the mission every day at home.

Chapter One

The pamphlet Papa had brandished when he'd surged excitedly through the front door those many months ago hadn't mentioned the monotony. It hadn't hinted about the stench, the endless rattling, or the insects and dust. To be honest, the pamphlet's pleading words had been more like a song, beseeching its listeners to travel. "To the West! To the West!" it cried. "There is wealth to be won!"

"They're giving land away, Winnie!" Papa had exclaimed. "Just giving it away, if we live on it for five years and build a house. Over one hundred acres in the Oregon territory! Isn't that something?"

Winnifred had smiled and nodded, but in that moment, she hadn't totally grasped just how drastically everything was going to change.

Now, as she trudged alongside Lenora, gazing at the ample rear of their milk cow and avoiding piles of dung, Winnie wondered what all the fanfare had been about. They'd been on the trail for three weeks now, and the only thing they'd had to look at along the way was livestock and prairie grass.

It was alluring in its simplicity, if one liked to watch grass tossing about like a rooted sea.

"Do you think we'll be stopping soon?" Lenora rubbed at her lower back with a wince.

The slant of the late afternoon sun was piercing, and

the brim of Winnie's sunbonnet was powerless against it. She squinted, holding up a hand to shield her eyes as she grinned sideways at her sister. "If we don't, you could always climb onto Millie."

Their milk cow twitched her tail with a grunt, as if she'd heard and was less than enthused about the idea.

Nora blanched and shook her head, similarly sheltered beneath her own bonnet. "I couldn't possibly! Lord only knows who might see."

Winnie shrugged and kicked at clods of soil as they walked, counting the plodding steps of Millie's hooves in front of them. "Does it matter? You're married now. You don't have to be perfectly presentable anymore."

Nora chuckled and shook her head. "If Jeb saw me sitting astride a cow with my skirts pulled up, he'd fall flat to the dirt."

She gave a sheepish look toward her new husband.

Jeb was prone to glancing toward her, as well, as if to reassure himself that his new bride hadn't dashed away into the tall grass. They'd only been wed a month, and he still looked like he couldn't quite believe his luck.

Winnie had nothing against Jeb Reed. In fact, she rather liked him.

Tall and gangly, he seemed to always be leaning this way or that, like a stalk of wheat. His reddish hair was continually mussed, perhaps from nervously running his fingers through it. Whenever he spoke, Winnie had to bend a bit closer to hear him properly. A strong wind could snatch his words away.

But he adored Lenora, and had pestered Papa for months for the chance to ask for her hand in marriage. Two weeks before they were set to depart for the outfitter's town of Independence, Missouri, Papa relented.

"Any man who's willing to follow a woman over two thousand miles deserves a chance," He'd winked at Nora.

Marriage suited Nora. She liked having someone to care for. She liked to fuss over people, holding hands and baking pies and gifting them with sincere words. Golden haired and brown eyed, she was a gentle breeze compared to Winnifred, who was more like a runaway horse.

The many differences between them had never bothered Winnie.

It wasn't that she didn't care for people, but it was never as natural for her as it was for Nora. Often impatient, Winnie found it easier to seek a course of action than to sit around, wringing her hands. She also had a habit of keeping her feelings close, perhaps too close. She was a lot like Mama in that way.

A bugle sounded at the head of the column, traveling down through the dozens of wagons like a sigh of relief. They would be stopping here tonight. There would be no need for Nora to ride the cow, after all.

Nora reached out to squeeze her sister's hand before heading for the wagon she now shared with Jeb.

Winnie stepped around Millie's rump and came up alongside Papa's wagon, slapping at her once-white apron to try to shed some of the intolerable dust.

Papa walked next to their team of oxen, slowing them to a crawl as the wagons ahead of them began getting into their positions for the night.

They always parked in a circular formation, so the smaller livestock could be rounded up and penned within the wagons, protected from predators.

The coyotes had been particularly cunning, sneaking close enough to snatch any careless chickens or young sheep.

Along with the dairy cow they'd brought from home and a new horse they'd purchased in Independence, they kept six oxen that would be hauling them and everything they owned over 2,000 miles to a place that Winnie had never seen.

She'd wanted to give the oxen all names, but Papa had warned against it.

"They aren't pets. They've got a big job to do, in getting us west. And they likely won't all make it there."

So the oxen remained unnamed.

"Winnie!" Elijah called when he spotted her from his seat next to Mama at the front of the wagon. "Look what Big John gave me!"

Her little brother stood abruptly on the wagon seat, holding something up for her inspection.

"Sit down, before you fall," Mama snapped.

Winnie moved closer to Elijah's seat, pulling her skirt up so there was no danger of it being caught under the wheels.

Mama's steel-gray eyes watched Elijah like a hawk until his bottom was firmly planted on the wagon seat.

He pouted a little. He was a sensitive boy, and Mama wasn't the gentlest of women these days.

But Winnie understood.

Only two days ago, a little girl had fallen from the sideboard and been run over by her own wagon wheels. Both her legs were broken before her father had been able to stop the team of oxen. She would live, but her cries of pain could occasionally be heard from within their jostling wagon. Travel would be agonizing for her, until she healed. If the bones had been set properly, she might walk again. If they hadn't, she would be crippled for life.

But Elijah was only six, and his new toy meant a great deal more to him at the moment than an accident that hadn't affected him directly.

"It's a horse." He proudly held the object out again for Winnie to see. "Big John said his name was Bandit."

The small horse was cleverly made from bundles of tightly woven prairie grass. Strips of leather had been tied around the hooves, rump, and neck to keep the horse together.

"He's a very fine horse." Winnie patted its back. "You must take good care of him."

Elijah clutched Bandit to his chest, and his brown eyes, so much like their father's, were bright. "I will."

Papa's decision to move west had been the hardest on Elijah. The youngest sibling by more than a decade, he'd cried and cried on the day they sold most of their belongings. Space within the wagon was precious, and with all the supplies they needed, his toys, rock collections, and tediously assembled stick cabins hadn't made the list of things to be brought along. He'd only been allowed to bring one toy, a wooden wagon Papa had made with working wheels. Elijah could pull it along by a rope attached to the front.

Winnie hoped Bandit lasted at least a few days. She was sewing a cowboy doll for Elijah, but downtime on the trail was scarce, and she was only about halfway finished. There was always something else that needed to be done: cooking, setting up tents, tending the livestock, mending clothes, keeping the fire going…the work was never finished.

Winnie didn't mind that either, most of the time. She'd been allowed to bring two new books with her for the journey, and so far, she hadn't had time to open either of them. But that was fine, for now. At least she wouldn't finish them too quickly.

Papa got the oxen maneuvered into their position for the night and began to remove their yokes and harnesses.

Mama hopped down from the wagon seat, and Winnie helped Elijah down as well.

"Get the tent, please, Winnie." Mama deftly untied the knots that held her cap on. "Elijah can help you with the bedrolls."

Winnie set to work, hauling the tent canvas from its storage and lining up the poles Papa had cut along the start of the trail.

Their parents shared the tent with Winnie and Elijah most of the time, though sometimes the siblings would just sleep under the wagon, especially in fair weather.

But there was a wind picking up, and the earthy smell of rain was in the air. It would likely be wet under the wagon tonight.

After the tent was more or less erected, Winnie milked Millie while Elijah spread their bedrolls inside the tent. She rested her forehead against Millie's warm flank, and the sounds of nearby conversation, crying babies, and hungry livestock faded somewhat as she relaxed into the familiarity of the task.

She missed so much about their farm. Like the calls of the piglets and the reassuring grunts of their big mama. She missed the clucking of the chickens when they were laying. And the smell of freshly plowed earth, waiting for seeds. She missed the bray of the donkey that alerted them when a neighbor arrived for a visit. And the touch of their dog's tail tapping happily against her skirt.

Papa had been selling off chunks of their farm for the past year, just to make ends meet. Times had been tough, and they'd taken on debt just to keep crops growing and animals producing. It wasn't sustainable, and he'd been looking for a way to get out from under the debt. When a member of their church in town had sent letters back from Oregon territory, singing the praises of its fertile valleys and farmland, Papa had seen the way out. The inspirational pamphlet he'd brought home had simply sealed the deal.

After discussing it with Mama, he'd put what remained of their little Missouri farm up for sale. The money they earned funded their long trip to the Oregon territory.

They'd sold all of their animals, too. Even Millie's little calf.

"I bet you miss your baby," Winnie murmured as she aimed the last of the milk into the pail. "But don't worry, she's in good hands with Mr. Higgins. He's a sweet old man."

Finished, she untied her bonnet and tugged it down to rest against her back, scratching at her dark hairline with a sigh of relief.

"Does Millie ever talk back?" A male voice chuckled.

Winnie leaned back to peer around Millie's swishing tail, and a smile crested like a wave across her cheeks. "Sometimes she does. But only if no one else is around to overhear."

Hal Clark dismounted his bay mare with a grin. He held the reins loosely, and the horse lowered her head to graze behind his shoulder. He pushed his hat higher off his forehead, exposing a tangle of tawny hair soaked with sweat.

"And do you keep her secrets? Or spread gossip around the campfire?"

Winnie stood, pulling the milk pail with her so it wouldn't be knocked over by careless hooves. "I'm sworn to secrecy."

Hal nodded and gestured toward his mare. "Ask Millie to teach Ol' Belle, then. Maybe she can tell me what she wants instead of trying to buck me off."

The horse raised her head abruptly, gave a huff, and went back to her grass.

Winnie laughed, and Hal smiled a bit as well before looking down and clearing his throat. "Well, I stopped by to see if you'd like me to turn Millie out to graze with the rest of the herd tonight."

Papa chose that moment to come around the back of the wagon, hands full of harnesses. Having clearly heard the last part of the conversation, he gave the young cowhand a welcoming nod. "That'd be fine, Hal, thank you. You can go ahead and take her."

"Yes, sir." Hal reached out to clasp Papa's hand in a brief shake, and then tipped his hat toward Winnie. "Smells like rain." He untied the cow's halter and climbed back onto Belle's saddle. "Big John wants everything buttoned up tight." He clicked his tongue, urging Millie ahead of the horse and out toward the rest of the grazing cattle herd.

Winnie looked up, assessing the dark clouds in the fading afternoon light. There was a brief flash of lightning in the distance, but the thunder that followed was weak.

There was still another hour or so before full dark,

and then the clouds would be invisible to them, swelling with their storm in secrecy.

"That cowboy sure does like Millie," Papa mused, bringing Winnie's thoughts back down to the ground. "That's the third time this week he's come by the wagon." He gave his daughter a knowing smile.

She ducked her head to hide her hot cheeks. "Hal's very thoughtful."

"He is." Papa rested a calloused hand on her shoulder. "But what do you think about him?"

Winnie eyed Hal's back in the distance, swaying with the motion of the saddle as he drove Millie out to the cattle that followed behind the wagons. "I like him, Papa. But I don't know if I'm ready to settle down just yet."

In the weeks since the hired cowhand had introduced himself at the start of their journey, Hal had been quick to earn respect. He worked hard, had a kind smile, and had a way of showing up just when help was needed.

Papa wasn't accustomed to hiding his opinions, so Winnie was well aware that he liked Hal, and perhaps even related to him. He'd said many times that one man with a good work ethic was worth more than a dozen who liked to hear themselves talk.

He turned and met her gaze squarely. His luminous brown eyes crinkled at the corners. "You know, I didn't have an acre of land to my name when I met your mama. She waited almost a year for me to get myself situated so we could be married."

"It's a wonder I didn't wise up before then." Mama came up on Winnie's other side. "Can you imagine waiting that long on a man? I nearly died an old maid."

But she smiled a bit wistfully, the steel in her eyes becoming more malleable.

Winnie looked between them, crinkling her nose. "Why don't you just say what you mean to say?"

They shared a glance, and Mama touched Winnie's dark braid before striding back toward Elijah, who was filling their cast-iron pot with twigs.

"We'll spend at least five months on this trail," Papa said at last, looking out at the horizon of lush April grass. "You've got plenty of time to decide."

"Do I?" Winnie would turn eighteen this winter. Nora was barely a year older, and already wed. She didn't want to turn out like Mae Cook, the daughter of their trail guide, Big John. Mae was twenty-two, and still unwed. She lived alongside her father on the trail, rode her horse alongside the men, and even carried a rifle.

It wasn't the freedom of trail life that scared Winnie. She admired Mae's willingness to live like a cowhand for the duration of the journey, and to make the most of that freedom. No, what scared her was what would happen when they arrived on the other side of the continent, and the expectations of society pressed in on them once more. That sort of freedom would be difficult to relinquish.

Papa smiled and patted her shoulder. "It's your heart, Winnie. And you've got a strong one. It'll let you know when it's time." He bent and picked up the full milk pail. "Now, let's go help your mama with supper."

Winnie winced a bit. She was already sick of beans and rice. But she followed Papa, her thoughts wandering back to Hal, and how much she liked it when he brought a finger up to tip the brim of his hat.

****

The rain was a torrent that night. The wind carried it through the camp, billowing the canvas of their tent in loud snaps that jolted Winnie from sleep. Elijah lay pressed tight against her side, and even Papa's snores were few and far between, as if he too was often awakened by the noise.

The lightning grew brighter and the thunder boomed louder. As the night wound stubbornly on, the storm rumbled above them, stretching like a giant beast.

The bedroll grew damp, and eventually she sat up with a sigh, careful not to bump Elijah.

She made sure the tent flaps were tightly closed, but some of the driving rain still blew in, despite her efforts. Tucking her knees to her chest, she edged as far away from the wet spots as she could.

Miserable, she ducked her head against her bent knees. Days on the trail were torturous after a poor night's sleep. Walking at least fifteen miles in the sun and dust was tiresome even after a full night's rest. But after a night like this, everyone would be in a sour mood before the midday meal even arrived.

She must have dozed at some point, because Winnie awoke to shouting. It was mostly overtaken by a roll of thunder, and she scrubbed at her face with her hands. If the night guards were shouting the morning call to wake the camp, then it was time to get up and get breakfast started. The long, wet night would soon be over.

But then the shouting came again. Closer this time. And it was not the same cadenced tone and pitch as the call to wake that she had come to recognize. This was more urgent, though she couldn't yet make out the words.

Lightning illuminated the inside of their tent, and

Mama stirred awake.

Scuttling over to the tent flaps, Winnie strained her ears against another wave of thunder.

At last, the words broke through the storm.

"Stampede!" A male voice cried. "On your feet! Stampede!"

Mama sat up abruptly, her dark hair spilling over her shoulders as she jostled Papa awake.

Winnie struggled to open the tent flaps, shielding her eyes against the rain that sluiced in with renewed force. Leaving Mama to wake Elijah, she took a fortifying breath and dashed out into the darkness.

It wasn't far to Nora and Jeb's wagon.

They parked beside one another each night and shared their fire and cookware. But it was pitch black. No lanterns burned, for they had to conserve the oil. The rain had drowned any lingering fires that might have lit her way.

She counted her steps, trusting in memory as lightning split the sky and gave her brief flickers of sight.

There.

"Nora!" Winnie called, struggling to be heard over the din of the storm. "Jeb! Get up, there's a stampede!"

The rest of the camp was shaking awake, throwing off the vulnerability of sleep. Families erupted from tents and wagons, shouting to wake neighbors who had not yet emerged. Horses that had not been set out to graze whinnied at all the commotion. Babies wailed as they were jostled awake.

Winnie reached the back of her sister's wagon and pounded on it.

Nora popped her head out, her long golden hair twining down toward her slim waist.

"Winnie! Climb in, you'll catch your death!" She reached a hand down to help her climb over the back wall.

Winnie vaguely realized she was sodden, her nightgown plastered to her skin.

The rain on her back ceased abruptly as the oiled canvas of the wagon sheltered her.

Nora snatched a blanket from their bedding to drape around her sister's shoulders and smoothed drenched hair from her cheeks.

"Where's Hank?" Winnie checked to ensure her nightgown was appropriately covered with the blanket.

Jeb's elder brother was also traveling with them to Oregon, but since Jeb was newly married, Hank slept in a tent and spent a good chunk of his time riding with the cowhands at the rear of the wagon train. But he could always be counted on to be at their wagons for supper, eating two plates of whatever was handed to him.

"He had one of the night watches," Jeb answered as he hurried to finish dressing. He slid the straps of his suspenders over his shoulders before turning to lay a comforting hand on Winnie's shoulder. "Stay in the wagon," he instructed, before turning hazel eyes upon Nora. "I'll go see if there's anything else to be done."

He settled a hat atop his head and pecked Nora on the cheek before shimmying atop their trunks to reach the back of the wagon.

"Be careful!" Nora reached a hand out as if she wanted stop him.

Jeb looked over his shoulder, and a flash of lightning illuminated his anxious expression. "You, too." He jumped down and vanished into the downpour.

"He'll be fine," Winnie said firmly, to herself as

13

much as her sister. "Papa will likely go with him."

"That doesn't make me feel better, Winnie." Nora groaned, pressing a hand to her stomach. "Oh, I hate this place. Nothing is safe out here."

Winnie wanted to comfort her, but she never stooped to lying. And if she wouldn't lie to her sister, then sometimes it was best to keep quiet. Nora was right, it was dangerous on the trail. And they had barely even begun.

They'd already made it over two big rivers: the Missouri and the Kansas. They'd been easily ferried across both; the most harrowing part had been waiting in line for their turn. But for most of the waterways ahead, they'd have to ford with the oxen or float the wagons across much more aggressive currents.

Winnie had heard stories of whole families being lost to rivers. People and animals were easily swept away into the rushing waters, and never seen again. She'd never been afraid of rivers before. But she'd also never been afraid of Natives before, and there were as many stories about the Natives on the trail as there were of fatal river crossings. Perhaps more.

Papa had told her that the Natives were just families, same as them, and most of the time they were civil, sometimes even friendly.

Big John and his daughter, Mae, had both kept company with Natives along the trail on their previous journeys across the country.

But there were more-gruesome stories, passed along firesides in ghastly whispers. Stories of fathers and mothers butchered, and children stolen. Stories of indiscriminate slaughter. Stories that made Winnie wake in the night with gasps of terror.

The dangers they faced would be beyond counting.

The unknown was like a phantom to Winnie. At times it beckoned excitedly, eager to show her things. Other times it loomed before her, a specter that could not be outrun or overpowered.

In the wagon, Winnie strained to listen for anything that might hint at what was going on outside.

Nora kept a hand pressed to her stomach, face sour as she took deep, measured breaths.

Mere moments passed before Winnie caved to the tremors that had steadily built within her. Sitting in blind ignorance for another heartbeat was intolerable. She clambered over a trunk, hissing when her bare toes smacked against a barrel of flour.

"What are you doing?" Nora reprimanded. "We're supposed to stay here!"

Winnie waved a dismissive hand blindly in her sister's direction. "I'm just trying to see what's going on."

She stretched and poked her head as far out as she could without getting poured on again. Rain cascaded a mere inch from her nose. She braced for a flash of lightning. She could still hear shouting, but it sounded farther off.

Most of their neighbors had likely taken shelter in their wagons, leaving vacant tents to be pummeled by the storm. And if they were very unlucky, by hundreds of hooves.

Illumination roared across the plain, and she glimpsed men on horseback, hats angled against the driving rain, galloping into the distance.

"No sign of the herd," she called to Nora. "The men are riding out."

Nora let out a relieved sigh.

Movement near the ground caught Winnie's eye, and she squinted, struggling to make it out. Whatever they were, there were a lot of them. They almost seemed to be jumping out of puddles. Another flash of light brought the phenomenon into detail.

Hail. Marble-sized chunks of hail slammed into the ground and bounced up again.

Before Winnie's eyes, the hail thickened, until it seemed it was not raining at all, but pouring stones. When the marbles gave way to hunks of ice the size of her palm, she drew back, shouting to Nora, "Find something to cover your head!"

And Nora, bless her, reached for a blanket.

Winnie spat an unladylike curse and surged back across the trunks, splitting a knuckle in the process.

The din was enormous, like the earth was being pummeled by giant fists.

A thud on the barrels behind her and a fresh curtain of rain confirmed her suspicions.

The hail was breaking through the hoop of the wagon. If either of them took a bad blow to the head...

Reaching her sister, who shook beneath her wool blanket, Winnie hauled an iron skillet over her head, and passed a pot to Nora, who looked at it incredulously before following Winnie's lead. They huddled together, and another chunk of ice broke through, skittering off the wooden dresser before lodging against the wagon frame.

"I hope they're all right in this!" Nora clutched the pot around her ears.

A few more chunks of hail came in, one missing Winnie's knee by inches. She glanced back at the wagon seat that was full of sparkling ice. If only they were actually precious gemstones, and not just frozen water. Then they could have afforded to get sweets and lemonade at every fort they passed along the route.

As quickly as it had begun, the hail quieted. The pummeling ceased, and the rain left behind sounded almost peaceful in comparison.

When she was fairly certain no more ice was going to fall, Winnie set the skillet aside.

"Do you intend to keep the pot as a hat?" She smirked at her sister.

Nora seemed startled to find the pot still atop her head. Sheepishly, she handed it to her sister. "Not quite my style."

They gathered the chunks of ice they could find and tossed them out the back of the wagon before they could melt onto Nora and Jeb's belongings.

Some rain still dripped down through the rips in the canvas where the hail had broken through; it would have to be mended in the morning.

Nora made sure the lids to the casks of precious food supplies were on tightly, so they wouldn't grow wet and spoil.

Winnie was at the back of the wagon, trying to examine her cut knuckle, when Hank rode up. She heard his horse before she saw him, and jumped a bit when his voice broke the serene patter of the rain.

"Hey there, Winnifred." It was more of a sigh than a greeting. "You and Lenora all right?"

"We're fine." She pulled the drooping blanket tighter around her shoulders. She doubted Hank would even notice her nightgown; his hazel eyes had the glazed and bleary look of someone who badly needed sleep.

Nora had lit their lamp, and rushed over to sit behind

Winnie, anxious energy fixed on Hank. "Is Jeb hurt?" she demanded.

"What happened out there?" Winnie asked at the same time.

As Hank looked between the sisters, the downward tilt of his hat brim poured a steady stream of water atop the back of his coat. "Jeb and your Pa are fine. Jeb took a tumble off his horse and cut his arm a bit. Make sure you fuss over it, because he's quite proud." Even Hank's smile was tired, with only a flicker of its usual luster.

He'd been on night watch for hours already when the stampede had broken out.

He likely hadn't slept since the previous night, and Winnie saw he was in no condition to ride out again. Though he would likely try, if they didn't intervene.

"Get yourself up here." Nora had reached the same assessment. "You're no good to anyone if you slide out of the saddle and sleep in the mud."

Hank started to protest, and Winnie hopped down from the wagon, splashing water.

The rain was much calmer now, and the horizon was gray. Dawn was unfurling.

Winnie tugged Hank's muddy boots out of the stirrups. "Give me your hat." She shielded her eyes to peer up at him. "And I'll see to your horse."

With a grunt that was both exasperated and grateful, Hank lifted his leg from the other side of the horse and slid rather gracefully to the ground. He patted his horse's neck and handed the reins to Winnie. "I know well enough not to stand in the way of the Hayes sisters when they set their mind to something."

He plopped his sodden hat onto Winnie's head, flicking the brim as he drew back. At least it would keep the remaining rain from her eyes.

"Nora is a Reed now." Winnie reminded him as he climbed up into the wagon, pausing on the edge to remove his filthy boots.

Nora took over from there, helping him with his coat and gesturing to the place where she and Jeb slept.

"Of course," Hank said. "Lenora Reed, my scrawny new sister."

Nora swatted at the back of his head, but he chortled to himself before slumping gratefully onto the makeshift bed.

"I'll see you at breakfast," Winnie called to Nora. She tugged gently on Hank's horse to get him walking. His dark head drooped, and he seemed as tired as his rider.

She led him around the side of the wagon before removing his bridle and securing his halter and lead rope. She removed the saddle and blanket next, huffing at its weight. She managed to get both under the wagon and out of the rain. Then she affixed a grain bag to his halter, and the sound of delighted crunching filled the air.

Task complete, Winnie trudged back to the wagon she shared with Mama, Papa, and Elijah. Their tent had collapsed, and the bedrolls inside were likely soaked through. Everything would have to be hung to dry. The thought of stringing the lines and hauling the heavy, wet blankets around made her want to take a nap.

Mama was sitting expectantly beside a lit lamp at the back of the wagon, already dressed for the day. Her gray dress didn't even look damp. Her cap hung on a hook inside, but her dark hair was already collected into a tight, no-nonsense bun.

Winnie felt like a wilted dandelion standing before

a thorny rosebush. And she'd forgotten to toss Hank's hat into Nora's wagon; it still stubbornly guarded her face from raindrops.

"I expect you're tired and chilled." Mama's back was straight as a pine tree. "And you deserve to be, after running off into a storm."

Winnie hunted for something to say that didn't sound defensive. "I only went to wake Nora and Jeb. I stayed with her until Hank came back with news"

Mama's rigid posture loosened, just a bit. "Nora is a wife now, Winnifred."

Winnie hauled herself up into their wagon, leaving Hank's wet hat hanging on the sideboard. "She was my sister, first."

Mama sighed and looked back at Elijah, who was asleep under a blanket on the table top laid across their barrels of sugar, flour, and bacon.

"I know it's been hard for you these past few weeks. We're all adjusting to this…change. But you can't run off like that. Nora has a husband to look after her too, now." She reached out and lifted Winnie's chin with her fingers. "But until you start a family of your own, it's still my job to look after you."

Winnie raised her eyes to her mother's, and her indignation dimmed. They had such similar features. The same dark-brown hair, though Mama's was beginning to show some silver. And they shared a steely-gray gaze. Nora and Elijah took more after Papa, with his golden hair and big brown eyes—eyes that wouldn't have looked out of place in the face of a doe or her fawn.

And now, in the stormy expression and the tight lines of her mother's mouth, Winnie read the remnants of concern there. Mama hadn't just been angry; she had been worried. Suddenly, Winnie thought of the little girl traveling in the rear wagon of their party with two newly broken legs.

She lowered her gaze. "I'm sorry."

Mama nodded, and the moment of understanding between them dissipated. "Let's get you some dry clothes, and then see what we can scrape together for breakfast. Your Papa and Jeb will be famished when they return."

Chapter Two

Dawn crept along the horizon, and the sun rose brightly, the storm already a distant memory to the rapidly clearing sky. It was apparent they would not be moving on at their usual time. The men who straggled back in exhausted pairs and small groups all gave the same brief explanation.

"They're still rounding 'em up."

Hundreds of livestock traveled behind the wagon train. They consisted of family milk cows, horses, any spare oxen, and steers that would be slaughtered along their journey westward.

Big John had said there were likely to be herds of buffalo along the trail, but they didn't have the time and resources to send out frequent hunting parties to bring meat back. They would take what came close to the trail, whenever they could, but it was important they not rely on it.

He'd relayed tales of earlier travelers who hadn't brought enough provisions with them, and ended up having to sell what little they had left just to make it to the Oregon territory. And once there, they had no tools to farm with, money to buy crops with, or livestock to tend. They'd given it all just to cross the Great Plains and mountain ranges with food in their bellies.

Big John was determined that would not happen to anyone who traveled with him as their guide. Each wagon in their company carried at least 300 pounds of flour, 200 pounds of bacon, 60 pounds of coffee, 100 pounds of sugar, and 200 pounds of lard. They carried sacks of beans, rice, dried fruit, and tea. Even with all that, they would still need to resupply at forts and trading posts along the route.

An experienced guide's knowledge of the trail and its hazards was irreplaceable. Just last winter, a party of wagons endured severe consequences after following a guidebook written by a man named Hastings, instead of hiring a real trail guide. They'd taken the author's suggested shortcut, and instead of saving time, encountered an untamed forest. They'd spent a month cutting through the timber to make space for their wagons to pass through. And a lot could change in mountain weather in a month's time.

The company of wagons, now being whispered about fearfully as "the Donner party," were blocked in by early winter snows before reaching California. The snowfall prevented them from traveling onward or turning back.

There were grisly stories whispered about their trials. The most horrifying was that they'd resorted to cannibalizing their own dead to survive the winter.

Tales like that spread quickly amongst the emigrants and their families. Bad news waited at every fort, and was dispatched in every posted letter back east. Everyone now under Big John's guidance knew the story of the unfortunate Donners.

Nobody wanted that to happen to them.

When they'd first arrived in Independence after selling their farm in central Missouri, Papa declined several offers to join up with guides who seemed less competent than his high expectations demanded. He wasn't going to trust the safety of his family "to just any man wearing a beaver hat," as he'd put it.

Winnie knew it was smart to travel with the livestock. But as the morning ground slowly onward and they still remained at a standstill, she found herself cursing cattle and their tendency to spook at loud noises.

Because every day they were delayed brought the possibility of a brutal winter on the trail another day closer.

While Elijah played with a pack of boys near his age, watched over by communal grandmothers, Winnie, Nora, and Mama patched the tears in the wagon covers.

Blankets were laid out in the sun to dry and hung from every available place.

Some families had tossed their bedding over their covered hoops, adorning the roofs of their wagons like a quilt shop.

The same bustle was happening at every wagon. The women had small fires going, started from dried buffalo chips that most used in place of wood. They worked on breakfast and mending anything damaged by the storm. Many of the men who'd already returned from trying to catch the herd were laid out under their wagons, hoping to get a bit of rest before they got the call to move on.

Winnie and Nora were folding the tent canvas when Mae Cook rode up, black hair sticking out in all directions under her weathered hat. "Hello, Mrs. Hayes." She dismounted. "Winnie, Nora."

"Mae." Mama wiped her hands on her apron. "How's it going out there?"

"We finally got them all. They're bringing them back now. I rode ahead to tell everyone to hitch their teams. Once they arrive, we're moving on."

Nora looked up at the sky, gauging the sun's placement. "It's near noon already."

Mae nodded, wiping at her dirty face with one hand. "Pa wants us to get about four hours in today, if we can." She looked as though she'd been in the saddle for hours. Her wool pants were caked with slowly drying mud.

Winnie winced, but four hours was far better than a full day, after such a restless night. "Was anyone hurt?"

Mae accepted a corn cake smeared with sorghum that Mama passed to her. "Thank you. Most are all right. Wore out, the lot of them. One of the cowhands was thrown from his horse and had his back broke by a bull that ran right over him. They rigged up a stretcher to pull him back."

"It wasn't Hal, was it?" A broken back…Winnie couldn't imagine the pain.

Mae shook her head, answering around a mouthful of corn cake. "No, it was Amos. The McClearys' oldest boy."

The knot that had clenched abruptly within Winnie's chest loosened a bit. "It's lucky that no one was else was hurt. Poor Amos."

"We're lucky they didn't run right over the camp," Mae licked her sticky fingers. "Thank you for the biscuit, Mrs. Hayes. I'd better go and make sure everyone gets ready to move out."

"I'll go and tell Mrs. McCleary about Amos," Mama stalled Mae with a hand on her elbow. "It's best that news like this…comes from another mother."

Mae nodded, looking relieved. "Please let her know that Pa is bringing Amos back himself."

Mama turned to Nora and Winnie. "I'll bring Elijah

with me to the McClearys'. Get Hank to help you hitch the oxen." She strode away, toward where Elijah and the other boys were playing a loud game of chase.

When Mama was gone, Mae took off her hat and shook out her long black hair with a wince. The snarls and knots made her look wild. "I feel like I took a bath in a mud hole and dried in a dirt devil."

"I suppose you've been cleaner," Winnie chuckled. "Come walk with us later?"

Mae plopped her hat back on and gave her a tired grin. "See you then." She led her horse to talk with the family at the next wagon, visibly straightening her spine.

Winnie enjoyed Mae's company on the trail. No one would ever replace Nora, but her sister was quiet, a bit timid, and well...feminine. Mae had some inner confidence that intrigued Winnie. She didn't seem to care that she was unwed, and likely to remain that way. She was kind to everyone, but she didn't coddle. She wasn't the type to languish alongside a sickbed, soothing hot brows. No, Mae Cook was a doer, not a woman well practiced at biding her time.

Winnie admired that about her. She'd had the disconcerting thought, on more than one occasion, that Mae's courageously authentic demeanor matched what Winnie felt stirring secretively within her own heart. The desire to drink that freedom in, like fresh, sweet water.

Taking hold of her wayward thoughts with a firm tug, Winnie helped Nora line their oxen up so that Hank could hitch them. The few hours of sleep he'd succumbed to had done him good. His hazel eyes were brighter, and a smile flashed often across his broad cheeks. With his help, the work was done quickly, and the three of them sat on stools around the smoldering fire, eating a lunch of leftover bacon and corn cakes from breakfast.

Hank was already on his third cup of coffee, and even Winnie, who didn't care for the bitter liquid, downed a cup.

When Papa and Jeb rode up, leading Millie along behind them, a bubble of tension Winnie had felt since before dawn finally dissipated and left her as a long, grateful sigh.

Hank stepped up to help his brother dismount, careful of his wounded arm.

True to form, Nora was there a heartbeat later, taking Jeb's forearm gently in her hands and examining the long cut there.

Jeb ducked his head, reddish hair tossing in the breeze. "I'm all right, Lenora. It's just a scratch." But there was color in his cheeks as she fussed over him, tugging him to take her seat at the fire while she went to find a cloth to clean the wound.

Papa wrapped Winnie in a brief hug while Hank tied Millie to the back of their wagon. The cow's bags were heavy with milk, and she was likely getting uncomfortable. Winnie hurried to milk her while Papa scarfed down the remaining lunch spread, and when she was finished, she hung the milk pail beneath the wagon. Most days, the trail was so bumpy that the pail would be full of butter by suppertime.

The dozens of families in their company waited alongside their wagons until Big John was safely through with the injured Amos McCleary, who groaned and thrashed his head atop the hastily built stretcher.

As agonizing as travel would be for him, they couldn't delay any longer. Winnie wondered if his family would choose to turn back. They were less than a month's travel from Independence. If not, she hoped that between his Pa and Doc Collins, they had enough whiskey and laudanum to keep him comfortable.

She watched as Doc hurried after Big John and Amos, leaving his wife and only son to drive their team of oxen. In his forties, Doc Collins was a man of limited patience, and had a face well acquainted with pained expressions. But he had a kind streak, especially toward children.

They were lucky to have a doctor in their party. They were also fortunate to have a midwife. There were at least four pregnant women in their wagon train, and birthing a babe on the trail would be dangerous work.

Winnie counted herself quite lucky to be unmarried, with no potential for pregnancy. Walking fifteen miles a day was tiresome enough already.

When the call came down the line to move out, it was welcome.

Winnie was stiff and tired, and the walk loosened her tight muscles. The four hours passed slowly, but they did pass.

Mae returned to join her and Nora, and they talked of things they craved as the afternoon wound onward—ice cream and strawberries, and sleeping in past dawn.

Setting up camp that night was a blur of firelight, biting mosquitos, and tired faces.

Winnie curled up with Elijah beneath the wagon as soon as the sun went down, letting Mama and Papa have the tent to themselves. Sleep claimed her easily, before she'd even finished her prayers.

****

Three days later, Winnie was walking with Elijah

behind the wagon when Hank and Hal rode up alongside them. They'd just set off again after their noon break, and Winnie's back was sore from carrying her complaining brother for part of the way.

"Hank!" Elijah crowed delightedly. Though it was technically only Jeb who had officially joined the family, Hank was Elijah's favorite new brother. And Hank took special care with the six-year-old, letting him tag along during chores and telling him funny and clever stories.

Winnie smiled at them both as they dismounted, though her gaze lingered a bit on Hal. She hadn't seen him since the stampede, and his pleasant expression was a welcome respite from her boring afternoon.

"We brought your mama some rabbits," Hank announced, swinging Elijah up to ride on his shoulders.

Hal led both of their horses alongside Winnie, and she looked hungrily at the handful of brown rabbits that dangled from Hank's saddle. They would be a welcome change to the dinner menu. Perhaps she and Nora could sew the hides into some mittens. Their warmth would be comforting on the brisk mountain mornings ahead.

"Any sign of buffalo?" Winnie asked Hal hopefully. They'd all heard the stories of the enormous herds that roamed the plains, but so far, they had only seen small family groups that moved hastily away from the approaching wagons.

"No." Hal pushed his hat farther off his forehead. His green eyes narrowed against the midday sun. "But as we're only a day or so away from Fort Kearney, I'm not surprised. They won't want to linger where there's a lot of people."

Winnie smiled excitedly at the mention of the fort. "And what about you?

"Me?"

"Do you think it'll be strange to see other people again, at the fort?" After spending nearly a month among the same faces, the idea seemed both exotic and silly.

Hal chuckled, ducking his head. "From what I've heard, Fort Kearney is small and not very well provisioned. We won't have any reason to linger."

Hank leaned into the conversation, holding onto Elijah's legs, which dangled on either side of his neck. "The most important thing we'll get at Fort Kearny is information. A few other groups started ahead of us, and if any of them ran into trouble up to this point, the people at the fort will know about it."

Winnie swallowed, adjusting her sunbonnet. "What kind of trouble?"

Hank shrugged, bouncing Elijah. "Not much, this early on. Sickness, maybe. Or bandits."

"What about Natives?" Winnie asked.

Hank shrugged again, clearly unconcerned. "There's no way to know."

A wave of clouds passed over the sun, and Winnie realized her steps had quickened. She took a deep breath and forced her steps to slow.

Hank slung Elijah from his neck and sat him astride his empty saddle, taking the reins from Hal. With a brief wave, he led his horse around the wagon, moving up to walk alongside Mama and Papa, who were leading the oxen. Out of the corner of her eye, Winnie noticed Hal considering her.

With only Belle left to lead, he narrowed the distance between them. "The Natives make you nervous." It was an observation rather than a question.

Winnie reached up to grip her elbows, a bubble of

shame expanding beneath her ribs. She wasn't ashamed of being afraid, but rather for being so judgmental. She'd never met a Native, and she shouldn't let that fact intimidate her so much. Papa had taught her better than to let gossip influence her opinions.

"Not knowing what to expect from them makes me nervous." she said at last. "I just wish I knew whether or not I should be afraid." She raised her chin to look into his eyes, which were the shade of the prairie grass around them, the green of growing things. She should look away, but she waited. Let him read what he could of the map her expression painted.

Hal looked away first, but his lips tilted up in a pleased smile. "I'm sure you've heard how Big John and Mae talk about the Natives. And they know more about them than the rest of us."

Winnie nodded, releasing her elbows and letting her hands sway with her steps once more. "Mae says the men are warriors, defending their territories from other tribes. She says their women sometimes appear along the trail route to trade with travelers. That they're usually friendly and curious."

Hal nodded. "I'm mighty curious, myself. I look forward to meeting some of these Natives, and learning more about them."

He stopped walking and reached for Winnie's hand. He moved slowly, so she could step back if she wished.

But she didn't. When his hand wrapped around hers, calloused and warm, Winnie looked up into his face, which had turned solemn and resolute.

"I want you to know—" He looked down at their joined hands. "—if we ever run into hostiles along the trail, whether they're Natives, or bandits…" He trailed off, as if casting aside words that weren't quite right, and searching for better ones. "I would stand between your family and danger," he finished. "And I just want you to know that."

His face began to warm with color, and he let go of her hand, pulling his hat down lower over his eyes. He clucked to Belle, getting her walking again.

Winnie lingered a moment longer, willing her heart to start beating again.

When it was apparent she was still breathing and not in danger of fainting from surprise, she jogged the few steps to catch up to him. "Thank you," she murmured, reaching out to give his hand one final, grateful squeeze.

Hal grinned at her, and they walked on in a companionable silence for a moment. She was searching for something else to say, but a gunshot fired through the air ahead of them.

The change in the relaxed atmosphere was instant. Screams of fear split the air, and Hal pushed Winnie to the back of her family's wagon, which Papa stopped as fast as the oxen allowed.

Some shouting echoed from the front of the wagon column, but no further gunshots split the air.

Hal left her side to draw his rifle from the scabbard along Belle's saddle, while Papa grabbed his from the front seat of their wagon.

As Hank ushered Elijah back toward Mama, two words were shouted down from the wagons in front of them.

"An accident!"

Winnie pressed her forehead against the wagon box with a sigh of relief. They weren't being attacked. It had just been a misfire.

Hal swung up into Belle's saddle, readying the reins. "I'll go see what happened." He nudged Belle to get her moving up through the wagons.

Hank went with him, the collection of rabbits bouncing aside his knees as they rode forward.

Nora joined Winnie from where she had been walking with Jeb, grasping her arm. "What happened?"

Winnie scrubbed a hand down her face, grimacing at the dust. "I'm sure we'll find out soon."

They joined the rest of their family at the front of their wagon, taking the opportunity to get a drink and splash some water on their faces.

Moments later, Hank came back down the line, his face pale and pinched.

He motioned for Jeb to come join them as he dismounted. As they all gathered around, including a few families from wagons close to them, Hank took a fortifying breath.

"Mr. Roberts is dead." He removed his hat, and the rest of the men followed his lead. "His rifle went off from the wagon seat. Struck him right in the neck."

Murmurs of shock and surprise spread through the group. This was only the second death they had experienced since leaving Independence. The first week, a young woman had stepped on a rattlesnake, and died three days later. Perhaps their good luck was about to turn.

"May he rest in the arms of the Lord." Papa bowed his head.

Winnie bowed hers as well, clutching her hands together against her ribs. When they had all finished praying, she sent up an additional plea that her papa not be taken from her in such a senseless way. That he never be taken at all.

"Well," Papa put his hat back on, "those of us with shovels should start preparing the grave."

They selected a spot only a few dozen yards from the trail, where there was a rare cluster of trees. The women and children spread out, searching for stones they would use to cover the exposed dirt of the grave.

Winnie watched where she stepped since the woman with the rattlesnake bite was fresh in her mind.

A half hour later, the rest of the wagon train had gathered beneath the few shade trees, and Big John stepped up to the cross that had been assembled from two sticks and pounded into the dirt. He held his hat to his burly chest, his thick head of wavy black hair exposed as he bowed his head.

"Lord, we give you our brother, Tom Roberts. He was a good father, a good husband, and an honest man. We pray that you show him the glory of your kingdom, where we know he has been received with welcoming arms."

Winnie couldn't help but look at what remained of the Roberts family.

Mrs. Roberts stood stoically, lips clamped and eyes vacant as she tried to hold onto all four of her daughters at once. The oldest was a few years younger than Winnie, and the youngest looked to be about two. She seemed confused as to why the others were crying, and her big eyes scanned the rest of the assembled travelers, as though searching for her father's face among them.

"We ask that you comfort the Roberts family, Lord, and that you walk beside them in their grief," Big John finished. "Amen."

An echoing "Amen," signaled the end of what

passed for a funeral on the westward trail. They were hundreds of miles from a real church.

None of them would ever lay eyes on this grave again. Tom's family would never be able to bring him flowers, or to sit in the grass and talk to him.

His body would lie here, all alone. Beneath a giant prairie sky.

The thought made Winnie sad, and she held Elijah's hand tighter as everyone walked somberly back to their wagons.

Those who were friendliest with the Roberts family trudged alongside the mother and her daughters, murmuring words of encouragement and solace. A man from another family took it upon himself to lead their team of oxen for the remainder of the day.

Winnie looked back once, and the cross above the grave was already out of sight. Only the few trees could be seen, a darker green smudge amidst the prairie.

Day to day, it seemed the scenery of the prairie hardly changed. It was incredibly misleading.

Now she had a sense of just how vast the territory they were attempting to traverse really was.

Two hours ago, Mr. Roberts had been leading his family toward what he'd hoped to be a prosperous future. And two hours from now, even the trees sheltering his freshly dug grave would be completely out of sight.

Winnie glimpsed the fluidity of life in that moment. It was like a river that couldn't be dammed, its rapids never slowed. Even when the waters seemed smooth and calm, they were still moving onward.

Early the next morning, only hours before they were to set foot at Fort Kearney, Mrs. Roberts loaded up her family's wagon. She set her youngest daughter in a sling upon her back. And without a word to anyone, she began driving the oxen back the way they'd come. Back to Independence.

Chapter Three

Fort Kearny was...underwhelming. The collection of small sod buildings on the south side of the Platte River didn't even have a fence for security. Bricks of soil and dense grass roots stacked up to rooftops where grass flourished under the sun and blew in the wind. A handful of wooden buildings were under construction, with various stages of logs lying in piles.

Pairs of soldiers in blue uniforms patrolled with rifles, but most were busy working on the new buildings.

"I'm astonished they call this a fort," Nora told Winnie as they walked together along its grounds. The wagons were mercifully parked for the day, only half a mile away. They'd take the day of rest, purchase any supplies or livestock they felt they needed, and enjoy the variety provided by new faces and voices.

Theirs was the only wagon train here, though another had passed through only 4 days ahead of them. As Hank had predicted, they had left news behind.

Lieutenant Woodbury, the engineer who had been sent to build the fort, had greeted Big John and those who had joined him on the fort's small parade ground, where the American flag was erected.

"I bid you all welcome." He'd assessed those of their party gathered around Big John. "We've just relocated, and as you can see, construction is still underway." He gestured to the collection of buildings around them. "But our general store is open, and you can purchase any provisions you may need. My men will personally guard your wagons and livestock while you are here."

The lieutenant's blue army uniform had looked like it would be sweltering in the rapidly approaching summer. But its golden buttons gleamed in the sun, and the embroidery adorning the stiff collar looked very official.

In comparison, their party looked like they'd been walking through dust for a month, with little opportunity for bathing. Which, of course, they had.

"The party that came before you asked me to pass along that they'd been making good time and not been set upon by any hostiles," Lt. Woodbury continued. "They stayed overnight and then continued on. We haven't had any wagons turn back thus far, though it is still early in the season."

Then he and Big John began discussing what provisions needed to be acquired, and Nora and Winnie peeled away to explore the fort on their own. Mama had told them ahead of time they had no money to waste on frivolities, and Nora knew that Jeb had put all his money into their wagon and supplies, so they only window shopped within the crowded, stuffy general store before returning to the fresher air outside.

It was just as well, because the prices within were exorbitant.

"Who in their right mind would pay a dollar for tobacco?" Nora shook her head incredulously. "Papa bought his for five cents in Independence!"

"We're not in Independence anymore," Winnie reminded her. In fact, they were already three hundred and seventeen miles away.

Feeling they had seen what there was to see, the sisters turned back for the wagons, eager for some lunch.

The laundry would be waiting to be done, but a full day of rest was rare, and their placement alongside the wide, shallow Platte River was too good to pass up. Perhaps Winnie would finally get to rinse some of the dust off her skin, too.

Hal and Mae stopped to wait for them.

"Don't worry," Mae chuckled upon seeing Nora and Winnie's less-than-impressed expressions. "Fort Laramie is much bigger. And it's only five weeks away."

The four of them headed back to the wagons, following the well-worn path, keeping the river on their right.

Winnie untied her sunbonnet and carried it in one hand. The breeze playing alongside the water felt good on her hair. They talked of the ridiculous prices of the goods at the store, and what they would have bought anyway had they had the extra money.

"I love peppermint candies," Nora admitted. "I'd have bought a whole bag full."

Hal made a face. "Not a chance. The licorice, on the other hand…"

"Lemon drops." Winnie sighed longingly.

Mae's sudden warning was at odds with their light-hearted conversation. She thrust a hand out, halting their progress. "Look."

Winnie looked, and her stomach lurched.

Three Natives watered their horses along a sandbar by the river, beneath the canopy of shade trees. Winnie's heart began to pound. Due to the nearness of the fort, Hal wasn't carrying his rifle. And neither was Mae.

"What do we do?" Nora whispered. Her hand gripped Winnie's and grew damp with sweat.

Mae removed her hat, letting it hang against her back. Her black hair moved loosely in the breeze. "We keep walking, and we don't do anything threatening. We smile and acknowledge them, and then we keep going until we reach the others."

Winnie looked to Hal.

He subtly shifted himself alongside Mae, putting Nora and Winnie behind them. He glanced back to catch her gaze, but she didn't see any fear in him. The curiosity he'd spoken of was bright in his green eyes.

Winnie forced herself to begin walking again. Putting one foot in front of the other was a monumental task. It was hard to get a full breath. She clutched Nora's hand. You can do this, she repeated to herself.

As they drew nearer, details became clear. There were two women and one man, who was kneeling to fill their water skins from the river. The women said something to the man as they approached, and he stood abruptly, striding forward to stand between them and the women.

Just like Hal, Winnie realized, and suddenly she wondered if it was possible the Natives were just as wary of them.

The man was shirtless, and a pale, jagged scar branched across one shoulder. His dark hair hung in two braids on either side of his neck, and there was a tomahawk at his hip.

The women stood behind him, each with their dark hair unbound. They both wore knee-length dresses made from some kind of hide, with delicate beadwork along the sleeves. The older of the two women stood just behind the man, an obstinate hardness to her narrowed gaze. The younger one, likely close to Mae in age, kept farther back, sheltered between the two horses.

Mae closed the remaining distance between them, and raised her hands before her.

Whether it was in greeting or to show she was unarmed, Winnie could only guess.

"Nawah!" Mae said cheerfully.

The man and older woman glanced at each other, perhaps in surprise.

"Nawah." The woman tilted her head and stepped around the man. She gestured to the horses behind them.

Winnie saw they were laden with bundled furs and leather bags. The knot in her stomach loosened a bit.

Mae smiled and nodded, pulling something from the pocket of her pants.

Winnie peered around Hal's shoulder to see what her friend displayed.

The piece of antler had two curved prongs, polished like ivory. Embellishments had been carved into it and darkened with wood ash.

The older woman took it from her, turning it with an assessing gaze. After a moment, she nodded, and turned to one of the horses.

The man pointed to Hal, and pantomimed shooting a rifle into the distance before looking to Mae with raised brows.

"I think he's asking if we have any rifles to trade," Hal whispered.

Nora gripped Winnie's hand all the tighter. She'd clearly not yet been put at ease by their attempts at civil communication.

Mae shook her head. "Sorry."

The word didn't seem to spark any recognition in the man, but he appeared to understand the shake of her head well enough.

The older woman returned, the younger one trailing behind. She held out a rolled hide with both hands, and Mae took it, bowing her head in thanks. The older woman smiled a bit, reaching out to touch Mae's dark hair with gentle fingers before moving away.

The man said something to the women, but if Mae understood what he said, she didn't translate. He led their horses from the sandbar and back onto the path that led to the fort.

"Goodbye," Mae said, holding the hide with one hand to wave.

Winnie and Hal echoed her gesture, and the younger woman raised a hand to them in return before the Natives continued to the fort.

"Let's go," Mae whispered, gripping Nora's elbow to tug her along.

Nora's breaths came in little pants, her brown eyes huge above her flushed cheeks.

Winnie reached up and untied her sister's bonnet, which was always too snug under the chin.

"They're gone, Nora." She soothed her sister, glancing over her shoulder to prove her words true. "Nothing happened; we're safe."

Hal kept behind them, but Winnie suspected it was more for Nora's sake than anything else. He clearly wasn't afraid.

Nora clutched her free hand up against her ribs, as Mae kept a firm grip on her other elbow. "I…hate this," She gasped. "I hate being afraid all the time."

Mae and Winnie shared a glance.

"There's no shame in being afraid, Nora," Winnie said at last. "The stories about the Natives make me nervous, too." She had never admitted that to her sister before.

Nora gave her a cutting look. "Don't lie. You're not afraid of anything, even when you should be."

Winnie's eyes narrowed. "Just because I'm not making a scene doesn't mean—"

Mae cut her off, intervening. "Nora, do you know what I did when I saw Natives for the first time?"

"How would I?" Nora snapped. Then her shoulders sagged a bit as she gave in. "What did you do?"

"I hid under Pa's wagon."

Even Winnie was surprised by that. She'd never seen Mae hide from anything. "You're joking."

"I wish I was. It was our very first trip on the trail, four years ago. Our wagon train only had a handful of families in it. I was certain the Natives that rode up had come to kill us all. So, I hid."

Hal broke the silence first. "Well, it seems they didn't kill you."

Mae smiled, and even Nora's lips twitched upward. "They had come to warn us of bad water up ahead. They didn't even speak our language, and they still saved our lives."

Hal let out a whistle. "That's incredible. And lucky."

Mae swept her hair back and put her hat on again, a shield from the midday sun. "I won't lie to you and tell you there aren't Natives out there who would rather kill us than let us cross over their land," she said to Nora, her gaze sharpening into something intense and a bit jagged. "But I can tell you this: of all the Natives that Pa and I have encountered together, over four different trips along the westward trails…. I've only seen one tribe commit violence."

It was Winnie who found herself asking, even though she knew she shouldn't pry: "What happened with that tribe?"

Mae pulled her hat down lower, hiding her eyes. Her voice was rough when she answered, flooded with emotion that had no place to hide among the banks of the shallow Platte River. "You don't want to know."

They walked in silence the rest of the way back to camp.

****

When they returned, they went straight to their wagon to relay the news of what they'd experienced with the Natives.

Papa and Elijah listened with rapt attention, and a little bit of jealousy.

"I want to see the Natives!" Elijah pleaded.

Papa assured him that he would get his chance, and thanked Hal and Mae profusely for keeping his girls safe. He shook the other man's hand soundly before they departed, promising him supper at their fire tonight to express his gratitude.

Mama had just come from checking in on the McCleary family.

Sixteen-year-old Amos had been kept as sedated as possible since breaking his back in the stampede, but after several days of having to increase the dosage to keep him comfortable, Doc Collins had decided not to administer any more laudanum for at least the next week.

"He'll have to get by on whiskey," Doc Collins had told Mama and Mrs. McCleary. "Or we'll run out and won't be able to afford to re-supply."

That might have been the end of it for Doc Collins, who was nothing if not a practical man. But Mama said Amos had been in a fury, raging and shouting obscenities that chased Doc away from the wagon as though the youth had been shooting bullets.

"I worry about him," Mama told Winnie and Nora as they did the family laundry along the riverside. "I think it would be kind of you girls to go and visit him. Pain like that can drive a person mad. He'd benefit from some distraction."

"But surely he's happy just to be alive," Nora mused. "Pain doesn't last forever."

Mama's face was troubled as she dunked one of Papa's shirts in their large washtub. Silt from the river had already settled along the bottom. "When you're in a lot of pain, time is fluid. Minutes can feel like days." She added a sprinkle of thin soap shavings and began scrubbing. "When I had you, Lenora, all alone with your grandmother on our little farm, I was certain the pain of it would kill me. And poor Amos doesn't even have a place where he can lay comfortably."

Winnie couldn't help but wince. She had no desire to endure childbirth, though she knew it went hand in hand with marriage. While inexperienced in that aspect of life, she was far from sheltered. Several of her friends back home had already had their first babies before her family had sold everything and left for Independence. She'd been present for the birth of two of them. The screaming, sweat, tears, and blood had done little to persuade her that she wanted such an experience for herself.

Nora's face soured; her cheeks sallow beneath her golden hair. She blew out a long breath. "If you think a visit will help Amos—" She took the shirt from Mama and wrung it out. "—then we'll go visit him. Won't we, Winnie?"

Winnie made a face, and Mama flicked some water droplets onto her in reproach.

"All right!" Winnie held up a hand to shield her eyes from the sting of the homemade soap. "We'll go and see him. At least he's not having a baby."

Mama rolled her eyes, and a bit of color returned to Nora's cheeks as the conversation moved from pain and childbirth to what they hoped to see and do at Fort Laramie, which was just over a month's travel away.

Fort Kearny was a reprieve from the trail monotony, but there had been nothing in the way of society for them to enjoy. As Mae had reassured them, Fort Laramie would be much bigger, better provisioned, and with a much greater range of goods and services for sale.

And once they passed Fort Laramie, they'd finally begin their ascent into the mountains, and out of the dust and wind blasted grass of the prairie.

****

True to their word, Nora and Winnie went to the McClearys' wagon to visit Amos while Mama and Elijah prepared their supper.

Mrs. McCleary was out tending her own cook fire and three younger children, and though she smiled warmly as they approached, her exhaustion was palpable. Her shoulders were stooped, as though beneath a yoke, and even her smile seemed pinched.

"Amos!" She set aside the spoon she'd been using to stir their stew. "You have visitors."

A groan came from within the wagon. "Send them away."

Mrs. McCleary pursed her lips, stomping over to the open archway of the wagon. "Winnifred and Lenora came to keep you company, and you'll oblige them like a gentleman."

There was a brief chuckle, cut off by a gasp of pain. "It's not as if I can run away."

Mrs. McCleary turned to the sisters with an apologetic grimace that tried to be a smile.

Nora gave the woman's arm an understanding squeeze. "It's all right. We won't overstay our welcome."

Mrs. McCleary gave a grateful sigh and nodded before returning to her cook fire and younger children, who were making faces into the pot at their intended dinner.

The back of the wagon was already lowered, letting in a bit more of the breeze, and Winnie helped Nora climb in before following.

Every step they took made the wagon box shudder, and Winnie's first glimpse of Amos was of clamped lips and glassy eyes. They sat as quickly as they could, on the first thing they could find. Even with the bit of breeze, the wagon was too warm, and held the tang of stale sweat.

"Hello." Amos sighed, at last able to release the tight lock of his jaw. The pallet he rested on was barely wide enough for his shoulders.

"How are you, Amos?" Nora slipped easily into the caretaker side of her that arose to every beck and call of someone in need.

"I'm half drunk." He gestured weakly to a dark glass bottle that rested near his head. "Forgive me. I can't manage without it. Hell, I can barely manage with it."

Nora barely glanced at the bottle, but Winnie reached out on a whim and brought it to her lips, taking a shallow swig before she had the chance to smell it. It burned all the way down, leaving a fiery trail that pooled unpleasantly in her stomach. She coughed before setting the bottle back down. "That stuff is awful."

Nora stared at her with barely concealed horror, but Amos actually smiled, the barest bit of light flickering in his dark eyes.

"It is, isn't it?"

They shared a moment of communal misery over its taste before Nora recovered, glancing only once at what passed for whiskey before launching her efforts into making passable conversation. "Have you been able to go outside? Surely the sights and smells of the camp are better than being cloistered in here?"

Amos nodded, sending a few beads of sweat along his brow sliding into his dark hairline. "Mama and Papa tried to move me a few days ago. But I passed out."

Winnie looked at the canvas overhead, and tried to imagine it being the only scenery to look at. It was a dismal thought. But she tried to find something encouraging to say. "Just think, Amos, once you've recovered, you'll be so happy to be out of the wagon, you'll never complain about sleeping in a tent again!"

Rather than laughing, as she'd hoped, his expression darkened. "Doc says I may never walk again. And if I do, I'll need a cane."

"And what's wrong with that?" Nora's voice turned unusually sharp. "Surely using a cane is preferable to never walking? Do you think the little girl who broke both of her legs is complaining about having to use a cane?"

Amos turned his face away.

Nora may have been pushing too far, but Winnie couldn't think of anything better to say.

"That little girl is hurting, just like you. And she's probably dreaming of the day when she can run after butterflies again, or swim in a stream. Try and think of the things you stand to gain, Amos, instead of what you're so afraid you've lost."

Amos stared at the sacks of flour and sugar on the other side of his makeshift bed, and made no reply.

"Don't just lay in here feeling sorry for yourself," Nora finished. "It will do you more harm than good."

"That's enough, Nora," Winnie interjected. "Leave him be."

Nora looked at her in surprise, as though she had forgotten Winnie was there. "I'm just trying to help."

Winnie knew that. Her sister always meant well. But Amos didn't seem to be in the sort of place where tough truths would be well received. They might well be a heavier weight than what he was currently able to carry. "Rest, Amos." She tugged on Nora's hand. "I'll ask around and see if I can bring you some better whiskey. Something that doesn't taste like someone just used the privy."

Nora gaped at her crude joke, but the chuckle that Winnie had hoped to hear from Amos never came. They made their way out of the wagon as gingerly as they could, but it still rocked under their weight.

"See you later, Amos," Winnie said once they were on solid ground.

"Goodbye," was his brittle reply.

They politely waved off Mrs. McCleary's offer to share supper, and made their way back to their wagon in silence.

Winnie was afraid they'd only made Amos's melancholy worse, and she was determined to think of something that would make him feel livelier.

Nora was silent and stony beside Jeb throughout their brief dinner, and though Hal stopped by as Papa had requested, he had barely finished his plate of bread and beans before giving his thanks and leaving to begin his night watch over the cattle herd.

When Winnie curled up with Elijah beneath the wagon that night, she thought of Amos, lying alone in his family's wagon. Was he able to sleep? And what would he do when he ran out of whiskey to drown in?

****

Another week on the trail passed without much incident. Mae took a turn scouting ahead with Hank, and Nora spent several days in her and Jeb's wagon, complaining of a headache and unsettled stomach.

Winnie worried about her, afraid they may have come across bad water, but no one else was sick.

Dysentery and cholera were sicknesses they'd all been warned of, but as the days passed and Nora's condition didn't worsen, it became apparent that whatever ailed her, at least it wasn't either of those.

Winnie and Hal tried to visit Amos, to see if his mood had improved. But Mrs. McCleary sent them away, telling them that he was sleeping and she didn't want him to be disturbed.

Winnie had asked around for some better whiskey, but most had already given the McClearys what they could spare, and she was forced to give up the idea. It wasn't as though there was a store nearby where she could purchase any.

She was walking with Elijah and Papa on the day that Amos's whiskey ran out.

Everyone could hear him, cussing and crying out with every jolt of the wagon, every bump of the trail. It grated on her nerves, but her irritation was tempered with sympathy.

"Is there anything else Doc can do?" she asked Papa, swinging Elijah's hand between them. "I hate hearing Amos this way."

Papa led the oxen, and there was finally a break in the dust as the other wagons spread out, trying to distance themselves from the noise coming from the McCleary wagon.

"Mrs. McCleary told your mama that Doc is refusing to give him any more laudanum. The last time he did, Amos wrenched the bottle from him and drank twice the amount he was told to. Hard as it is, Doc has to think beyond Amos and his pain. He has to conserve his supplies."

Winnie understood. But she also knew how she would feel, if it were her brother suffering like that. By now, she'd be desperate for anything that would offer him some relief.

When they made camp that night, Winnie checked in on Nora before supper. Jeb met her outside the wagon with a big smile. She took that as a sign her sister had been in a better mood today, and not griping at anyone who ventured near.

"Need anything?" she asked the pair of them. "I can bring by some of the bacon and biscuits."

Nora poked her head out, and though she looked pale, she appeared otherwise herself. "Don't even mention bacon right now." And then she disappeared again, clapping a hand over her mouth.

Jeb chuckled, shaking his head of reddish hair. "Your poor sister. Make her get out tomorrow, even if she doesn't want to. It'll do her good."

Winnie promised she would.

It rained that night, a soft, peaceful rain that lulled Winnie to sleep beside Elijah in the tent with their parents. It was the kind of rain that spun into a refreshing, cool mist. The kind of rain that filled the soul with a sense of calm and solace.

She slept so soundly that when the gunshot echoed through the camp, she thought it was a dream. She found herself sitting up before she was fully awake, and glimpsed Papa ducking through the tent flap with his rifle as Mama took up a defensive position in front of her and Elijah.

Elijah stirred at the commotion, but didn't wake. He curled farther around Winnie's legs, sheltering his face into her nightgown.

For a long, tense moment, Winnie and Mama waited to hear another gunshot. Or a warning cry to arm themselves against an attack.

Neither came.

Distantly, Winnie heard what she thought was weeping, but the rain made it hard to be sure.

Remembering how Mama had reprimanded her the night of the stampede, Winnie stayed put, and rested a hand on her brother's sleeping chest. She counted his breaths, she counted raindrops. She counted anything that proved time was still passing, and not frozen from her fright.

At last, Papa returned, though it had only been five minutes at the most.

"What happened?" Mama urged as Papa sat heavily on their bedrolls and removed his wet boots.

"The McCleary boy is dead," Papa murmured.

Winnie strained to hear properly.

"Shot himself."

"Amos?" Winnie ignored the soothing hand that Mama placed on her back. "He wouldn't!"

Papa shook his head, wiping lingering rain off his face with a sigh. "I'm sorry, Winnie. But he did."

Mama placed a hand on his cheek. "Is Mrs. McCleary…?" She trailed off, voice quivering.

"She's exactly as you would expect," Papa answered. "But Big John is with them. And Doc Collins."

Winnie was unsure where the surge of violent anger came from. Amos had not been a particular friend to her, nor had she known him long. But he had been a part of this strange new world, a young man pitted against the wilds of the west, just as the rest of them were. He had deserved better.

"If I was Mrs. McCleary," she hissed, "I'd shoot Doc in the foot and tell him to get away from my wagon. It's his fault this happened! If he'd just given Amos the laudanum, Amos would be sleeping peacefully right now."

Papa sagged back to lay atop their bedroll, crossing an arm over his eyes. "Don't judge Doc until you've been in his place, Winnifred."

"I'll judge him as I see fit," she snapped. "And so will God."

Papa rose up on one elbow like he wanted to argue, but Mama placed a hand on his chest, shaking her head. "That's enough. Let's say a prayer for Amos."

Winnie folded her hands and listened to Mama's kind words as they swelled within the tent. Words about forgiveness and acceptance and about the end of all pain. But in her mind, she kept hearing Amos's fearful words: "Doc says I may never walk again."

They had proven true. He never would.

Prayers completed, the three of them lay down once more.

Winnie tried to focus on the rain and on her sleeping brother's tiny snores, but Mama and Papa's quiet exchange went straight to her ears, as though some greater force insisted that she hear.

"How did he even do such a thing?" Mama whispered. "The poor boy couldn't even sit up. He couldn't have gripped a rifle. And even if he had, he wouldn't have been able to reach the trigger."

"He didn't use a rifle," Papa replied.

"What? But you said—"

"He used a pistol."

There was a long pause before Mama spoke again. "I didn't think Mr. McCleary had a pistol. Did he buy one at Fort Kearny?"

"No."

"Then how…"

Papa's voice was thick when he answered, and so low that Winnie was convinced she must have heard incorrectly. "Somebody snuck it to him. Probably earlier today."

"Lord," Mama whispered. "Who would do such a thing?"

"Someone who saw the boy's suffering and wanted him to have a choice."

"You can't possibly think that was the right thing to

do!" Mama admonished.

Papa's reply was a long time coming. "I don't know what to think. If he was our boy…I just don't know."

Mama's hiss of disapproval was the last sound Winnie heard before that soft, mournful rain drew her back under. She slept until the call to wake sounded, as though the cloaked figure of death had not hovered over their wagons that night, and stolen one of them away.

****

Like the funeral they'd had only a week before for Tom Roberts, Amos was laid to rest without much fanfare. Once stones covered his freshly dug grave, the gathered families sang a sad, sweet hymn.

Winnie and Nora stood together, and though Winnie knew the things Nora had said to Amos hadn't been the bullet that killed him, there was still resentment in her heart. It was unexpected, and new. The sisters rarely quarreled, or even had cause to disagree.

She couldn't help but wonder what might have been different, had she been able to find the right words to say that afternoon. If she had been able to make him laugh more, or if Nora had been able to find a kinder route to distance him from his own self-pity. Perhaps he would have stayed.

But as the hymn ended and the gathered families began to disperse to prepare to head out for the day, Winnie left Nora and made her way to the grave where Mrs. McCleary knelt, her husband and three remaining children gathered around her. She watched as Mrs. McCleary reached out to lift a rock, clenched a handful of the soil from her son's grave, and pulled it tight to her chest.

Winnie cleared her throat, ignoring the burn in her

eyes and chest as she fought for the words she'd walked over to give them. "I'm sorry for your loss. I wish we'd been able to do more to help him."

Mrs. McCleary had the strength to actually smile at her. "So do I, Winnifred. Thank you."

She didn't say that Amos was with the Lord, or his pain had finally ended. She didn't comfort herself with scripture. She just clutched that bundle of grave dirt, aware that like the Roberts family, she would never see the grave of her loved one again.

Struck by sudden inspiration, Winnie said, "Wait a moment. I'll be right back."

She rushed to their wagon, barely noticing that Hal was there, talking with Papa while Elijah played with Bandit, the toy horse. She went straight to the trunk she and Nora kept their few possessions in, digging beneath the half-finished cowboy doll for Elijah, the practical dresses and coats, until she found what she was searching for underneath.

She'd sewn the cloth bag as a place for her brother to keep the most prized rocks of his rock collection. There were only five rocks in it, and she wrapped them carefully in her spare bonnet before taking the small bag and closing the lid of the trunk.

Hal was there when she jumped down, eyes going to the cloth in her hands, patterned with spring flowers. "Is everything all right?"

"I want to give this to Mrs. McCleary." She held the bag up before turning and making her way back to Amos's grave.

Hal followed her, stopping just a step behind and removing his hat.

Winnie reached out and pressed the cloth bag into

Mrs. McCleary's free hand. "I want you to have this. So you can take a part of him with you."

Mrs. McCleary looked down at the small bag, and then at the dirt in her grip. Her smile slipped, and a single tear traced down one plump cheek. "Thank you." She choked on the words.

Winnie held the bag open for her, and grains of dirt tumbled against her fingers as Mrs. McCleary carefully poured it in, then cinched the ribbons closed at the top.

When Winnie turned to go, leaving the family to their grief, Hal was still there.

His eyes held brightness, and a look of wonderment. "I'm proud to know you, Winnifred Hayes," he said at last.

Winnie took his offered arm and leaned her head against his shoulder for a moment as they walked, not caring who saw, or what they thought of the gesture. Because to her, it was like a spot of cool shade in a merciless summer day. Or a warm hearth to sit beside during a winter storm.

Knowing what it meant to her, she cared less about how it appeared to others.

Hal said nothing more, only smiled a bit as they walked on.

Chapter Four

Over eighty miles after leaving Fort Kearney, they finally crossed the south fork of the Platte River, slowly fording its wide maze of sand bars and islands. Luckily, it had been a dry season so far. Snowmelt had been slow to arrive from the mountains, and the river was sluggish.

A few wagons got bogged down in the sandy bottom of the riverbed. The owners tossed out some unnecessary furniture, and with a lot of pushing, they made it safely to the other side. Only the children got wet past their knees.

Immediately following their crossing, they encountered California Hill.

After they'd spent nearly six weeks traversing flat ground, this felt like they were climbing a mountain.

The oxen moved slowly, laboring the entire mile of the ascent, pulling each family's nearly two thousand pounds of gear and supplies upward.

At times, Winnie was certain their wagon would begin to roll backward, and she found herself holding her breath.

Big John had assured them this was the best way to reach the oasis known as Ash Hollow, which also gave the best access to crossing the north fork of the Platte River. They'd follow the north fork to Fort Laramie.

A steep downgrade funneled into Ash Hollow. The drop was so intimidating, even Mama seemed nervous, which was a rare and always unsettling occurrence.

It took them two whole days to get all thirty wagons down. It was so steep, each wagon had to unhitch its team of oxen and lead them down separately. Once the animals, women, and children were safely below, the men locked the wagon wheels with chains. Then they lowered each wagon down from the top of the hill with ropes, preventing them from tipping over or racing down the hill to crash at the bottom.

The long, grueling two days were stressful to Winnie, watching the men grunt and heave as they lowered wagon after wagon down.

Most resorted to wrapping strips of cloth around their hands to protect them from the ropes.

Even then, Winnie and Nora still tended to Papa's, Jeb's, and Hank's torn and bleeding palms each evening.

They lost one wagon in the descent, when a chain unexpectedly came loose from a front wagon wheel, tearing a rope through the hands of several men. Lopsided from the momentum, the wagon fell sideways, pulling the remaining ropes free, and then flipped the rest of the way down the hill. No one was badly hurt, but many of the supplies within were damaged, and the wagon box split from the frame. One whole barrel of the family's bacon, packed in bran so it wouldn't spoil, had broken open.

The entire wagon train ate bacon for dinner that night, to keep it from going to waste.

Several other wagons also needed repairs, most to the axles and wheels. They lost another day at the base of the hill waiting for those repairs to be completed.

Big John warned everyone they might encounter camps of a few Sioux Natives there, as it was their territory and a well-regarded camping spot. There'd been few clashes between emigrants and the Sioux, he assured them. If everyone kept their heads about them and remained calm, they wouldn't have any trouble.

But there were no Natives to be seen when they at last crossed into the wooded canyon, traversing its floor to choose their own camping spots along its famously sweet spring water. They kept a loose version of their wagon circle, but with more space and privacy than usual. And at last, there was plenty of firewood. They didn't need to collect a single buffalo chip.

The first thing Winnie and Nora did was take Elijah to the spring a short distance from where they'd parked their wagons beneath a grove of ash trees. The sisters took their boots off, soaking their feet in the cold water, while Elijah delighted in floating sticks and leaves downstream, chasing them along the bank.

Winnie braced her hands behind her and tipped her head back, listening to the bird calls echoing through the trees overhead.

Bright coneflowers, golden tickseed, and cowboy roses grew in clusters among the lush grass.

"This feels like Heaven," she said dreamily to Nora.

Nora had pulled her skirts up to her knees, sunning her pale shins, and laid back with a sigh, leaving her feet submerged in the water. "If Heaven is anything like this, I won't much mind going there."

Winnie looked over. It was the most relaxed her sister had seemed in weeks, and it warmed her heart. She reached out and took Nora's hand, and together they listened to the birds, the flowing water, and Elijah's laughter.

She must've fallen asleep, because Winnie woke to

Nora pushing on her shoulder.

"Supper's ready. There's going to be music and dancing after."

Winnie shoved her boots on excitedly, snatched her sunbonnet from the grass, and followed her siblings back to their wagon.

Millie was grazing contentedly, and though it was usually Winnie's chore, Papa had taken pity on her and already milked the cow for the evening.

Hank and Jeb were sitting back against the wagon wheels, shoveling cornbread and bacon into their mouths at an impressive pace.

Nora went to sit with Jeb, who had saved a plate for her, but pushed her food around far more than she chewed it.

Mama watched them with a little furrow between her brows, as though she was trying to untangle a snarl of yarn with only her mind.

Winnie ate so fast, she barely tasted the food. It was common enough for families to wander to neighboring fires and share some conversation before bed, but they hadn't had a good music session since their first night on the trail. And she adored music.

She couldn't play a single instrument, and could barely keep time or dance properly. But music was a grand distraction, a conduit to giddiness and sorrow in equal measure, depending upon the composition. It was its own language, and though she didn't speak it herself, she felt it more deeply than most.

Nora was passable on the piano, and had taken lessons from a widow in town, but she'd stopped going before they left for Independence, and had never mentioned missing it. There was no way they were fitting a piano into their wagon anyway, even if they had owned one. What a sight that would have been!

In the center of their loosely gathered wagons, the two Wilson brothers who played the fiddle began to tune their instruments, starting with a series of scales.

Mama saw that Winnie was near to bursting with excitement, and took her plate with a smile. "Go on, then." She reached up to tuck a stray piece of dark hair back into Winnie's braid. "We'll be along shortly."

Winnie glanced back at Nora, but she was leaning against Jeb's shoulder, holding his arm between her hands, and didn't seem interested in moving at all, much less dancing.

Mama bumped Winnie with her hip. "Get going! I'll convince her."

Winnie grinned and made her way to the center of camp, enjoying the May evening air that snuck cool caresses along her cheeks. It was just crisp enough for her to be glad of the long sleeves of her dress. She'd only packed three dresses, but she liked this one well enough. It wasn't scratchy, and the round neckline didn't itch. Those things were far more important to Winnie than keeping up with the current fashions. The frontier was hardly the place to consider restricting a woman's movement for the sake of beauty to be a wise idea. That suited her just fine.

Campfires lit the ground in as large a circle as could be managed, and a handful of long torches had been hammered into the ground. Those who had stools brought them to sit on, others laid blankets or rested atop fallen logs.

The Wilson brothers had stopped tuning their fiddles and were talking animatedly with Big John, who had brought out his harmonica. Mr. McCleary, of all people, was sitting nearby with his banjo. Last time, Mrs. McCleary had sung with him, but there was no sight of her now.

Winnie spotted Mae and made her way over, greeting those she knew along the way. She unabashedly watched for Hal, but didn't spot him in the crowd. Children ran by, shrieking with laughter, and she dodged out of the way.

Mae greeted her warmly, stepping aside to make room for her among their waiting neighbors. "Where's Nora? Still not feeling well?"

Winnie shrugged. "Mama says she'll convince her to come."

"Well then, she'll be here, because I'm convinced that your mama could wring water from a rock."

Winnie laughed. Her mother's stubborn streak ran deep and true. Painfully deep, at times.

She was about to ask if Mae had seen Hal when the Wilson brothers struck up their first song, a lively polka.

Mr. McCleary and Big John joined in, and then the camp was clapping along, happy to be in a pretty place, to have good health, plentiful food, and music.

Across the circle, Winnie spotted the little girl who'd been run over by her wagon, sitting on the ground between her mother and father, healing legs carefully laid out before her.

She clapped along with everyone else, bobbing her head to the cheerful music.

Winnie felt a fleeting hope stir beneath her ribs, that wherever Amos was now, he could hear it too, and could dance if he wanted. She wondered if perhaps Mr. McCleary was hoping the same thing, as he strummed his banjo with a faint smile on his face. She looked away when she glimpsed the tears that lingered alongside his smile.

Big John took his harmonica from his lips long enough to call out, "Don't just stand around, everybody! Let's have some fun, we've earned it!"

A few good-natured cheers rang out, and suddenly everyone was moving. Husbands danced with wives. Grandmothers twirled with granddaughters. Mothers stomped with sons and swayed with babies on their hips. Friends spun each other in circles.

Mae took Winnie's hands and swung her into the crowd, laughing.

And maybe it was the music, which swelled from within, filling up the parts of her that so often felt forgotten on the trail. Or maybe it was the cool air, and the wildflowers, and the memory of the spring water running over her feet. But Winnie felt lighter than she had in weeks, and young and invincible, as though a company of angels had crossed shields in the sky above them to guard them throughout the long night.

Without warning, she felt a tap on her shoulder.

"May I cut in?" Hal winked at Mae.

He wasn't wearing his hat, and his tawny hair had been combed. It looked like he'd even put on a clean shirt; the white sleeves were rolled up his forearms, and not even dusty. He held his hand out to Winnie.

Mae backed away, cheeks flushed and eyes alit from laughing.

She looked beautiful in that moment, and Winnie couldn't fathom why Hal was looking at her instead of Mae.

But she was grateful for it. Not just for being seen.

No, plenty of people saw her, every day. But only Hal looked at her with a combination of bashful admiration and calm assurance, rolled into one contrary expression.

Winnie took his hand, and he spun her around and around, laughing every time she stepped on his boots.

She tried to apologize, but he shook his head good-naturedly.

"Do you have any idea how many times I've been stepped on by a horse?" he teased. "I don't even notice your stomping!"

The musicians launched into a new song, and cheers went up as people recognized it. They began to sing along with the opening verse.

They danced past voices Winnie recognized, and she turned her head to find that her family had arrived.

Jeb pulled a protesting Nora into the crowd, and Mama twirled Elijah around and around by one finger as Papa stomped his feet, singing at the top of his lungs.

Even Mae spiraled by on Hank's arm.

For a moment, all the smiling faces were so surreal. The happiness was so vibrant, so loud after weeks of grit and steady, gradual progress.

Hal was singing too, and Winnie wished she could hear him over everyone else. She imagined his voice as a steady, simple croon, soothing cows from the saddle through a long, watchful night. She drew herself back from the noise and motion of everything going on around them, focusing on the feel of his hand holding hers, guiding at the small of her back or turning at her elbow.

She'd wondered what it would be like, to touch him so casually, to not need an excuse. His body was flushed with warmth, the muscles of his arms pleasant under her grip.

He wasn't taking advantage of their closeness, but he wasn't quick to let go, either. His hands lingered where they could, just long enough to draw her attention and make her realize she wanted there to be more.

If she intended to follow her initial desire to remain unattached and free for the duration of this long journey, then Winnie was in trouble. She liked Hal, trusted and enjoyed him, and the feeling seemed to be growing with every mile they crossed. If she wasn't careful, she'd find herself in love with a cowhand, trading the freedom she admired in Mae for a new husband and other responsibilities.

But just then, dancing with him, it didn't seem like such an unfair trade.

The musicians finally wound down into a slower song, letting people catch their breath.

Hal kept holding Winnie's hand and led her to the fringes of the crowd, finding them seats along a fallen tree carpeted in moss.

"I have a question to ask you," he said without preamble, pausing only to take a fortifying breath. "I've counted myself lucky to be your friend these past weeks. But I've realized that I would like you to be more than a friend. Much more."

Winnie's heart leapt with excitement even as her stomach sank with trepidation. Was he about to ask for her hand in marriage? It was too soon. Her mind wasn't made up yet. If she said "No," he would likely end whatever was burgeoning between them. Her thoughts swam and tumbled over one another, panicked. What should she do?

She was so busy inside her head that she almost missed his actual question.

"Winnie, I want to ask your father if I can court you. Officially. What do you think?"

She was so relieved that for a moment she simply stared, letting go of all the responses she'd been struggling to form to answer a question he hadn't even asked. Her mind cleared, emptying of the worry. Of course, Hal would know better than to ask for her hand so soon. He knew her better than she thought. Perhaps better than she knew him.

"Winnie?" For the first time, he sounded unsure.

She realized she'd been staring at him, with Lord only knows what expression on her easily read face. Quickly, she squeezed both of his hands. He was offering her time. Time to know him better. Time to know herself better. Time to decide which future version of herself to let go of.

Impulsively, she pulled him up, off the fallen tree. He was bigger than her, easily eight inches taller, but he let himself be led, as though he'd go wherever she asked. His green eyes were vulnerable, cast in shadow by the campfires.

"Let's go ask him," she said.

Hal's face brightened, as though a candle had been lit within. "Right now?"

"Right now." She began to pull him back through the crowd, winding between groups of people telling jokes, sharing tobacco, and dancing.

"I haven't practiced that part yet!" He protested sheepishly, but he kept hold of her hand.

Winnie spun to face him, bumping her chest with his own before he could stop. "You practiced asking me to court you?" It was so endearing; she felt a sudden urge to kiss him.

He ducked his head just a bit, as though he was wishing he'd worn his hat, to better hide his expression. But then he raised his chin. "Maybe I wanted it to be perfect."

She smiled at him. "It was."

He swallowed and put one hand gently along the side of her neck. "All right then. Let's go, before I lose my nerve!"

Winnie found her parents, who had moved a bit farther from the cluster of dancing.

Mama was holding Elijah, whose head lolled sleepily against her shoulder.

Papa was talking to Jeb and Nora, who looked like she could barely keep her eyes open.

They stopped before her family, and Hal tried to let go of her hand, but she gripped it tighter, sending him a wink.

"Hal has something to ask you." Winnie flashed him a sideways grin. "But he hasn't rehearsed it yet, so he's a bit nervous."

Hal shook his head, narrowing his eyes with mock indignation. "You're making me rethink this, Winnifred Hayes."

Papa watched the two of them with a barely concealed smile, while Mama kept her gaze locked on Hal's face.

Nora leaned back into Jeb, who propped his chin on her shoulder.

"I'd like your permission to court Winnie," Hal blurted.

Winnie couldn't tell if it was only the firelight, or if his cheeks were reddening.

Papa looked between them for a long moment, and

Winnie saw he was fighting to keep from laughing. He kept tapping the heels of his boots against the ground. "I assume you're happy with this arrangement, Winnie?"

He was undoubtedly remembering their talk about her heart, and that he believed it would tell her when she was ready. Gesturing to her and Hal's joined hands, Winnie smiled. "I suppose he's tolerable enough."

"Tolerable." Hal scoffed.

At last, Papa's big laugh escaped him. "You have my permission, Hal. And it's about time! Now you can finally stop having to ask about Millie every time you come by the wagon!"

Everyone laughed, even Hal, though he ducked his head a bit in embarrassment.

It was a lighthearted moment, but to Winnie, it was also swollen with possibility. Like the westward trail they traveled, several new paths were being laid along her horizon. All that remained was for her to experience the moments that awaited between now and then, and to make the right choices.

They spent another hour there, as the stars came out, enjoying each other's company and the ebb and flow of the music's mood.

Abruptly, Big John stopped blowing into his harmonica, and thrust his hands up.

"Everyone, quiet! Listen."

The music stopped at once, though it took a moment longer for conversation to end. And then, they all heard it.

Drums.

Winnie strained her ears, and Hal tilted his head back, staring at the expanse of stars overhead.

People began to whisper.

"They're making music with us." Big John grinned, breaking the seed of unease that had sprouted like a thorny weed. Raising his harmonica, he added, "We have nothing to fear, except not giving our best! C'mon, boys!"

And the Wilson brothers sawed away at their fiddles, and Mr. McCleary beat at his banjo, and Big John blasted the harmonica, merging once more with the drums of the Native tribe, which echoed off the walls of the canyon around them.

There was no way to tell where they were coming from, but Winnie wasn't afraid. Big John wasn't afraid, Papa wasn't afraid, and neither was Hal. And so she wasn't, either.

She remembered the Native woman giving Mae the hide in exchange for her polished piece of antler, and wondered if the drums were maybe another kind of gift. A gift of physical presence without the threat of proximity.

They were a wild call into the night that proved the travelers were not stranded and alone beneath the vast prairie sky. They were a gift of music, an acknowledgement of being heard.

Winnie listened, tipping her head back with Hal to watch the sky, and with her family around her, she was far from afraid.

****

Leaving Ash Hollow the next morning felt like saying goodbye to an old friend. Winnie kept glancing back, as if the elation and comfort she'd felt the night before was something that could be spotted, watching them go from between the trees. She sternly reminded herself that as long as she had her family and friends, and their freedom, such feelings would always be accessible to her. They weren't tied to a place or a time, no matter how special the place had been.

Nora had said she would walk with her that day, which made Winnie hopeful that her sister was well and truly past whatever illness had stalked her, draining her energy and appetite. But Nora was unusually quiet, offering succinct replies to whatever questions she thought to ask. Even bringing up Hal and his blunt but sweet courtship proposal had done little to animate Nora.

After about an hour, Winnie gave up, and they slipped into a companionable silence, each walking with their own thoughts and fears as much as with each other.

At the noon break, Mae rode up while they were finishing their lunch. After dismounting and passing quick greetings to everyone gathered around to eat, she turned to Winnie. "Would you like to ride ahead with me this afternoon? Pa asked me to scout for tonight's camping spot."

Mae was very much dressed as a scout that day, wearing pants and a long-sleeve shirt to protect her skin from the dust and sun. Her hair was practically braided back from her face, and with her black hat on, she would've passed for a man to anyone looking on from a distance. Her rifle hung in a sling alongside her saddle, and she wore her father's pistol in a gun belt with extra ammunition around her hips.

Cowhand, indeed. Mae Cook could have sauntered into a saloon dressed like that, and no one would have protested.

"May I go?" Winnie begged Papa, who was finishing a cup of coffee.

Mama turned to look at him also, eyebrows rising

incredulously as a moment passed and he didn't say no.

"I've seen you shoot, Mae," Papa said at last, setting down his cup. "So, I know your rifle isn't for decoration. But I'm still not overly comfortable with the idea."

Winnie opened her mouth to argue, but Mae spoke first. "We're supposed to stay within sight of the wagon train. We'll use the same system as the cowhands if we run into trouble—two shots into the air if we need help, and three shots to warn of an attack."

Papa braced his hands on his knees and then stood, adjusting his stirrups. He gave Winnie a long, hard look, as if weighing her and Mae against several invisible foes. Finally, he smiled and held his hands up in a gesture of surrender. "Go on, then. Enjoy your ride."

Mama threw her hands up, muttering under her breath about fathers and daughters as she turned to scold Elijah into finishing his lunch.

Winnie threw her arms around Papa and gave him a tight squeeze before bouncing back. "Thank you, Papa!"

Papa gestured to their wagon. "You'd better put on a pair of pants, yourself. And be careful."

Short of breath with excitement, Winnie raced to climb into the wagon, and traded her long skirt for the only pair of pants she owned. Mae was waiting patiently when she emerged, still pulling her hair back into a bun on the back of her neck, the way Mama wore hers most days.

It was strange and freeing to be wearing pants. To feel her legs striding independently and not have them be constricted by fabric. She liked it, but she wasn't sure she should like it at all. It felt a little too bold. It showed more of her shape than her dresses did.

Papa had sent Hank to retrieve his horse from the

rear of the train near Millie and the rest of the herd, and the pair of them finished tacking up as Winnie approached.

The bay gelding, affectionately named Lazy Louie, had been purchased along with their oxen in Independence. He was sound and solid, and even Elijah could ride him. But he wasn't a quick mover.

Winnie hoped Mae wasn't counting on racing the wind or the river like heroines in a novel, because the only thing she'd pass while riding Lazy Louie would be insects in the grass. If she could even get him to stop trying to eat the grass as they went.

Papa helped her into the saddle, and she marveled at how easy it seemed to mount in pants.

Hank handed her his rifle, which set Mama to muttering again.

Winnie clearly heard the word "foolish," but dismissed the rest.

"Point, aim, and shoot," Hank instructed with a wink. "But don't shoot Mae, please. I'd hate to have to break in a new friend after all the effort I've already put in."

Mae rolled her eyes, nudging her horse into a walk. "As if you could."

Winnie took the rifle from him and slid its strap over her head and across her chest, letting the weapon rest against her back. "I did grow up on a farm, you know," she reminded him. "I've shot a rifle before."

Papa patted her knee affectionately. "Of course you have. But fence posts are a far cry from moving targets. Better to let Mae take the shot, if something happens."

Winnie sat straighter in the saddle and tried not to let her confidence deflate. Papa didn't give false praise, but he wasn't one to hold back compliments on a job well done, either. Maybe they'd be lucky enough to bring some wild game back. See if he told her to let Mae take the shot, then!

"Take care." Papa waved.

"See you soon." Winnie waved goodbye to Elijah before urging Lazy Louie to catch up with Mae's horse.

They were greeted by everyone as they passed, even though most were putting away the remains of lunch and preparing to move again.

Mae knew everyone by name, but since she was their trail guide's daughter, that didn't surprise Winnie.

What did surprise her was that most of the families also knew her own name. Even though some of them called her "Miss Hayes" instead of Winnifred, she couldn't help but feel a bit as though they were riding down the main street of the small Missouri town where she'd grown up and not along a westward trail full of strangers.

But after spending more than six weeks on the trail together, she supposed they weren't strangers anymore. If anything, they were neighbors, as though they occupied a small, nomadic town.

Mae led Winnie to the front of their company, where Big John was finishing loading his and Mae's wagon with practiced efficiency. His wavy black hair was slick with sweat, his hat tossed aside during the noon break.

"Winnifred is coming with me," Mae announced as they grew closer. "Her pa was all right with it."

Big John's eyes lingered on the rifle slung across Winnie's back. "Yes, I can see that. Well done, Winnifred. I'm sure Mae will be glad for the company this afternoon."

Mae gripped the reins atop her thighs, as though eager to be off. "Any last instructions, Pa?"

Big John wiped his forehead, and shaded his eyes to look up at his daughter. "You shouldn't run into any trouble here; we're still in Sioux territory. If memory serves, there's a little stream not too far ahead. If you find it in time, we'll set up camp there. Make sure you're back well before dark."

Winnie and Mae nodded their understanding.

"Follow the sun into the West." Big John winked at Mae.

"Taste the freedom of her skies," Mae replied.

Winnie recognized it for what it was, a ritualistic farewell between a father and daughter who had crossed the country four times together. Who knew what dangers they had faced in the wilderness?

There were many untold stories between this pair. But what had happened to Mae's mother? She hadn't yet dared to ask. Perhaps she would today.

As they started out, Winnie settled for what seemed like an easier question. "What was that about? What you and Big John said?"

Mae shrugged, tugging her hat lower down on her forehead. "I was quite a bit younger on our first trip across. I had a lot of fears. Remember what I told you about the first time I ever saw Natives?" She looked over sheepishly.

"You hid under the wagon."

Mae gave a nod and looked ahead, her eyes taking on a solemnity that spoke of old wounds. "I was scared of everything. I think…. I think I grew up watching my mother be afraid of everything." She paused. "I didn't realize there was another way to be, if you were a woman."

Winnie stayed silent. She hadn't imagined their conversation getting so personal so quickly, and she was afraid to say the wrong thing and send Mae's loyal heart back into hiding.

"Two Sioux Natives approached us during our first trip along the trail, not far from where we are now. They were brothers, seeking experience as guides. My father hired them, and paid them well in exchange for leading our small group and teaching him their language."

"Was Big John wealthy back then?" Winnie hoped to soothe some of the rawness from Mae's voice. Most wagon trains split the cost of a guide between all the families. If Big John had been able to afford the salary for two guides, after already purchasing all their supplies...

Mae grimaced, sticking out her tongue. "He still is. My mother came from old money back east. An old family with a good name."

Winnie couldn't believe her ears. That her best friend, aside from Nora, was an heiress to east coast money. And here she was, wearing pants and a pistol, covered in dust in the middle of nowhere. And Big John, rather than wearing suits and putting on airs, chose to live out of a wagon for half of each year.

It was strange. And remarkable.

"What were their names? The brothers?"

Mae looked a little surprised she had asked. "Chatan and Tatanka Ptecila." Her voice was smooth around the names, like a stream flowing around well-worn rocks.

"What does that mean?" Winnie was fascinated.

"Hawk and Little bull, loosely translated. Anyway, my father was curious and eager to learn, and so they told him a lot of stories. One story was about a group of warriors who went to visit the sun, to ask it for great gifts. He passed the story on, and something about it stuck with me, I guess. After that I talked to the sun every morning. Asking it not to lead us astray. I suppose it grew into a reminder between Pa and me. To view the sun and the trail that followed it as gifts."

"What happened to them? To Chatan and..." Winnie stumbled over the second name. "Tatanka Ptecila?"

Mae looked down at her hands for a moment, loosely holding the reins. "They died after we reached Oregon City. Within days of each other. Natives catch sickness easily from white men." She said the last part in a removed, carefully distant voice.

"I'm sorry about your friends." It didn't seem like nearly enough. "What about your mother?"

Mae blinked and looked over at her, as though she'd forgotten Winnie was there. "Mama and my little sister, Lucy, got very sick. So did a few others in our group. Chatan and Tatanka Ptecila went out and brought herbs back that they claimed would help with the sickness. My mother was terrified of them. She thought they meant to poison us all. She wouldn't let them near her, or my sister. When Pa tried to force her, she aimed his pistol at him and threatened to shoot him and his 'heathen friends.' "

Winnie tried not to look too shocked. She was almost certain she failed.

"Mama and Lucy died the next night," Mae finished. "Most of the people who took the herbs from Chatan and Tatanka Pteccila recovered. Not all, but most. If Mama had just been able to see past her fear, and her prejudice…"

Winnie wanted to say something. But what could she say in the wake of such a tragic story? What could she possibly offer that hadn't been said before?

Still, she hunted for words that might comfort her friend. Seeking to center herself, she focused for the first time on their surroundings, and not on Mae. They were farther ahead of the wagon train than she'd thought. They weren't even in the dust anymore.

Winnie blinked at the realization, and it wasn't a blink to clear her vision. She hadn't been free of dust in weeks while on the move like this.

The grass around them, once so flat, was now beginning to rise and swell in little hills. The details were crisp and clear, not smudged in a haze of billowing dust clouds.

There were trees in the distance on both sides of them, now. It was no longer an endless sea of grass devoid of timber or rocks. Nothing was endless, it seemed. Not even the prairie.

Finally, Winnie found what she wanted to say. "I'm sorry your mother couldn't overcome her fear."

Mae's grateful smile was full of warmth. "So am I."

"Will you tell me the story? About the Natives who went to visit the sun?"

Mae took a swig of water from her canteen and wiped her lips with a sleeve before launching into the tale. "One day, six warriors who were the best of friends went together to ask their chief's permission to take a long journey to find the sun, and visit it where it touched the land in the West in the evening."

Winnie listened, and they rode on.

Chapter Five

The friends passed the next several hours on horseback, taking care to always keep the wagon train in sight. The wagon canopies were so small in the distance, they resembled a herd of sheep.

Mae recounted many stories from her native friends—outlandish tales of trickster coyotes, nature spirits, and ancestral guides who took the forms of animals.

As they hunted for the stream that Big John had spoken of, the wilderness around them seemed to come alive.

Winnie knew it was because of Mae's stories, but she couldn't help herself. The afternoon sun gilded the tree tops, and she found herself searching their branches and trunks for a glimpse of curious eyes or a wily smile.

When they ventured from the swath that had been cut by hundreds of wagons before them, the prairie grass grew tall enough to brush the bellies of the horses. It wasn't hard to imagine something crouching there, peering at them between stalks of grass.

The wildflowers seemed brighter, the colors more vibrant. The biting flies that lingered around the livestock were long gone, and for the first time, Winnie thought she could see why people had begun to venture west.

Maybe it was the break from the monotony. Maybe

it was the novelty of riding Lazy Louie instead of walking. Or just maybe, Winnie was finally beginning to actually see the wilderness, instead of only resenting it for its hardships and the simple fact that it wasn't the farm she'd grown up on.

With that thought, she felt that she had found the root of the matter. The heart of the cause for the blinders she'd worn the past month and a half, which had kept her from finding anything about the trail worthy of its renown. She bore resentment. A bit of anger. Reluctance.

Papa had decided to bring them across the wilds to Oregon territory. He had spoken to Mama about it beforehand, but he'd been the driving force behind the idea. And months later, the animals Winnie had helped to raise were all gone. Millie's little calf. The piglets that Mama Pig grunted with so affectionately. The chickens that had followed Winnie around the yard when she did her chores.

All were gone now, except for Millie, the milk cow.

The simple life she'd known had been traded for the uncertainty of the westward trail, and she saw now that she had been determined to endure it, but also determined not to find anything about the scenery of their travels very pleasant or worthwhile.

With her stories, Mae breathed life into the trees, curiosity into the rabbits and squirrels, and omnipotence to the birds, and Winnie removed the blinders she'd been wearing. She saw the true feelings that had lurked there, ducking behind the exhaustion, the cautious excitement over her relationship with Hal, and the irritation over small inconveniences.

She'd been grieving the home she'd lost. And she'd never even known it, until now. It wasn't until those wounds began to close over that she even acknowledged their existence.

"We should be getting close." Mae drew Winnie out of her introspection.

They climbed a rise, and the curves of the North Platte River were visible again as it wound past on their right. When they summited the hill, Winnie pulled on Lazy Louie's reins, drawing him to an abrupt halt.

"Oh," Mae breathed. "That's incredible."

Winnie agreed, but she didn't speak. She was too busy taking it all in.

They had indeed found the spring, feeding swiftly down into the North Platte. But the reprieve promised by the spring paled in comparison to the buffalo herd that grazed there. There had to be hundreds of them, drifting among the tender grasses. The buffalo were massive, even from their vantage point.

Some had babies with them, which were almost reddish compared to the dark brown of the adults. The babies seemed so small next to their mothers, but Winnie was sure that up close, they'd be bigger than any dog she'd ever seen.

Slowly, so as not to startle them, she pulled the strap of Papa's rifle over her head. She'd never shot anything from horseback before. And she wouldn't try to take one of the mothers with a calf. But she guessed that one buffalo would feed all the families in their company tonight, and the thought of fresh meat made her stomach clench.

"Do we need to get closer?" Winnie asked Mae, who had yet to draw her rifle from the sling alongside her saddle.

"Definitely. Let's make our way down along the

trees on that side."

They dismounted and began leading their horses down the hill, walking on their far side so the horses' bodies hid them from the buffalo.

Reluctantly, Winnie settled the rifle against her back once more. She'd never been on a hunt before, though Elijah had started going with Papa last year. She wondered if her little brother had ever felt the same nerves that she was feeling now.

When they reached about half-way down the hill, the buffalo still seemed unaware, or uncaring, of their presence. But Mae halted mid-step, thrusting a hand out behind her to warn Winnie of something.

"What is it?" Winnie whispered over Mae's shoulder, her breathing fast and shallow. "Do they see us?"

"Someone does."

"What do you mean?"

Mae just pointed, and Winnie followed her friend's finger down the line of trees, looking for anything out of place. Five pairs of eyes locked on her as she registered what she was seeing.

The Native men were all on horseback, standing silently in the last available shade of the tree line. Many were shirtless. All wore bows with quivers of arrows. A hunting party.

"Winnie, turn your horse around, and walk back up the hill," Mae said. "Don't mount up until you're at the top. I'll be right behind you."

Winnie studied her friend for a moment, trying to keep her heart from drumming out of her chest.

Mae's dark eyes were narrowed, her face taut with concentration. As though she was trying to read the

Natives' intent solely by their apathetic, watchful expressions.

Winnie didn't fail to notice that the other woman had not yet called out a greeting.

"What about the buffalo?"

"The tribe will view it as an act of hostility if we fire on the buffalo now. They're on the tribe's land. It would be stealing."

"It's not stealing," Winnie protested. "These buffalo don't belong to anyone. We've just as much right to take them as the Natives!"

Mae shook her head, clearly losing her patience. "That may be the way that you see it, but the Sioux would not agree. The buffalo are the lifeblood of the Sioux people. They provide for everyone in the tribe."

Winnie still hesitated, glancing back at the Natives in the shade. They looked more than somber, they looked displeased. Whether that was because Mae and Winnie could spook the herd of buffalo and ruin the Natives' hunt, or just because they were outsiders, was impossible to know.

"Kola," Mae said to the Natives, taking a single step closer while putting her hand to her chest. "Kola."

"What does that mean?" Winnie hissed. She disliked feeling ignorant of the conversation.

One of the men shook his head, gesturing to the young women. "Wasicu." His voice was pleasant, low and smooth like a calm lake.

Mae clearly recognized the word. Her dark eyes took on a look of hurt, as though she had been struck somewhere deep within.

Then, astonishingly, the man said something Winnie recognized. English words.

"Go, now." He pointed back the way they'd come. "Go, wasicu."

Mae took a step back, lowering the hand that had been on her chest. "Get going, Winnie," she repeated. "Wait for me at the top of the hill."

"But…"

"Go!" Mae snapped.

Huffing her irritation, Winnie tugged on Lazy Louie's reins, pulling his head up from where he'd seized the opportunity to chomp mouthfuls of grass. She marched up the hill, certain she could feel the eyes of the men upon her back, and equally certain that if she dwelled on it, she would begin to tremble with fear.

She focused on her indignation instead, because it was a blade wielded outward and not inward, as fear was. Fear could gut her from within. Fear made people act like animals caught in a snare: wild and without reason.

She would not be caught in a snare today.

She looked back once, to be sure that Mae had followed.

The Natives had not come any closer, but Mae had also not moved away.

She looked to be exchanging flurries of words and hand gestures with one of the men, but Winnie was completely ignorant of whatever they might be saying.

She slowed her pace, but continued up the hill. She was nearly halfway up it, now. Her indignation had cooled, and she cast about for something else to think of, to distract her from the very real fear of feeling an arrow burst through her exposed back, or through her friend's vulnerable chest.

Mae had said that her friends, Chatan and Tatanka Ptecila, had been Sioux.

And Big John had mentioned they were still in Sioux territory, as they had been in Ash Hollow the night before.

The Natives below might have known Mae's friends, before they'd left the tribe to be guides. They also could have been among the ones who'd played their drums alongside the dancing fiddles of the wagon train.

Winnie wanted to believe that these Natives were decent folk, as the trading trio they'd encountered at Fort Kearny had seemed to be. But her distrust and wariness ran deeper than she'd realized. It was a struggle not to ride down the hill, snatch Mae up into the saddle, and gallop away with her foolish friend.

She reached the top of the hill, stepped into the stirrup, and swung a leg over Lazy Louie's back with a wince. She wasn't accustomed to hours in the saddle, and her muscles were already sore. She turned the horse so she could see back down the hill, just in time to see Mae mount up, making a final hand gesture that seemed none too gentle. Then her friend cantered up the hill, not looking back even once at the hunting party.

"Let's head back," Mae said a bit breathlessly as she passed Winnie. "Pa will be waiting."

"What did you say to them?"

"Does it matter?" Mae answered tersely.

Winnie reached again for her indignation, but it sputtered and went out, heedless of her summons. She knew that if Mama cooked beans or rice for supper, she would be sullenly imagining fresh buffalo meat instead. But it seemed she couldn't stay irritated with Mae when she was also grateful her friend was alive and decidedly not kidnapped.

She took a last look down at the Natives before

turning to follow Mae. They were all watching her, like a parent might assess a willful child who had just been warned not to do something. She wondered what they would do if she aimed her rifle at the buffalo, and then immediately dismissed the thought.

She wasn't Mae. She had so little experience with Natives, and if they responded the way Mae had said they would, she'd deserve what she got for not listening.

Mae didn't waste time. She urged her horse into a canter, and then a gallop, easily outpacing Winnie and Lazy Louie, who was admirably living up to his name.

For a moment, Winnie feared she'd be left behind, but Mae circled back a moment later, pulling back on the speed so that Louie could keep up.

Winnie half expected her to heft her rifle and fire three shots into the air, signaling about the Natives, but she didn't. She wasn't sure if it was because Mae trusted the Natives behind them not to attack the wagon train, or if it was because she feared spurring them into violence with the gunshots.

A few minutes of hard riding had them reaching the outriders on the fringe of the wagon party, acting as its first line of defense.

Hank saw them coming fast and hard, and pulled his horse up to wait as they approached.

Winnie was gulping air when she slowed Lazy Louie to a walk, unaccustomed to the feeling of riding so fast. She should really be grateful she hadn't fallen out of the saddle. She was a mediocre rider at best, with neither the grace nor the passion to be truly accomplished at it. As Lazy Louie blew out a big sigh and tossed his head, she realized he probably hadn't gone so fast in a while, either.

The pair of them were well out of their depth. What had she been thinking, riding off alone with Mae and the illusion of safety that two rifles and a pistol produced? Those men could have overpowered them and done whatever they wished. They could have cut them into so many pieces that even the coyotes wouldn't have been tempted by the remains.

Winnie realized she was shaking, still gulping down air, and she was rapidly letting her fear be overtaken by anger, just to feel more in control. "We could have been killed," she snapped at Mae's back. "What were you thinking, trying to talk to them? You're lucky they didn't drag you into the woods!"

Mae glanced back at Winnie, dark eyes narrowed. Her expression was taut, like a rope under strain that could fray with the slightest touch of a blade. "Do you want an apology? For not letting you kill a buffalo to prove yourself to your Pa? For not cowering in the presence of savages?" The last word was laced with mocking disdain.

Winnie was close enough now to see Hank eyeing the pair of them warily, oblivious to why they argued but shrewd enough to know something significant had occurred.

She replied stiffly, all too aware of Hank's presence. "You called them savages, not me."

Mae rolled her eyes. "I put words to the look on your face. That's all."

Winnie looked away, feeling her cheeks flush with either embarrassment or anger. Likely both.

Hank let out a whistle that dropped in pitch like a stone. "As much as I'd love to hear more of this fascinating exchange, is there something we need to know?"

Winnie kept her mouth shut, letting Mae step into her role as the guide's capable daughter who had no qualms about issuing orders.

"Form up as many of the hands as can be spared, and space them throughout the wagons." Mae gathered her reins again. "We ran into a small party of Sioux alongside the stream out on a buffalo hunt. I don't think they'll bother the wagons, but Pa would want us to be prepared."

Hank gave a stiff nod, sparing a sympathetic look for Winnie as he turned his horse away and spurred him toward the wagons to gather the rest of the cowhands.

She wondered if that would include Hal, or if he was already riding with the herd. What would he think of her decision to ride ahead with Mae?

"I'm going to speak to my pa. You can come if you want. I'll understand if you don't."

Mae's tone wasn't soft, and neither were her eyes, but Winnie interpreted it for the olive branch that it was. Rather than shutting her out, her friend was giving her a chance to continue to be involved in the afternoon's action.

If she wanted to be.

Winnie's decision was immediate. She clicked her tongue to Lazy Louie. "Let's go."

They found Big John at the head of the column, leading his oxen on foot just like the rest of the men did.

Mae jumped out of the saddle before her horse had even fully stopped, with the ease of frequent practice.

Winnie rolled her eyes and plopped down to earth with a wince and barely concealed groan.

Immediately, Lazy Louie began trying to rip up

mouthfuls of grass, as though he felt he'd suffered terribly in the brief hours they'd been away and was owed a reward.

"What did you find?" Big John didn't miss the strained look on his daughter's face.

"There's a band of Sioux warriors by the stream. A buffalo-hunting party. There's a herd there."

Big John removed his hat just long enough to finger comb his hair before settling it back into place. "Did you speak to them?" He didn't sound outraged by the idea.

"I told them we weren't seeking the buffalo, but we intended to camp along the stream."

Big John nodded, chewing on the inside of his cheek thoughtfully. "Good."

"Hank is rounding up the cowhands and placing them among the wagons."

Big John waved a dismissive hand. "They won't attack if we give them and the herd some space. But still, it's important that everyone feel safe and secure."

"You still intend for us to camp at the stream?" Winnie surprised herself. She'd never questioned Big John about anything. It wasn't her place. "What if the Natives return with more men?"

Mae looked sideways at her, as though she wanted to say something snide, but Big John spoke first.

"If the Natives approach us, then I will go speak to them. But let's not load bullets for a battle not yet upon us."

Winnie nodded stiffly, though the thought of keeping camp in the spot where the hunting party expected them to be was more than a little unnerving. It would be easy for them to wait until nightfall, to sneak through the trees, to come upon the sleeping families in the night…

She stomped down on her racing fears, as though squishing a wasp that had been trying to sting.

"Winnie, it's best that you go to your parents now, and let them know you're safe and sound. And a certain cowhand was asking after you, as well." Big John winked at her, already privy to the knowledge that Hal had officially obtained permission for their courtship.

Oh, her Papa loved to talk, all right. He was more of a proud gossip than Mama ever was.

But Winnie wasn't angry. She mustered a smile for Big John. "Yes, sir."

She gripped the reins to aim Lazy Louie to go and find her family's wagon, but thought better of it and turned back to Mae. Her friend was watching her, a distance in her eyes.

"I'm sorry if I offended you. I don't think all Natives are savages."

Mae's expression softened, and she nodded.

But as Winnie nudged Lazy Louie into a walk and then a trot, she couldn't help but feel that she'd badly disappointed her friend. And she may have disappointed herself a bit, as well.

The buffalo were gone when they set up camp along the stream that evening, and so were the men who had been hunting them.

Hal and Hank slept in a tent with their rifles outside of Nora and Jeb's wagon, and Winnie slept fitfully alongside Elijah in the tent with her parents.

Not even an owl broke the calm serenity of the camp that night.

Her fears did not manifest. The Natives never returned.

All was well.

****

Winnie kept her distance from Mae over the next few days, trying to let her emotions settle, like silt sinking to the bottom of a pond that had been disturbed. If she was being honest, she was angrier with herself than she had ever been with Mae. Worse, she was ashamed at her behavior. She'd taken the ancestral stories and heart-felt experiences Mae shared with her and chucked them into the bushes at the first opportunity, choosing to wield ignorance and common misconceptions about the Natives in the same way that a drunkard might swing an empty mug of ale to keep others at bay.

She'd been shown otherwise, twice now, and still she dropped what she was learning of the Native people to clutch at her persistent fears, instead. And as several days went by without speaking to Mae, Winnie wondered what she might be able to do to set it right. She was not content to let their friendship pass into a chilled and unremarkable civility.

Luckily, a welcome change in the scenery uplifted her spirits, and reminded her to be gentler with herself. She was not who she had been when they left Independence, and she wouldn't be who she was now when they arrived in Oregon territory. It was hard work, metamorphosis. Just as it was hard work, inching across the prairie, grinding mile after mile into dust beneath their wheels and their feet.

She was learning that things could change fast on the trail, even as one despaired that the scenery, the work, and the routine might never change again.

"Would you look at that." Nora shaded her eyes as she gazed upon the monoliths of rock that had been the talk of their wagon party for nearly three days. "It really does look like a courthouse. Much grander than our tiny one back home, though."

Indeed, Courthouse Rock was grand. A monolith of stone jutting hundreds of feet above the prairie, it was the larger of the two rocks that now dominated their horizon. Jailhouse Rock, the smaller one, was so close to the Courthouse that from a distance they appeared to be one.

"Big John says that next we'll see Chimney Rock and Scott's Bluff. And they're even more spectacular."

Nora nodded, smacking her sleeves to dislodge dust that had settled in the folds there. "The only reason I'm excited to see any big, old rock is because Fort Laramie is on the other side."

Winnie was also excited to finally reach the fort, though probably for different reasons. Nora would undoubtedly want to ogle the fabrics, as she had been talking of sewing herself a new dress for several days now. Winnie was mostly hoping that Hal would seize the opportunity to ask her to stroll about the shops with him, as though they were a normal courting couple, taking a turn around the town arm in arm.

She'd made a few hints to him about such hopes already, rather shamelessly. But he had been tight-lipped about any such plans, likely just to watch her squirm excitedly over the possibility.

"I've heard some of the cowhands whispering about an establishment at the fort called the Hog Ranch." Nora leaned closer conspiratorially. "It's a bordello!"

Winnie cheeks blazed. "What an unflattering name! I hope it's not referring to the appearance of the girls in its employ." She also hoped Hal had never even heard of the place.

Nora agreed, her own face turning pink. "Is it wrong that I'm secretly hoping Hank will poke his head in just so I can ask him about it after?"

Winnie barked a laugh in surprise. "Since when are you curious about bordellos?"

Nora shrugged, picking up the hem of her skirt to do a dainty twirl. "I'm a married woman now, you know." She gave a little wink.

Winnie ignored the implication that Nora was now privy to the furtive activities that went on within bordellos while she herself remained wholly ignorant of them. She was too busy enjoying her sister's good mood. The weariness that had plagued Nora for the past few weeks seemed to have abated, and there was a spark of life and humor in her sister's eyes again.

"It's heartening to see you in such good spirits." Winnie took Nora's hand in her own and gave it a squeeze. "I was worried about you."

Nora's smile compressed into a line, and a guilty look flickered across her face, one Winnie might have missed had she not known her sister so well.

"What aren't you telling me?" She let go of Nora's hand. "Aren't you feeling better?"

Nora sighed and reached out to grip Winnie's shoulder, pulling her sister into her side. They adjusted their stride so they could walk without their hips banging together.

"I am feeling better. I'm just fine."

Winnie leaned away to eye her with suspicion. "If you're fine, then why are you taking such care to soothe me? Have you finally let Doc Collins examine you? Did he find something?"

Nora looked up at the sky with what might have

been exasperation. "Heavens, Winnie, I'm not sick! I'm going to have a baby."

A flood of elation and relief filled her. "A baby! Really?"

Nora grinned. "You're going to be an aunt."

Winnie flung her arms around her sister, squeezing her tight around the middle. When she pulled back, she chuckled. "No wonder you want to sew a new dress. This one won't be fitting you when we arrive in Oregon territory!"

Nora blew out an exaggerated sigh. "Don't remind me. Before long I'll be as huge as Mrs. Blake."

Mrs. Blake, one of the pregnant mothers on their journey, was in her last weeks of pregnancy. What her husband lacked in height he seemed to make up in virility, as they already had four children under the age of six.

"Are you going to be waddling around like she does?" Winnie teased.

Nora swatted her arm, pretending to be offended. "I shall never waddle." She stuck her nose high into the air and adopted a nasally voice. "I'm far too proper a lady."

The pair of them dissolved into giggles, and Winnie spared a moment to send up a silent prayer of thanks.

"Does Mama know?" she asked when they'd recovered themselves.

"She'd suspected for a couple of weeks already. A mother's intuition, I suppose."

"And Papa?"

"He clapped Jeb on the back so hard he nearly knocked the poor man over. Jeb blushed so badly, Mama teased him about forgetting to wear his hat to protect his face."

Winnie chuckled. She could only imagine poor Jeb, being congratulated by his in-laws for successfully performing his husbandly duties.

"Have you been to see Widow Simmons yet?"

Widow Simmons was the midwife of their party, and easily as prized among the women as Doc Collins was. She was nearly into her sixties, but her three daughters and their young families had all joined her to make the trip to Oregon territory. Her oldest, Moira, was her apprentice, at her side during all births and examinations with the intent to one day take over the duties.

Nora waved a dismissive hand. "I spoke to her briefly, but it's too soon for an examination; I'm only a couple of months along. She told me to help her care for the other ladies from now on, to gain some experience. She claims it will help settle my nerves."

Winnie had doubts about that, but she kept them to herself. Nora was a worrier by nature, a handwringer. She doubted seeing precisely what lay in store would ease her sister's mind. But Widow Simmons was the midwife, not Winnie. Perhaps she knew what was best.

Winnie linked her arm through Nora's, looking again toward the towering Courthouse Rock. If such a leviathan could be pried from the earth and raised to the sky by the mighty hand of God, then anything was possible. Even becoming an aunt, it seemed.

"You know what I just realized? Elijah will be an uncle! And he'll only be six years older than his niece or nephew!"

Nora smiled. "Uncle or not, it'll be good for him to have another playmate in the family." She leaned over to whisper in Winnie's ear, "And if Hal becomes your husband, maybe Elijah will be lucky enough to get two!"

Winnie poked her sister in the ribs, conscious as she did so of the new life that was growing below those delicate bones. "Don't name my future babies just yet, if you don't mind."

Nora gave her a knowing look. "You can pretend you're not sure if you're going to marry him. But I know better."

Winnie kept her gaze on Courthouse Rock. "Oh really? How so?"

Nora rested a hand over her stomach. "Because I know your heart. And it's been walking alongside his for a while, now."

"Is that what marriage is?" Winnie teased, "Just a walk through life?"

Nora smiled once more, eyes taking on a pensive look. "It doesn't have to be. It can be a leap, or a dance, or a race. It can have a gentle, tugging current, like a stream. Or it can burn hot for a short time and leave nothing but ashes behind."

Winnie was taken aback. Her elder sister wasn't usually a poet, or a crooner of words. "That's beautiful."

Nora shrugged. "There's lots of time for thinking out here. With all the open space, sometimes I feel like my thoughts float right out of my head, and just disappear into the sky."

Winnie knew exactly what she meant. "It is a marvelously big sky." She tipped her face up. "Isn't it?"

Nora looked down, focusing on the strides of their feet. "I'd prefer a roof," she said at last. "Something to shield us from the storms and the sun."

"Your baby will be born in Oregon territory," Winnie assured her. "In a house that Papa and Jeb and

Hank have built for you. Not out here. You don't have to worry."

Nora's lips twitched up. "Of course. You're right."

But her sister was worried, and probably would always be. Winnie changed the conversation back to Fort Laramie; to peppermint candies they could sample, and sweet-smelling bags of lavender that Nora could hang in the wagon to ease her sleep.

Nora wondered aloud how much fabric she should buy to get a head start on making clothes for the baby.

The rest of the afternoon passed that way, beneath the distant prairie sky that Mae loved, and Nora feared.

Winnie wasn't totally sure yet which she would come to claim. But she was starting to have an idea.

Chapter Six

Fort Laramie was all that Fort Kearny had not been. It was much better established, having been built over a decade earlier by fur traders in need of an outpost in the west.

Most of the fort's structures were made of adobe brick, lined up in a neat row that made Winnie feel as though they'd stumbled upon the main street of a town.

Circles of wagons were parked near the river, and a few short rows of teepees formed an encampment on the other side of the fort.

Big John said they were likely Sioux, or possibly Cheyenne or Arapaho, keeping their own seasonal trading post alongside the fort.

Once they had secured a place for their wagons and their livestock, most of their party followed Big John on foot into the fort to see what manner of services were for sale or for hire.

As he gestured along the main street, recalling what was typically there and exclaiming over new establishments, Winnie couldn't help but notice the hungry looks in the eyes of her neighbors.

They were hungry for food, yes, for anything that didn't travel in a barrel or get scorched over a campfire. But there were other hungers—for conversation, the exchange of money, the delight of items of comfort considered luxuries on the trail.

She thought of the bordello Nora had mentioned, and blushed at the thought that it would satisfy a particular hunger, as well.

When their crowd of neighbors began to disperse and wander to different areas of the fort, Winnie kept an eye out for Hal from where she stood with her family and Jeb.

Mama handed a few coins to each of them, closing their fingers tight around the money earned by the sale of their farm.

"Be mindful of what you buy. Don't waste your money on something overpriced. I'd tell you not to waste it on sweets, either—" She looked pointedly at Elijah. "—but I'll save my breath."

Elijah bounced on his feet, looking ready to scale the nearest wall to better see what he could buy with his sudden fortune.

Papa recognized that he was about to bust and took his hand, steering him away. "Let's leave the women to their shopping." He winked over his shoulder at Mama. "Your old papa needs to see about getting a new pipe."

Elijah was all too happy to go with him and leave his sisters behind, puffing his chest out as though he were a young rooster given an important, manly task.

"Do you want to come with us to the clothier?" Nora asked Winnie. "You can help me pick out the fabric for my new dress."

"I'm partial to blue, myself." Hal appeared behind Winnie's shoulder and answered as though Nora had been speaking to him. "Sky blue, maybe with some lilac ribbon."

Nora pursed her lips thoughtfully, playing along. "You've an eye for frontier fashion, Hal?"

Hal bent a leg in a shallow bow, removing his hat and sweeping it outward in a graceful gesture. "Unfortunately, if an outfit doesn't require suspenders, I find myself at quite a loss." Straightening, he turned to Mama. "Mrs. Hayes, do you mind if Winnie walks with me along the fort? Or if you'd prefer, I could accompany the three of you."

Mama assessed him for a moment, face unreadable, but the sheer number of travelers, shopkeepers, and tradesmen seemed to assuage any lingering doubts she had about propriety. "All right, Hal. Be sure to meet us back here in an hour."

Hal withdrew a pocket watch from his pants, marking the time. "We will. Thank you, Mrs. Hayes."

Mama and Nora walked away, presumably to find the clothier shop that would sell fabric for dresses, trousers, and shirts.

Winnie had no need of those things, as her three dresses were all still in good repair, and last she'd checked, the sewing basket she shared with Nora was still sufficiently stocked.

She and Hal retraced their steps to start at what she imagined to be the beginning of Main Street, so they would be sure not to miss anything. The bustle of the fort was a welcome background, and her excitement about what they might see and what she might choose to purchase with the money Mama had given her was like a floating bubble of delight in her chest.

The only thing that wasn't entirely welcome was the smell. Livestock, unwashed bodies stale with sweat and sun, and manure all mixed together to form a rather potent perfume.

"I've never seen your watch before." She gestured

toward Hal's pocket. "Was it a gift?"

He pulled it from his trousers, running a thumb over its open face. The numbers were in an elegant script, the second hand stubbornly marching at its steady pace.

"I don't usually wear it. Scared something will happen to it, I guess. It was my father's."

"How old were you when he passed away?" He'd mentioned it briefly in the past, but they'd never looked it fully in the face. It wasn't exactly idle chatter.

"I was nine."

Winnie tried to imagine what that would feel like to a boy only three years older than Elijah was now, and failed miserably. "What happened to him?"

Hal placed the watch back in his pocket, tucking its golden chain out of sight. "He and my brothers worked as hands on my uncle's ranch. I wasn't allowed to go with them yet because my mother wanted me to keep up with my schooling. So, I wasn't there when it happened. He was out riding fences when something spooked his horse. He was thrown and broke his neck. My oldest brother was with him and saw the whole thing."

They passed a shop selling bridles and saddles, along with saddle soap, brushes, and expensive polish.

They were all items she thought Hal would appreciate, but he barely glanced at them.

"I'm sorry," she said finally. "That's horrible. But at least he wasn't alone."

Hal nodded, though she noticed his hand drifted once more to the pocket that cradled his watch.

"It was a long time ago."

"Will your mother come visit you in Oregon?"

"I was hoping she'd decide to make the journey with her second husband, Arthur," he admitted, rubbing at the back of his neck. "I'm sending some of my salary back to help purchase their supplies. I don't know what my brothers want. They've got families of their own to consider. But if my mother made the trip, I'd offer my house to her and Arthur. Until they got settled."

He looked at Winnie, green eyes unabashedly gauging her reaction.

"Are you asking if having your family come live with us would cause problems? If we were married?" Winnie asked incredulously.

Hal met her gaze with slightly furrowed brows. "Would it?"

Winnie couldn't shake her head fast enough. "Family should be close to one another. Of course I'd want that for you."

Hal smiled then, as if a weight had been removed from his shoulders. "Thank you, Winnie."

They passed a general store, but it was far too packed with people to tempt them inside.

Hal purchased some rifle ammunition from the gunsmith, claiming he wanted some extra for hunting once they made their way into the mountains.

"I've heard stories of huge brown bears. And deer that stand taller than a man!"

Winnie had a hard time believing that, but she was also beginning not to trust her instinct to dismiss anything she hadn't seen firsthand. Who knew what beasts and undiscovered oddities lurked in the mountains of the west?

They wandered into a tiny bookseller's store, and Hal examined the titles with her, listening as she gestured to the few she'd already read and enjoyed.

More than half of the shop was dedicated to maps

and guidebooks, and the remaining space was taken up mostly by adventure stories, books that would appeal to men reading around campfires at dusk.

Hal picked one up, examining the print and embellishments on the cover.

Winnie saw the cost of the book and winced. "Perhaps that one will have to wait until after we get to Oregon territory."

Hal nodded and placed it back on the shelf. "I suppose books are a luxury at the moment, aren't they?"

Winnie nodded, thinking of the two that were still unread in the trunk she shared with her sister. They were nearly one-third of the way to Oregon now, and she hadn't even cracked one open.

They left the bookseller empty-handed, but continued to partake of the sights and sounds of the thriving oasis that was Fort Laramie.

She knew many of the faces they passed, but the delight and excitement in their expressions brightened them into something almost new. Whole families shopped together, eager and awed by the seeming luxuries that surrounded them. The people who were not a part of their wagon train were almost like paintings— every detail examined and pondered over.

They passed livestock for sale—more of the same mules and oxen that had been touted in Independence.

The horses were outrageously expensive. Stalls held fishermen selling their catches from nearby lakes and streams. Butcher shops sold beef and pork along with wild game, already dressed for cooking. A millinery displayed an assortment of straw and felt hats, but Hal just tapped the brim of his old hat with familiarity and moved on.

As they went, Winnie took every chance to study him, to see what caught his eye and what went unnoticed. They stopped to post the letter for his mother, and it was strange to think that it would likely be months before it reached her hands. Had he mentioned her in his letter, and what might he have said if he had?

They passed woodworkers before their carving benches, and more replacement parts for wagons than one could imagine being used. Wagon wheels, axles, and tongues were stacked high. Iron rims, used to cover the wooden wheels, lay alongside buckets of sticky tar.

Hal stopped her before a storefront boasting refreshments like lemonade, coffee, and tea. "Would you care for a drink?" He gestured toward the sign.

Winnie had a particular weakness for lemonade, and the sun had grown hotter as they wandered the fort. She didn't try to hide the enthusiasm from her smile. "That'd be nice."

Although a few tables were within the store, it was clear the proprietor intended for most of the patrons to enjoy their drinks outside.

Hal returned from the counter with two glasses of lemonade.

Winnie drained hers in a few gulps, the tartness of the lemon and the sweetness of the sugar like a blast of gunpowder on her tongue. "Oh!" She sighed happily, clutching her empty glass. "I've missed lemonade!"

Hal, not to be outdone, tossed the remains of his back as well. "I've missed anything that isn't water or pitch-black coffee," he joked. "Would you like another?"

Winnie really would, but she tried to be polite. "Please, don't spend more of your hard-earned money."

Hal held up a hand, stopping her protest. "It is hard

earned. But the look on your face is well worth it."

Winnie blushed a bit.

He laughed.

"Don't worry. I promise not to stare."

He returned with another pair of glasses, and they took their time with the second batch, taking small sips.

"I have some exciting news." Winnie leaned a bit closer as the door to the shop opened and a pack of children made their way to the counter excitedly. "Nora is pregnant."

Hal raised his glass and clinked it against hers with a grin. "Congratulations, Auntie Winnie! Jeb must be thrilled."

"He is, but I think he's also quite nervous about the whole thing."

Rather than blustering about how childbirth was the burden of all wives and not anything to lose sleep over, Hal's face turned contemplative. "I can't say that I blame him. It can't be an easy thing, risking the one person you love most in the world, in order to gain another. I'd be nervous, too."

He was carefully looking anywhere but at her.

"Do you think it's worth it?" Winnie shoved aside the inner censorship that tried to scold her about manners and propriety. Childbirth was not something ladies discussed with men. "There's so much that can go wrong."

As though he sensed the worries for her sister that she hadn't dared to examine too closely, Hal reached for her free hand. "I've watched my brothers with their wives and my nephews. They became a part of something bigger than themselves. I'm not sure you can understand it fully until you experience it."

Winnie gazed at him, her lemonade forgotten.

"But I think that kind of love is worth any risk."

Winnie felt an unexpected urge to kiss him, right there in front of everyone trying to enjoy their drinks. She found herself setting her lemonade down on the counter, though a few sips remained. She kept his hand and reached toward his face with her other hand, brushing her fingers into the tawny hair that curled beneath his ears.

His green eyes locked onto her with an awareness that made her dress feel much too tight, and her lungs too small.

Winnie realized that she was leaning in, closing the space between their faces with an intense curiosity. She'd never kissed anyone on purpose. Will Thompson had grabbed her by the shoulders and kissed her on a dare when they were twelve, and it had done nothing to tempt her toward repeating the experience.

But Hal Clark was a far cry from freckled Will Thompson, who'd been sweating with nerves.

"Winnie," Hal whispered, his other hand coming to rest on the small of her back as though a rope had pulled him in and tied him there.

The pack of children who'd come in a few moments before chose that moment to push and excuse their way back to the door, and Winnie was jostled out of their path, her hand pulled down from Hal's hair.

"Sorry, miss!" The last boy called carelessly as he closed the door behind them.

Hal gripped her elbow, steadying her and keeping her from bumping into the two older women behind her, who exchanged whispers behind their glasses of tea.

At last able to take a full breath and come to her

senses, Winnie realized what they must have seen.

What had she been thinking? To nearly kiss him here, in front of neighbors and strangers alike? She'd have been scolded for her behavior by her mother, if gossip had spread around their camp.

Resisting the urge to shake her head clear, Winnie gave Hal an apologetic smile as she reached for her glass and downed the rest of her lemonade in one swallow.

His jaw worked, as though he very much wanted to say something, but instead he pulled his pocket watch out and glanced at it. His eyebrows rose. "We're due to meet your family in ten minutes," he warned. He clearly didn't want to be late after their first outing.

Hal pocketed his watch as they returned their glasses and stepped back out onto the busy street, heading back the way they'd come.

At least four wagons and their teams could pass alongside each other on this thoroughfare.

Ahead on their right, Winnie saw a swinging sign overhead that declared the establishment "The Hog Ranch." She couldn't help but gape at it as they approached. How taboo would it be to stick her head around the doorframe and take a peek inside?

"I've heard of this place," she said as they passed. "I expected they'd have more customers lined up."

A collection of chairs sat on the wooden porch, but only two men waited in them, facing each other across a checker board.

Hal looked at her with wide eyes, and the red that flamed his cheeks was all Winnie needed to see to know that he knew exactly what the Hog Ranch was. "Have you ever been to a bordello?" she asked innocently, clasping her hands behind her back. "My sister mentioned it to me."

Hal made a choking noise that he covered with a hasty cough. "She did?"

"Yes," Winnie said sweetly. "She overheard some of the cowhands talking about spending their money there."

Hal ducked his head, rubbing at the back of his neck. "Well, I wouldn't doubt that."

"Do you think Hank is in there?"

Hal laughed, his whole head tilting back. "Oh no," he declared. "Not a chance."

"Why not?"

Hal raised his brows at her. "You haven't noticed the way he looks at Mae? That man would rather sleep on the hard ground the rest of his life than for her to find out about him setting foot in a place like that and ruin his chances."

Winnie stared at him, the bordello forgotten. "Hank...fancies Mae?" She'd never seen any hint of it. They spent so much time together that they'd appeared to be good friends, and nothing more. Mae had never mentioned anything to her of intentions toward anything else. "Does Mae know?"

Hal shook his head. "I doubt it. Hank keeps his feelings close."

Winnie let that information soak in as they kept walking. They passed a physician's tent, with a line of people outside hoping to purchase liniments, tinctures, and teas for various ailments. She saw a sign advertising laudanum, and her thoughts wandered darkly to Amos McCleary.

Ironically, a saloon was next to the medicinal tent. That likely provided the doctor with a fair bit of work, just due to proximity. Bawdy singing sounded from within, and the clanging of something akin to a horribly out of pitch piano.

Much too soon, she saw Mama and Papa waiting with Elijah at their appointed spot. Winnie had been enjoying her uninterrupted time with Hal. It was nice to talk for more than a few minutes between chores, and to feel like they were actually a part of civilization again. Proof that they weren't stuck in some limbo between the east and west coasts. She'd been so enthralled, she hadn't spent a single coin.

Hal, ever the gentleman, walked them straight up to her parents, a genuine smile on his face.

"Howdy, Hal." Papa reached out to shake his hand in greeting. "Have a nice time?"

"Yes, sir, thank you."

"Would you care to join us for supper?"

Winnie could tell that Mama wasn't only asking out of politeness.

"That's kind of you, Mrs. Hayes, but I still have an inquiry to make with the blacksmith." Stepping back, he saved a last, broad smile for Winnie. "Thank you for the pleasure of your company, Miss Hayes."

Winnie gave an unladylike snort at his mock formality. "The pleasure was mine, Mr. Clark." She wanted to say more, but she was all too aware of their audience, and she saw the same truth in his expression before he turned away with a rueful twist of his lips. Until later, then.

Once Hal had walked away, Elijah tugged on Winnie's hand, demanding her attention. "Look what Papa let me get!" He held up a sack of penny candies. "Do you want one?"

Of course she did. Elijah let her pick one, instructing her to close her eyes and blindly select a flavor. When she pulled her hand out and opened her eyes, she winced. "Black licorice! Yuck."

"I'll eat it!" Elijah snatched it from her hand and popped it into his already sticky mouth.

"Don't eat it so fast, you'll make yourself sick," Mama cautioned.

But Winnie doubted her brother cared. He'd likely eat it all today, be unwell at dinner, and grumble all through the night with a stomach ache.

And she wouldn't blame him one bit.

****

At their wagon that night, she caught up on the gossip others had collected during their time inside the fort.

The wagon train that had been four days ahead of them upon reaching Fort Kearny was still here, taking what they considered to be a well-earned respite. In order to keep from bunching too closely to Big John's party, they had agreed to leave first thing in the morning, while the rest of them would wait until the next day.

That meant Winnie would have another chance to go into the fort to spend the money that Mama had given her, which was exciting. She'd been toying with the idea of getting something small for Hal, as a thank you for the lemonade, but unless something jumped out at her while browsing, she didn't have any ideas. He was the type who used everything he had, having little need for items without purpose. The pocket watch from his father was the only thing she'd seen of his that was more sentimental than functional.

He hadn't shown any interest in a new hat, and it

wasn't really appropriate for her to get him a new shirt, even if she did guess the right size. Perhaps she could look into something he could keep in his saddle. A little trinket that would mean something to him.

At last, she had an idea.

The following morning, after the other wagon train had already pulled out, Winnie set aside the cowboy doll she'd been working on. It was nearly finished, and she was stitching the hat on. After that, she only had to add the eyes and a smile. "Papa." She drew his attention from where he sat, cleaning his rifle. "Would you come with me to the teepees? I'd like to see what sort of things they have for purchase."

Nora, who was leaning against Jeb's knee on the other side of their breakfast fire, sat up a little straighter. "Do you really think that's a good idea? Surely you could spend your money on something to support our fellow frontiersmen in the fort, instead."

Winnie scoffed. "You mean the handful of men with a complete monopoly on all the resupply items for every wagon crossing the country? I think they're managing just fine."

Papa set his rifle aside, rolling his head a bit to stretch his neck. He'd been bent over the weapon for quite some time. "I don't see any harm in going to take a look."

"It could be dangerous," Nora protested. "Jeb, tell them." She nudged him in the ribs with her elbow.

Jeb glanced between his wife and his father-in-law. "I don't think there's much danger, Lenora," he said finally, clearing his throat to banish an errant squeak. "The men of the fort wouldn't allow the Natives to stay if they weren't peaceful and fair in their dealings."

Nora rolled her eyes. "Peaceful, indeed. Until they decide not to be." She clasped her hands tightly in her lap.

Winnie wanted to tell Nora that she was being closed-minded, but her own recent actions with Mae were too fresh in her mind, and she wasn't in the mood to feel like a hypocrite. Instead, she tucked the nearly finished cowboy doll into the sewing basket and brushed grass from her skirt. "Can we go now, Papa?"

He stood, reaching for his hat as he nodded. "I expect we can make it back by lunchtime."

He leaned his immaculate rifle against the wagon wheel, rather pointedly, she thought. As though making a statement to Nora about the fact he didn't feel it necessary to carry the rifle to the Natives' trading post.

Sometimes actions went further than words with her sister. Words could be hasty, ignored, or forgotten. Actions were the true root of words, even those left unspoken.

With an overly cheerful wave to Nora and Jeb, the former crossing her arms and glowering, they set off.

They walked briskly to the teepees along the edge of the fort.

She supposed they'd walked enough in the six hundred forty miles they'd traveled since leaving Independence to become efficient at it, if nothing else. Anyone who'd had any pudginess around their middle would likely boast of needing their clothes taken in before long, if they hadn't already.

When they reached the short rows of teepees, they paused, taking in the sight.

"Would you look at that," Papa said. "Imagine being able to pick up and move your house anytime you wanted. Seems pretty similar to our wagons, don't you think?"

Winnie looked up at him in surprise, but he was right. The teepees were made with buffalo skins instead of canvas, and they used straight poles to support the structure instead of wooden bows, but it was impossible to deny the similarity.

They weren't the only emigrants who had ventured to see what the Natives had brought to trade.

The Wilson brothers who played the fiddle were there, and so was the midwife's eldest daughter, Moira Simmons. She appeared deep in conversation with a Native woman about a cluster of herbs she was examining.

Winnie remembered Mae's story about her Sioux friends bringing back herbs that had healed most of the sick in their wagon party, and how her mother and sister had died after refusing to take them. She vowed, then and there, to never speak a word to Nora about witnessing Moira's apparent interest in Native herbs and medicine. She wouldn't take the chance that Nora would balk at the unfamiliarity if there was a dire need.

A handful of other Native women had laid hides out atop the grass, far enough away from their teepees to maintain privacy.

Papa followed Winnie as they walked slowly among the hides, looking at the items for sale. The women were accompanied by a handful of watchful, middle-aged men who sat together, wearing the same expressions of boredom that Winnie had seen on Papa's face during trips to the general store that ran too long. It was the look of suffering worn by men everywhere when they would rather be somewhere else.

Mercilessly, she speared deep into her feelings, assessing her reaction to the Natives' presence. She noted every breath, whether it was too fast or too shallow, and any quiver that might betray the resurgence of her fear.

She found nothing. Her breaths were light and unhindered, her pulse slow and steady. The drop in her stomach that preceded panic was hiding somewhere far away. Whether it was because Papa was with her, or because the men at the fort so greatly outnumbered these few Natives, Winnie had no idea. But she was heartened by it. It made her feel less like a hypocrite and more in control.

Winnie assumed some of Natives spoke passable English, as Moira appeared to be having no problem conversing with the woman selling the herbs. She found what she had been hoping for, and stopped to admire the assortment of blankets.

"These are beautiful," she said to the Native woman that knelt beside them. "Did you make all of these?"

The woman nodded, wrinkles deepening around a well-worn smile. Her black hair bore streaks of gray, and it pooled over her shoulders like a wave when she bent to run a hand along the blankets. Some were made of painted buffalo hide, and others appeared to be handwoven cotton. Each bore several colors and geometric patterns.

Papa stood at her shoulder as Winnie fingered the coins in her pocket, willing the blankets to be within her budget. It was the one idea she'd come up with for Hal, something both beautiful and functional, something he could appreciate as thoughtful and still deem worth packing up before riding out every morning. And with his curiosity about the Natives, something handcrafted seemed to be the perfect gift.

"How much for this one?" Winnie pointed to the blanket that most caught her eye, a zigzagging pattern dyed in beautiful reds and oranges, like a captured sunset. The fact that the dyes were likely derived from roots, berries, and leaves made the bright colors even more remarkable.

The woman gathered the blanket up and held it out to Winnie, letting her touch and examine the wool. The weaving was tight and strong. The woman held up one finger and gestured to the blanket.

"Only a dollar?" Papa echoed Winnie's own surprise.

The woman nodded. "Yes." She didn't stumble over the English word, though it lacked the melody of the few Native words that Winnie had heard.

Winnie supposed that unfamiliar languages would always sound magical to those who couldn't speak them. Just a bit forbidden and impossible to attain. Learning a new language seemed such an immense undertaking, like walking into the ocean to learn how to swim.

Winnie had two dollars in her pocket. She held them out to the Native woman, a mix of quarters and half dollars. "Your blanket is very fine."

The woman shook her head, but began picking through the coins in Winnie's hand, selecting those she needed. "One dollar," she repeated.

"But—"

"Thank you," Papa interrupted. "That's kind." He gave Winnie a look that told her not to push about the amount of money.

The woman folded the blanket up and passed it to

Winnie.

The men watched the exchange with bored faces.

Winnie realized this was likely one of a dozen daily exchanges, and tried not to take it personally.

As she followed her father back to their wagon, she mused out loud, "Why do you think she didn't take the two dollars? Who wouldn't want more money for their work?"

Papa had tucked the blanket under his arm to carry it for her, and withdrew it once more, running a hand over it. "It seems she didn't think it was worth that much. She didn't want to cheat you."

"I feel that I'm the one who cheated her. I wanted to pay her fairly."

He smiled and reached out to squeeze her shoulder. "It's good that you value fairness. What's important to remember is that your perception of what's fair might not always match another's."

Winnie sighed. "I suppose we do tend to project our own expectations onto other people, don't we?"

Papa chuckled. "If by 'we' you mean the human race, then I'd have to agree with you."

She tucked that tidbit away for future inspection. "How disappointed do you think Nora will be when we return without a single wound from an arrow?"

"Oh, I suspect she'll look quite a bit like a man who just lost his hand at cards." He chuckled good-naturedly.

As they drew even with the shops of Fort Laramie, Winnie's stomach gave a loud complaint about its emptiness. It was near lunchtime, by now. Again, she fingered the remaining money in her pocket.

Papa looked sideways at her and raised an inquisitive brow, likely having heard her stomach.

"Should we stop by the general store so you can drag back a heavy bag of sweets?"

She grinned from ear to ear. "Absolutely!"

Chapter Seven

Several days after leaving Fort Laramie behind, Winnie found an opportunity to give Hal the blanket.

He and Hank had both been busy, leading extra hunting parties alongside the trail, keeping the herd at the rear in order, and serving as outriders that scouted ahead, among other endless tasks.

At last, Hal came by the family wagon, just as Nora and Winnie were scrubbing plates and putting away the remains of supper.

"Howdy, Mrs. Hayes." He addressed Mama first, removing his hat to hang it tiredly by his leg. "I'm sorry to come by so late."

The sun had not yet set, but it was late June, and they were all getting used to closing their eyes to sleep before dusk even fully settled around them.

Winnie looked up at the sound of his voice, saw the exhaustion on his face, and rushed over, taking his arm to steer him onto Papa's vacant stool.

"Never mind the time, Hal." Concern lit Mama's steely eyes. "Let's get you something to eat. Hot food is near as good as rest, they say."

Winnie assessed him in the fading light, cataloging the drying sweat stains on his shirt, the disarray of his hair, and the fact that he hadn't yet summoned the energy to put his hat back on his head.

Nora appeared behind his shoulder with a full mug

of milk, fresh from Millie's milking only an hour before.

"Thank you." Hal said took the mug and drained it in one long gulp. He handed it back to Nora rather sheepishly. "I brought you some pheasant to cook, Mrs. Hayes." He rubbed his eyes. "But I've just realized I left them tied to Ol' Belle's saddle."

Winnie spied the horse at the front of the wagon, her lead wrapped loosely around the wagon tongue that the oxen occupied during the long, hot day.

"Can I go get them?" Elijah bounced into view ahead of Papa and Jeb, who had finished putting away the oxen's harnesses.

"Mind you don't get blood on your shirt," Mama managed to say before Elijah raced off to his task.

"I'll help you pluck them," Hal murmured to Winnie. "It's not my intention to bring you more work so late in the evening."

Winnie rolled her eyes and placed a hand on his arm. "I think Nora and I can handle a few birds, Hal. You need sleep more than we need your help."

"And the fresh meat is more than welcome," Nora chimed in. "Thank you."

Papa reached them and extended his hand for a shake. "I'm much obliged to you Hal, for helping to provide for my family."

Hal lurched up from the stool and grasped Papa's hand. "You're welcome, sir. I'm sorry it's not more. I've been given most of tomorrow to go hunting, and I'm hoping to bring a deer back."

Elijah, having retrieved the pheasants with a little bit of help from the much taller Jeb, returned with his prize. "A hunt?" He crowed excitedly. "Can I come too?"

Hal opened his mouth to reply, but Mama spoke

first. "I doubt Hal will be able to catch anything at all if he's busy looking after you."

"What if I came, too?" Winnie offered, surprising even herself. "I could keep Elijah occupied while Hal does some tracking. Maybe we could even find something else worth bringing back. Some berries, or mushrooms."

Hal looked at her in surprise, but he didn't protest her idea.

"Stay away from mushrooms," Mama warned, looking pointedly at Elijah. "Many are poisonous, and they're likely different varieties than what we're familiar with."

Winnie raised her hands in a gesture of surrender. "No mushrooms, then. Can we go?"

Mama looked to Papa, brows raised, and he pulled her over to the corner of the wagon for a brief, whispered exchange.

"I had no idea you cared about hunting," Hal murmured as they waited for her parents to finish.

"I don't, really," Winnie whispered back. "But it's an important skill to have out here, don't you agree?"

"Of course. But it could be dangerous."

Winnie laid her hand on his arm again, squeezing gently. "Don't worry, I'll protect you."

Hal chuckled. "You know, I believe that you would."

He angled his head toward her, and the setting sun bathed his skin in oranges and pinks. His green eyes crinkled up a bit at the corners, betraying the gentle smile that turned his lips up. He still hadn't put on his hat, and Winnie reached up to run a hand through his hair, deftly easing wind-tangled knots with her fingers.

"You did that at the Fort," Hal murmured, leaning a bit more into her touch and closing his eyes. "I like it. Feels like coming home to relax at the end of a long day."

Winnie's chest seemed to swell, and her pulse fluttered at the base of her throat. Rather reluctantly, she pulled her hand from his hair. "I got you something." She seized their brief pocket of solitude. "I'll be right back."

She rushed to the back of their wagon and tugged the blanket from a trunk. She pulled it out from behind her back as she approached Hal, surprised to find herself a bit nervous.

"This is for me?" He took it, turning it over in his hands, examining the colors and the fabric. His eyes were a bit wide, as though it had been a long while since he'd been given a gift.

"I wanted to get you something, but I also wanted it to be practical. You may already have one, but—"

"It's wonderful." Hal interrupted, smoothing out her anxious flood of words. "I'll treasure it. Thank you, Winnie." He shifted the blanket to beneath one elbow and held his free arm out to her in invitation.

She folded into his side, sighing as he slid his arm around her and tugged her close. She didn't care that he smelled of sweat and dust and gunpowder. She pressed her cheek against his chest, feeling his heartbeat, and smiled as it quickened.

"Thank you." He bent to place a silent kiss on the top of her head.

Jeb pointedly cleared his throat, reappearing around the side of their wagon with Nora, who looked more than a little smug.

"Winnie's been dying to give you that for days." She smiled at Hal. "Now I can finally stop listening to her worry over how she can slip it to you without being too forward."

Winnie blushed and reluctantly pulled away from Hal's side, allowing the cooling evening air to come between them.

"You can slip me anything, anytime." Hal winked at her.

Winnie blushed even more.

Elijah, having followed Jeb and Nora, plopped the pheasants down next to the dwindling fire and began pulling out feathers. When they had collected enough of them, they could use them to sew a new pillow.

"So, are you going to marry my sister?" Elijah eyed Hal. "Then you could be my brother, too, like Jeb and Hank!"

Hal laughed, not bothered in the slightest by the boy's bluntness. "That's up to your sister." Leaning closer, he mock-whispered behind his hand, "Put in a good word for me, will you?"

Elijah grinned and nodded before turning back to the feathers.

At last, Mama and Papa had come to an agreement about the proposed hunting trip. Winnie began smiling as soon as she caught sight of her mother's face, stern eyes narrowed in the way that indicated she meant business.

"You can go." Mama folded her skirt neatly and knelt beside Elijah to begin plucking her own pheasant. "But there's a condition."

"What condition?"

"You have to take Nora or Mae with you," Papa said. "It's fitting to have a chaperone."

"Mae!" Winnie and Elijah blurted in unison, as

though it had been rehearsed.

Nora folded her arms stiffly, looking miffed. "You could have at least pretended to discuss it first!"

Winnie fought to keep the smile off her face, and could tell Hal was doing the same.

"Lenora, do you actually want to get up before dawn and go traipsing through the dark forest?" Jeb reached up to rub her shoulders.

Nora raised her chin. "That's not the point."

Papa bent beside Elijah and Mama, selecting his own pheasant and getting to work. "Let's get these dressed, and then we'll go to bed. Dawn isn't in the habit of waiting."

True to his word, Hal stayed until the last bird was plucked and ready for the cook fire. They covered each with coals and set them to roast.

When they parted ways to sleep, Hal took Ol' Belle to the other side of Jeb and Nora's wagon and pitched his tent where Hank usually did.

Hank was on night watch with the herd, and Winnie caught herself looking over at the canvas of Hal's tent more than once before she managed to fall asleep, snuggled up with Elijah beneath the wooden planks of their wagon.

****

It was still dark when the call came down the line to wake the camp.

Winnie was already up and dressed in the pants and shirt she'd worn on her outriding adventure with Mae. As she finished braiding her hair back out of the way, her parents emerged from their tent.

Papa strode off to gather their oxen while Mama began removing the tent poles and neatly folding the canvas.

Nora had not yet emerged from the wagon she shared with Jeb, as she was snatching every bit of spare sleep that she could these days.

But Winnie caught glimpses of Jeb as he began his routine morning chores.

She got Elijah dressed, and then milked Millie, who stood patiently, as always. The earthy smell of the cow soothed some of her nerves, and she rested her forehead against the cow's warm flank, taking calming breaths.

It wasn't that she was afraid, exactly. Winnie trusted Hal, and she trusted Mae. But even back home, people got lost in the woods. They got injured and couldn't make their way out again. Wild animals were unpredictable, even when you knew which animals to expect, which she didn't. Not in these new lands she'd never seen before.

After departing Fort Laramie, Big John had told them they would be leaving the vast bison herds and the open grasses of the plains behind. They would be replaced with untamed forests, mountain cats, massive bears, and increasingly dangerous terrain.

Even the flora would begin to change, Big John claimed. They would soon be seeing trees, flowers, and other plants they'd never seen before, as though they were entering a new world.

It was this new world that made Winnie leery, and the thought of encountering something dangerous away from the security in numbers that the wagon train represented. She was doubly glad that Mae would be the one accompanying them, and not Nora. Her sister was a comforting presence after a crisis had occurred, but was less so in the midst of one.

Mae, on the other hand, had proven herself to be a fast thinker, with a stubborn will and brave spirit. She was the one to have by your side if you found yourself backed into a corner.

Hal wasn't anyone to scoff at, either. Leaner than Hank and sturdier than Jeb, his size wasn't incredibly intimidating, but his calm demeanor could be. Winnie had yet to see him truly frazzled. He was like a giant tree, with roots so deep, no amount of wind could unsettle him.

Winnie had finished the milking and was packing some hardtack biscuits and a canteen into a satchel when Hal came to collect her and Elijah.

He and Papa saddled Lazy Louie, and once again, Hank arrived back from his night shift in time to give Winnie his rifle.

Hank looked exhausted, even in the watery light of dawn, and she hoped he'd be able to steal even an hour of unbroken sleep from within the cramped wagon as it jostled and bounced its way along the trail.

"Good luck," he told her tiredly, helping Elijah to mount and sit in front of her. He ruffled Elijah's golden hair. "Be careful out there, little man. Listen to your sister."

Elijah made a face. "I'm the man of the house when Papa isn't around—he told me so."

"All right, man of the house." Winnie rolled her eyes as she settled the rifle across her back and took hold of the reins. "Let's get going."

Papa patted Lazy Louie on the rump. "Come back by the noon break, understand? I don't want to chance anybody losing their way in the dark."

"Yes, sir." Hal jumped onto Belle's back with ease.

The blanket Winnie had given him was tied into place behind his saddle.

"Take care of them, Hal," Mama called as the horses began walking. "And Winnifred, don't let Elijah wander off like he likes to do!"

"I'll keep a close eye on him, Mama," Winnie promised.

Elijah turned and made another face at her, and she gave him a little pinch along the ribs. "Sit still, and behave," she warned.

Mae was waiting for them when they made their way out from the circle of wagons, already mounted on her horse.

"Good morning," she greeted them warmly.

The last remaining nerves Winnie felt skipping around her stomach vanished.

She'd recounted their argument to Hal days ago, and he now rode ahead, letting Winnie fall into place alongside Mae. He discreetly gave them a chance to talk before starting their day together. Kind and considerate, he had a unique and remarkable kind of strength. Winnie found herself more in awe of it with each passing day.

"I'm glad your Pa decided to let you come," Mae said. "These forests are beautiful."

Mae fixed her eyes on the tree line that loomed perhaps half a mile in the distance. It was a shadowy specter in the dim morning light, slowly being revealed as the sun rose in the east. A daily beacon, lighting the way they had come.

Winnie summoned her courage, taking a deep breath that rose against Elijah's back. "I want to apologize for the way I acted," she said. "After we encountered those Natives. I don't...I can't allow myself to fall back into old fears. I'm sorry."

Elijah glanced back at her curiously, no doubt wondering what she was referring to. Though he was aware that the natives were a potential threat out here, Papa had taken great care to ensure it had not been blown out of proportion. The boy was too young to put much stock in the whispers of adults, while also being too old to huddle around Mama's skirt.

Unlike Winnie, who had internalized each fireside warning and let her imagination run, her brother focused on what was in front of him. How much longer did they have before that wonder of childhood began to fade away?

"I'm sorry too." Mae met Winnie's gaze. "I shouldn't expect you to have the same feelings as I do when you haven't had the experiences I've had. And I'm sorry that I snapped at you."

Winnie smiled, her grip on the reins loosening as she relaxed. "Then it's forgotten."

"Not forgotten," Mae corrected. "But learned from. It's good to keep learning new things, don't you think?"

Winnie pursed her lips thoughtfully. "I can't say I've always felt that way. Our farm wasn't exactly full of new experiences. But now that we're out here"—she gestured to the hills and impending forest—"I feel like I learn something new every day."

"Thank goodness for that." Hal pulled back on Belle to ride alongside them once more. "It'd be dreadfully boring, otherwise. Tell us some of the things you've learned on the trail, Elijah."

Elijah launched into a chaotic tale of toxic plants he'd learned not to touch, knots he'd learned to tie, and new meals he'd helped Mama to cook over the fire.

Winnie grinned at the back of his golden head, as his excitement seeped into her like the rising sun into her skin.

At last, they broke the barrier of plains and forest, crossing beneath the first of the overhanging branches. They had to move into single file, and wordlessly Hal took up the rear, leaving Mae to scout ahead, with Winnie and Elijah nestled in the middle.

Winnie had gotten used to the relative quiet of the prairie. It was a lonely place, seemingly devoid of life in some parts, even when one thought they knew where to look. The only sounds were usually human ones: conversation, turning wagon wheels that jostled the many possessions within, and the vocalizations of the livestock.

Aside from thunder, wind, and the cries of carrion birds, there hadn't been much to disturb the isolating peace of the prairie.

In comparison, this forest was blaringly alive.

Birds called to one another, as if announcing the rising of the sun and the start of a new day, full of new opportunities. The breeze made branches scrape and clack together, occasionally sending dead limbs crashing down to the dense bed of pine needles and other fallen debris. Squirrels raced up trees to avoid the horses, barking at them from the safety of their perches.

"I feel like Kit Carson!" Elijah grinned. "Hal, if you get a deer, can you help me make a fur hat?"

"Of course." Hal chuckled. "But you know, Kit Carson is more than just a mountain man. He helped make maps when he came this way. Lots of maps."

"I'd like to learn how to draw maps someday," Winnie mused.

Mae grinned. "Maps are just scraps of paper. You're living any explorers' dream, right here, right now."

Winnie looked at her across Elijah's head. "Have you drawn a map before? To show all the places you've been?"

Mae shrugged. "Sure, I have. I sketch in a journal. I try to draw each new animal I come across."

"You draw?" Winnie hoped she didn't sound rude, but she was surprised. She rarely even saw Mae sitting down, unless in a saddle.

But Mae only laughed. "Sure, I do! I guess it is kind of odd. The girl who rides like a cowhand also likes to sit by the fire and draw."

Behind Winnie, Hal's voice was thoughtful. "It's not odd. We're all much more than how others perceive us."

"Papa says we can be anyone we want." Elijah sounded pleased to be included in such a grownup conversation. "He says that's why we're all going to Oregon."

Winnie smiled wistfully. "You can grow up to be just like Kit Carson, if you want to."

Her brother twisted around in the saddle, nodding enthusiastically. "I do! Starting with my fur hat."

"I'll do my best to get you one," Hal promised.

Their conversation dwindled as they pressed farther into the forest, which grew shaded and dimmed as the canopy thickened. They were going uphill, though the grade wasn't too steep and seemed completely manageable for the horses.

Winnie glimpsed strands of spiderwebs glinting between the trees, sparkling with morning dew. The yellow, unblinking eyes of an owl peeked out from within a hollow tree.

Mae pulled her horse up, stopping abruptly.

Crashing sounded to the side of them, and Winnie glimpsed the haunches and raised tails of deer as they bounded away, breaking through branches and brambles.

"We should continue on foot." Mae turned to Hal. "We're making too much noise."

He agreed, and they picketed their three horses together, tying their lead ropes around a fallen pine tree that skirted a small clearing.

"I'll try to circle around that herd we startled." He crouched and checked the supply of ammunition and gunpowder he wore in a leather pouch. "If I don't run into them, we'll keep going."

"If we hear shots, I'll ride ahead to give you a hand," Mae said. "You might need help lifting it. Pa and I have seen bucks with a spread of antlers near as big as a man."

Hal's eyes widened, and he nodded. "Fair enough." He looked to Winnie, and then to Elijah, who was already busily hunting for sticks to begin assembling a miniature cabin. "Stay close to the horses. Keep your rifle with you. If you get separated from Mae and you need help, fire two shots into the air."

Winnie mustered a smile, despite the nerves that stirred in her stomach. She was committed now, and there was no way she was leaving. Not with her friend and her future husband already ensconced in these wild woods.

As she looked into Hal's eyes that were nearly sparkling with excitement and purpose, she finally gave in to the reality of what her heart had known since Fort Laramie. Hal Clark would be her husband. She was certain of that, now.

Her husband. What a strange notion. And yet, somehow no longer strange at all.

"We'll be careful," Winnie told him. "And you be careful, too."

Mae pointedly joined Elijah, combing the floor of the clearing for suitable sticks. She led Elijah a bit farther away, and when both their backs were turned, she muffled a forced cough into her hand.

It was hardly a subtle signal, and yet Winnie found herself grinning. Her parents had allowed her to select a far more lenient chaperone than Nora would have been.

Hal took advantage of their brief seconds of privacy, reaching a hand out to tug gently on the end of her dark braid. "I like you in pants." He leaned closer and brushed a kiss to her forehead. "But you're beautiful no matter what you wear."

Winnie blushed, and reached for him almost involuntarily, but he was already moving away.

He glanced back with a wink that conveyed how much he wished they had more time and more solitude.

Winnie's pounding heart was evidence of just how little she cared about propriety in that moment. She was lucky Hal had a strong grip on his manners.

She would've followed him into the trees in an instant, if he had only asked, leaving Mae and Elijah to amuse themselves while she discovered just where those soft, pliant lips of his would come to rest next.

But· he continued moving away, his stride lengthening, and the placement of his boots deliberate and silent.

The hunt had begun.

Winnie forced herself to blow out a long breath, trying to focus her thoughts away from Hal and toward deer stew and sausage. Her stomach was easily riled these days, and was growling within moments. She should've eaten a bigger breakfast, but nerves had made that seem foolhardy.

She went to Lazy Louie and pulled her satchel from his saddle bags, retrieving the hardtack she'd packed. It was hardly palatable, its insides coarse and brittle. She often softened them with milk, but she hadn't packed any this morning.

The less-than-savory snack redoubled her hopes of finding wild edibles. After checking the rifle at her back and looping the strap of the canteen around her neck, Winnie approached Mae and Elijah.

"Shall we go for a berry hunt? We could make some jam to go with our biscuits." The thought made her mouth water and her stomach grumble, as though offended by the hardtack that now resided there.

Elijah looked up from his stick cabin, which was already well assembled, lacking only a roof and supporting beams.

Her brother was quite the builder. Of course, being the only surviving son of the family, he'd been helping Papa with woodworking and such since he was big enough to know the sharp side of a saw. He had a knack with tools, and a clever mind.

Briefly, Winnie wondered what their other brother, Ezra, would've been like now. If he'd survived past infancy, he'd have been near ten this summer. ·

Ezra'd only lived for twelve days, but Winnie could still feel the strange pull and awe that she experienced, tracing his tiny toes and fingers. He'd been so small. So precious. So vulnerable.

When he sickened and died, Winnie and Nora had

cried for days, huddled together beneath their quilt at night. Papa had wept, resting his head in his hands atop the kitchen table. But they never heard Mama cry for Ezra. Not once.

"Heartless," Nora had whispered cruelly, in the dark hours of the night. "Mama is heartless."

But Winnie knew better. Their mother grieved so deeply that shedding tears would've served no purpose, brought no relief. The pain was too embedded. It would never rise to the surface. It would never be visible to others.

That was just Mama's way.

Now, looking at Elijah, Winnie was so grateful to have him. She pulled on the ends of his golden hair, growing long and brushing the worn collar of his shirt. "What do you say, man of the house? Can we finish your cabin later?"

Elijah stood, brushing dirt and bark off his pants. "Sure. Mama will be happy if we bring her some berries!"

"Stay close." Mae stood as well. "There could be large animals around."

"What else is there besides deer? Are there bears?" He sounded far more hopeful than nervous as they began walking away from the clearing.

"There are," Mae confirmed. "Smaller black bears and even bigger brown ones. The golden mountain cats are so quiet that you don't know they're there until you hear the scream of the animal they pounce on."

"Great," Winnie muttered. "And I was just beginning to feel relaxed."

Elijah was enthralled. "What else?"

"There are deer that stand taller than a man, with

huge antlers. We've also seen antelope, running faster than any buffalo. And wolves that hunt together in packs, chasing down their supper."

"Wow," Elijah breathed. "I really am just like Kit Carson! I want to see all those animals!"

Winnie rolled her eyes. "Don't get your hopes up, little brother. Let's focus on berries first, all right?"

Mae handed Elijah a bag she'd been wearing over her back, sewn from deer hide. "You can put anything you find in here. Whatever you don't eat, I mean."

Elijah took it eagerly, and they began to comb the surrounding area for anything Mae knew to be edible.

"We want a dark-purple berry," she instructed. "Almost black."

They went at a slow-but-steady pace, keeping the horses at their backs and the sun to the east. It couldn't have been more than eight in the morning.

"What about these?" Elijah called excitedly, pulling on the branches of a bush full of clusters of bright red berries. Their flesh was smooth and shiny, almost waxen.

Mae bent closer to examine them, and then pulled away abruptly. "Not those. Those are poisonous."

"How do you know?" he demanded, likely sore about his first find not being one he would get credit for.

"I was there when someone who ate them died," Mae said curtly.

Elijah rapidly let go of the plant, his pout vanishing.

"Let's keep looking." Winnie prodded him onward. "I'm sure we'll find something."

They lifted leaves, peeked under logs, and peered around massive trees. They found plenty of mushrooms, but Winnie heeded her mother's warning, and didn't let Elijah touch them. Some of the trees were cloaked in vines with massive thorns. They pricked her finger when she reached out to touch one.

"Those would build a tough fence," Elijah said. "Nobody would try and steal Millie if she was behind all those thorns!"

"I wish I'd had one of those fences awhile back," Mae said. "Elijah, did I ever tell you about the time some Shoshone boys stole Pa's best horse?"

He shook his head no, and they followed her through the woods as she recounted the story. Winnie was sure Mae made some embellishments, as it was unlikely any horse could run faster than a bullet, but her brother listened so intently that she just went along with it. A tall tale never hurt anyone, after all.

Winnie was wiping sweat from her brow when they finally came upon bushes loaded down with dark-purple berries. Some were missing, and others had already fallen to the ground and smashed. Most of the bushes grew up to her chest height, though some were smaller.

"You can tell other animals have been eating these." Mae sounded like a school teacher as she pointed. "That's one of the ways you can tell they're safe to eat. But if you're not sure, you can rub it against your skin, and wait to see if it feels strange." She demonstrated, plucking a berry and rubbing it against her forearm, staining the skin purple. "If it tingles or burns, best not to eat it."

"Where'd you learn that?" Elijah asked.

"A Sioux friend of mine."

"Is he in Oregon?" The boy pressed. "Could I meet him?"

Mae swallowed, dropping the crushed berry to the forest floor. "Sorry, but no. He's dead."

Winnie wondered whether it was Chatan or Tatanka Pteccila that Mae referred to. She wanted to ask, but was conscious of Elijah's young ears, and didn't want him to ask more prying questions.

"Let's get to picking!" she said instead, a tad overly cheerful.

She and Mae took turns handing Elijah berries until all their hands were stained purple. He ate nearly as many as he managed to get in the bag, but Winne was eating her fair share as well, so she didn't reprimand him. They were delicious, sweet and tart, and most importantly, fresh. The dried fruit they'd bought in Independence couldn't even begin to compare.

Suddenly, the loud crack of a rifle broke through the air. It didn't sound too far away, angled northwest of them. It seemed Hal had not had to stalk the deer for long before finding them.

Winnie waited for a breathless moment to make sure there wasn't a second shot, which would have indicated trouble. When none came, she unclenched her stained hands and turn back to the berries.

"I'm going to ride ahead and help him," Mae said. "Will you be all right here for a little while?"

Winnie assessed the forest around them, and the number of berries still left on the bushes they'd found. "Go ahead. We'll meet you back by the horses."

Mae nodded, clutching the butt of her rifle to keep it from swinging against her back as she jogged toward the clearing where the horses were tethered.

Once her friend was out of sight, Winnie began to feel less comfortable. But she reasoned with herself, not wanting to leave so many berries unpicked over something as silly as nerves. She had nothing to fear here, she told herself sternly. Hal and Mae were only moments away if she needed help.

This wasn't anything she couldn't handle. The only animals they'd encountered who seemed to even notice their strange presence were squirrels. At that moment, two small brown birds perched above them, just waiting for them to wander off so they could get at the berries themselves. Winnie resolved to leave plenty for them.

They weren't the only ones trying to stay alive.

Eventually, Elijah grew weary of picking berries, and his stomach too full to eat any more. He took to gripping the branches and shaking them, dislodging a cascade of berries down to the ground where he could gather them more easily.

"Must you do that?" Winnie scolded. "You're getting them dirty, and we may not have water to wash them with." They didn't always get to make camp along a stream, and sometimes the river was too far down an embankment to reach safely. When that happened, they had to rely on the water barrel packed in the wagon.

"I'm tired." The excitement in Elijah's voice had deteriorated into a whine.

"Let's finish with this bush and then we'll go back to the horses," Winnie conceded. She certainly didn't want him to be whining the whole way back.

They resumed picking, and with the end in sight, Elijah stopped complaining.

A nearby grunt made Winnie jerk her head up.

"Did you hear that?" She glanced her brother.

His wide eyes and open mouth told her that he definitely had. Winnie's heart sped up, its pleasant background pumping bellowing to the center of her awareness.

"It could be nothing," she murmured. But still, she waited, straining her ears. She wished Mae hadn't so vividly described the creatures that roamed here.

A huff reached her ears, closer than the grunt from before. Like a mighty exhale. Branches shifted as something moved through them.

Winnie gripped Elijah's arm. "Let's go," she mouthed. She started backing up, keeping her eyes locked on the bushes in front of them.

"But I want to see what it is!" Elijah raised his voice as she tried to yank him closer. "Let me see!"

He wrestled out of her grip, and the full bag of berries nearly spilled to the ground.

Winnie caught it, tossing the strap over her head the way Mae had done.

"Elijah!" She hissed. "Come back!"

Her brother pushed aside branches, eager to get a look at what was on the other side.

Winnie raced for him, just as a startled yelp burst from only a few feet away.

"Look!" He grinned. "I think it's a baby."

Sure enough, a dark brown muzzle and close-set, round eyes poked out of the bush nearest him.

Elijah reached out, intent on stroking its fur.

"Don't!" Winnie finally reached him and snatched his hand back. "Don't touch it!"

He turned to glare at her. "You can't tell me what to do. I'm the man of the house when Papa is gone, remember?"

Winnie ground her teeth together as she strove for patience.

The bear cub pushed the rest of the way through the bushes, its gangly limbs propelling it to the nearest patch of unharvested berries, where it began cheerfully stripping whole branches of fruit with its teeth.

"Do you think Mae has ever drawn a baby bear?" He tried to get closer. "I bet I can!"

"Elijah," Winnie warned. "Get back here. Or I swear, I'll tell Mama how you behaved."

He looked at her sullenly, already close enough to the cub to reach out and touch it. "Go ahead." He reached out and grabbed a handful of the bear's dark fur.

A shriek of surprise left the bear, and it darted around Elijah and into the bushes, knocking him over as it went. It kept calling, the tone rising in pitch. The sound sent the birds that had been waiting for berries careening through the air, anxious to get away.

Winnie stomped over to her brother, ready to throw him over her shoulder, when she heard a deep, menacing growl.

"Oh." She gasped, adding a curse word she'd heard Hank use once.

The musky scent of the bear hit her before she saw it. Like its last meal hadn't ever fully been washed off its thick fur. Panicked, she scrambled for Elijah, pulling him to his feet.

The adult bear charged through the bushes without warning, her massive paws striking powerful blows to the ground as she barreled toward them.

Even as she panted with fear, Winnie marveled at the sight of it, of how details could be frozen so adeptly into the mind.

The mother was massive, the talons of her feet long and wickedly curved. The dark brown fur of her face and chest stuck up in wet tufts, likely from pushing through the damp vegetation.

Her brown eyes fixed upon them, and there was nothing in them but instinct. To protect? To challenge?

Winnie didn't have time to guess.

She gave way to instinct as well, acting on pure adrenaline. Shoving her brother behind her legs, she swung the rifle around, grateful Hank had told her to always keep it loaded.

The bear charged, and Winnie closed one eye, forcing a breath out in a whoosh to steady her aim. She clumsily clutched for the trigger.

The resounding bang exploded through the forest, and blood spurted from the bear's front shoulder. Enraged, it slammed into Winnie, knocking her clean off her feet, right over Elijah's head.

Elijah scrambled backward, scuttling on his hands, shrieking.

"Winnie!" He screamed.

The bear raised a massive paw, then both, standing up to her full, astonishing height. She roared, her open mouth exposing a row of teeth sharp as knives.

Winnie, now sprawled on her back, tried to force air back into her lungs. The heels of her boots scraped uselessly against the forest floor. At last, she got a full breath and rolled over, reaching for the gun that had been flung out of her grip.

She didn't have enough time to reload. Not even close.

The bear's front paws slammed back down to earth, nearly crushing Elijah, who had turned over and was scrambling on hands and knees to get away.

The sound he made when the bear sliced her claws down his leg nearly stopped Winnie's heart. Resolutely, she surged to her feet, gripped the barrel of the rifle, and swung the butt of it with all her might into the bear's face.

It snorted and whined, pawing at its muzzle with momentary confusion.

At last, Elijah got his feet under him. Blood streamed down his left leg, and it dragged as he stumbled toward her. His wails seemed muted, somehow dim compared to the violent breathing of the animal before them.

Winnie doubted the blow to the bear's face had done much damage, but she wasn't going to let her brother die without a fight. She would fight with her own teeth and nails, if she had to.

Recovered from the shock of the blow, the bear charged her, knocking her over once more.

She rolled, trying to get out from under it, but was trapped between the bear's feet. It bellowed again, and the sound seemed to rattle the insides of her skull. She clapped her hands over her ears.

The weight of a paw pressed into her back, and she began to kick, thrashing her legs. The rifle was out of reach, and next to useless without a bullet in it, anyway.

The weight of the bear drove its claws into her back, and Winnie felt her skin split. "Run!" She screamed to Elijah. "Run!"

Far better for her to die than him. Better that Mama and Papa not lose another son.

The hot breath of the bear blew against the back of her head, and she had a startling moment of clarity. The bear hadn't attacked them until the cub had cried out. What if the mother had just been protecting her baby?

Just as Winnie was trying to protect Elijah.

As the bear huffed around her head, she stopped

kicking. Though her body went limp, her thoughts had never flown so fast. Was she hallucinating? She wished she'd had more time with Hal. And with Mae. She wished she could be there to hold Nora's hand when she had her baby.

She wished, she wished, she wished.

Then there was a gunshot.

And another.

The bear roared, and the painful pressure on Winnie's back vanished. She had enough awareness to scramble forward, fingers clawing through the leaves and other debris along the forest floor. She could barely see through the hair across her eyes.

The bear's roar turned into a terrible whimper, and then a guttering sigh.

The ground beneath Winnie shook as the bear slumped to the ground, crashing heavily on its side. It did not move again.

Someone called her name, over and over, but it swam disjointedly around her as though she was submerged in water. She shook her head, illogically trying to clear her ears. Some of the hair shifted away, freeing her vision.

Hal's frantic eyes came into focus, green pools in a face as stark and pale as a desert. "Winnie!"

She mumbled his name, then seemed to choke on the very air she breathed, and flopped over. She immediately arched off the ground, desperate to relieve the pressure it placed atop the slices on her back.

Hal's hand gripped her behind the neck, steadying her. "It's all right," he insisted, though it plainly wasn't. "It's all right."

"Elijah?" Winnie reached back to clutch at Hal's

shirt. It was damp with sweat, slick against her palm. Or was that blood? She couldn't tell.

"He's okay," Hal soothed. "Mae has him."

Winnie leaned over and was abruptly sick. Berries and terror were sour in her mouth. When she was done, she spit a few times, trying to clear the bitterness.

Hal clung to her free hand, a reminder that he was with her. He pulled her hair back from her face. "I'm going to carry you," he murmured into her ear. "I'll be as gentle as I can."

And though he was gentle, he was also swift. He swept his hands beneath her knees and neck, hoisting her up against his chest.

The contact made her back burn, but it wasn't as bad as it could have been. She was lucky to be alive. She was lucky Elijah was alive.

But the bear. Winnie craned her neck to see.

The corpse of the bear lay in the berry patch. Its fur shifted slightly in the breeze, but no breath rose beneath her flanks. The mother was dead.

Winnie heard keening from the bushes.

"The cub." She tried to point. "It'll be all alone." In that moment, the thought seemed to crush her chest. "It'll die, too."

Hal pulled her closer, as close as he dared without hurting her further. "I'm sorry. There's nothing to be done."

Winnie let her head sag back against his chest. And at last, with the keening of the cub so stark and innocent in her ears, she began to cry.

Chapter Eight

The ride back to the wagons was a surreal blur. Every jolt set Winnie's back aflame, as though she'd been lashed with a whip of fire. She rode in front of Hal, who kept one arm around her waist to hold her steady. His other arm urged Belle as fast as she could go.

The horse was heavily burdened, carrying the pair of them. She struggled with the extra weight.

Mae rode ahead with Elijah.

Hal had told her not to wait.

They weren't much lighter, with the gutted carcass of the deer Hal had killed slung behind the saddle. But Elijah's left leg was still bleeding.

Winnie saw traces of it along the tall grass that had brushed him as they darted past.

Mae had bound it with strips from the bottom of her shirt, but the fabric could only absorb so much.

As they rode, and Mae and Elijah galloped ahead of them, Hal talked to her. He told her about the deer he'd killed, how it had looked right at him before he'd convinced himself to pull the trigger.

He told her how he and Mae had been nearly back to the clearing, with the deer slung over Mae's horse, when they'd heard Elijah's scream.

His voice hitched when he told her that the bear had been enormous, and he'd been certain Winnie was dead, lying motionless between its massive legs, which were

144

thick as tree trunks.

She didn't reply, just gripped the hand and forearm that encircled her waist.

Arriving back at camp was just as tumultuous. The noon break had just begun, so everyone was at leisure, getting something to eat or taking a rest. Heads turned and voices exclaimed as they pelted by on horseback, wasting no time with pleasantries.

"Doc Collins!" Mae shouted, searching for his wagon. "Doc Collins?"

"Here!" The doctor ran into view, waving his arms above his head. "What happened?"

Mae dismounted first, cradling a dizzy looking Elijah in her arms. His eyes rolled, trying to focus.

Winnie felt the bite of true fear. That he could die when they'd gone to such lengths to save him was an unbearable thought.

"It was a bear." Mae rushed Elijah toward Doc Collins's wagon. There was a collective gasp among those who had gathered at the commotion.

"Someone get Mr. and Mrs. Hayes," Hal instructed. "Tell them to come."

Mr. McCleary took off running for her parent's wagon. The man who had lost his own son in the night, lost him to pain and misery, was the one who moved the fastest.

Winnie's heart ached at the thought. But her concentration ebbed when Hal handed her down to an onlooker so he could dismount. The pain in her back was intense. She could feel the blood on her shirt. That sparked a moment of irrational anger. It was her only shirt!

A moment later she found herself sitting in the shade

alongside Doc Collins's wagon, bent over with her head between her knees as Mrs. Collins sponged gently at her exposed back with a wad of wet cloth.

Hal knelt in front of her and held her hand, but kept his eyes averted.

Her front was still covered, but her back was bare from the waist up, the shirt pulled nearly over her head. It was a lot of skin for a woman to show, intentional or not.

Mae, having been relieved of Elijah by Doc Collins, stood guard next to them and waved away anyone who got too close.

Winnie could hear Elijah crying from within the wagon, and the soothing tone of Doc, trying to keep him still long enough to examine his leg.

Mama arrived first, breathless and sweating.

Hal moved aside for her, and she dropped to her knees at Winnie's feet, her hands fluttering from her daughter's bare shoulders to her hands and back again. "What happened?"

Her dark eyes were as wild as Winnie had ever seen them.

"They startled a bear," Hal said. "Winnie saved Elijah's life."

Papa arrived then, skidding to a stop in time to hear the last part of Hal's statement. Sparing a second to assess Winnie, and finding her under competent care, he lurched for the back of Doc's wagon, and was then out of sight.

"Of course she did," Mama breathed. "My brave girl." She clutched Winnie's cheeks.

Winnie weakly lifted a hand to grip her mother's wrists. "I'm all right, Mama," she croaked. "Just a few scratches."

Mama barked a laugh and rested her forehead against Winnie's. "A few scratches, indeed!" She seemed to come to her senses then, and realized that Mae and Hal were still beside them. "Which of you killed the bear?"

"Hal got there first." Mae answered without hesitation. "I fired a second shot, but his aim was true."

Mama reached a hand out to Hal, who clasped it in his own. There was blood on his skin. "Bless you," she said. "We won't forget what you've done for our family."

Hal tried to smile, but his lips trembled. "I-I'm sorry I didn't get there sooner." His face crumpled. "This is my fault." He swayed on his feet, as though he would fall over himself.

"Sit down, young man," Mrs. Collins ordered. "We have enough patients to care for as it is!"

Hal sank down, folded his knees, and pressed his forehead against them. "I'm so sorry, Winnie," he repeated, his voice muffled.

"I'm going to check on your brother." Mama tactfully disentangled herself and pulled away. "I'll be back."

Winnie could hardly believe that her mother had left her with the man she was courting, and with her shirt nearly pulled over her head! Even with Mrs. Collins still tending to her back, laying strips of linen over the wounds, Winnie was stunned. But Hal was her concern now. "Look at me," she told him.

He tried to protest.

"I'm perfectly presentable," she insisted. "Look at me."

At last, he obliged, and the distress on his face made Winnie take a deep breath to steady herself.

Though her back was exposed, his eyes never left hers.

"This isn't your fault." She adopted the soothing, gentle tone she had heard him use time and again with spooked horses. "I wanted to come. Elijah wanted to come. It isn't your fault." She reached a hand out to him, and he threaded his fingers through her own. "We're going to be fine…thanks to you."

Hal shook his head.

She could tell he was about to argue, but she cut him off. "You saved my brother's life. And mine. If you hadn't already had my heart, you'd certainly have it now." She watched with out-of-place amusement and tenderness as her words sank in, and registered in his expression.

He straightened, clutching their joined hands to his chest, pulling himself the barest bit closer. "I have your heart?" He repeated it softly.

And though her back blazed, and she could still hear her brother crying as they stitched the gash in his leg, Winnie smiled. "You definitely do."

Mrs. Collins broke the awed silence that swelled between them, no doubt rolling her eyes behind Winnie's back. "Young folks these days," she muttered. "Simply no sense in them."

****

Less than an hour later, seeing her well cared for, Hal left camp with a group of men on horseback.

Each led a pack mule. They would return in a few hours, likely right at dusk, needing every minute of daylight to skin and butcher the beast he had felled in the forest.

Winnie lay on her belly atop a blanket beside their cook fire and watched them go, her gut churning with guilt.

Leaving the bear untouched was wasteful. More than ever, they needed to ensure everyone in their party had enough food. Some families had lost dried goods to rot or mold, or due to poor stitching and busted linen. The bear was already dead. Butchering her was the smart thing to do, and it would help to keep them all fed.

But she was immeasurably glad she didn't have to be there to see it. And she doubted whether she'd be able to keep down a single bite, if it was offered to her.

"I'll keep an eye out for the cub," Hal had reassured her, as the men prepared to leave. "Mae said that another bear might take it in and raise it as her own, if it seems likely to survive."

Winnie had just nodded, well-aware that the damage had already been done, and no amount of lamenting over the outcome would change things. She didn't have it in her to blame Elijah, who slept deeply beside her, thanks to Doc.

She laid her hand atop her brother's back, and had never been more grateful for the rise and fall of his breathing.

****

More than a week passed before Winnie could lie on her back without hissing from the pain.

But she was better off than Elijah, who had been ordered to stay off of his leg by Doc Collins, lest he bust his many stitches open and ruin what Doc considered "his best sewing work by far."

Her brother had to ride in the wagon, jostled and

annoyed by everything that banged and clanked around him, or ride astride one of the oxen as Papa walked beside them. Neither was what he deemed to be fun or exciting.

Despite what had happened to his leg, Elijah was happy to recount their exploits to any and all who cared to listen.

At least once a day, a pack of his friends would sprawl around him, either at noon break or at suppertime, and beg him to tell them the story again.

"There I was," he would begin, "Ready to fight that bear with my own hands, just like Kit Carson would have done…"

By now Winnie simply winced and tuned him out. She wished others would do the same. Their encounter with the bear had been the talk of the wagon train this entire week. While her brother loved the attention, she shied away from it, happy to make any excuse to escape when people came near with the gleam of gossip in their eye.

Nora had seized upon every excuse to dote upon Elijah, and often walked alongside the wagon to patiently listen to his stories and badly constructed jokes. She had started laying a hand atop her slowly swelling stomach at times, almost absentmindedly, as though reassuring herself that the life she bore was really there.

Winnie found herself watching her sister, curiosity growing. If marriage always led to babies, and she felt she was ready to marry Hal…did that mean she was also ready to have children?

She didn't know.

She tried to push it from her mind, but it wasn't a thought so easily banished, with her sister practically glowing, and Jeb acting as though the sun rose and set with his pretty, pregnant wife.

July arrived, and the days grew long and hot as they wound their way through what Big John called the Black Hills. The heat was becoming harder for the livestock to bear, and it was no longer uncommon for oxen to drop without warning, causing delays until they could be dragged to the side of the trail. They lost more time butchering the animals, unwilling to waste the meat and leave it to spoil in the hot sun.

Winnie hated that the animals making their journey possible, pulling so much weight, day after day, were dying in such a way. It broke her heart. It wasn't fair, and there wasn't a single thing they could do about it.

"We need to lighten their load," Big John announced one day, after the sixth oxen that week dropped from sheer exhaustion. "At this rate, they won't make it across the mountains."

During noon break, he advised everyone to go through their possessions, and remove what was not absolutely essential.

Jeb and Hank hauled all the trunks and furniture out of Nora's wagon, while Nora daintily sorted through their belongings and tried to decide what needed to be kept.

Papa and Hal did the same with the family wagon.

Though Winnie tried to help, she couldn't lift much weight without feeling the slowly healing slashes in her back strain and sting.

As soon as the trunks were out, Mama set to opening things, ruthlessly tossing into a pile whatever couldn't be kept.

Winnie's grandmother's porcelain china was laid

out, and Mama selected a single set to keep, which consisted of a dinner plate, a saucer, and a tea cup. The rest would be left behind. Elijah's toy wagon was to be left behind, as well.

When Elijah put up a fuss, Papa promised to build him a new one when they reached Oregon.

To cheer him, Hal returned moments later and gifted Elijah with the fur hat he'd been promised, skillfully crafted from the hide of the deer Hal had killed.

The sewing was quite a bit better than Winnie would have expected. She'd had no idea Hal had such a deft hand with a needle and thread.

"Who do you think mends my clothes and blankets," he teased. "Ol' Belle?"

But even Hal's attempt to lighten the somber mood didn't last long. So many of their belongings were being left behind. So many memories. Things that had been carefully wrapped and packed nearly a thousand miles away. And now they were about to be left here, to the July sun and the wind blowing through the hills.

Winnie saw Mama carefully fold up a collection of Ezra's baby clothes, which she'd saved in a drawer for the past decade. She placed all but one of them inside the hutch Winnie's grandfather had made.

"Are you all right, Mama?" Winnie reached out to touch her arm.

Mama turned, clutching the remaining set of baby clothes to her chest, and hastily wiped at one eye. "It's hard to leave your brother's things," she admitted. "I feel as though I'm leaving him, too."

Papa overheard and strode over, gently taking the baby clothes from Mama's grip. "You've given up enough." He turned and placed the tiny bundle of fabric into a trunk that had already been sorted through and returned to the wagon.

Some things, however useless, were simply too precious to be left behind.

The end of the noon break was a relief. Decisions that had been agonized over had to be hastily concluded as the wagons began to pull out.

Winnie set both of her books, still unopened, atop her grandfather's hutch. She wondered if anyone who came along behind them might have the time to read them, as they deserved.

Nora was noticeably upset as the wagons pulled out, and Winnie drifted over, wrapping an arm around her sister's waist to help steer her forward. "They're just things, Nora," she soothed as they began walking. "They can be replaced."

Nora glanced back at the pile of belongings she'd given up, tears snaking down her cheeks. Many of the wedding gifts she and Jeb had been given, including a beautiful ceramic washbasin, embroidered towels, and cookware, were being left behind.

Winnie even glimpsed Nora's wedding dress nestled among them. Trailing sleeves of lace blew forlornly in the wind.

"Who will we be, when we get to Oregon?" her sister whispered, "When we've given up so much?"

"We'll be alive. And we'll be together."

Nora sighed, resting a hand on her stomach. "Yes," she agreed at last. "We'll be together."

Somehow, they all kept walking.

Winnie glanced back once, and the assortment of goods left along the sides of the trail looked astonishingly like an open-air general store. No one had left any food behind, as every last bit would be sorely needed, but anything else one could think of had been left to lighten the load.

There were piles of clothes, spare wagon parts, various items of furniture, and farm tools. There were bundles of wire, rope, and jars of nails. There were dishes, Dutch ovens, rocking chairs, and even a crib.

She wondered if the crib had belonged to Mrs. Blake, who was due to deliver her fifth child any day. Where would the babe sleep? She supposed it wasn't her business, and she doubted it would be restful for a newborn to sleep in a jolting wagon, even within a lovingly made crib.

Nora gave Winnie's hand a squeeze, and then resolutely quickened her pace so she could walk alongside Jeb.

He held an arm out to her when she reached him, and leaned down to kiss her cheek.

Winnie walked on alone, for some reason unwilling to follow. She didn't want to intrude on the picturesque vision that Nora and Jeb presented, walking hand in hand beside their team of oxen as dust swirled around their feet.

Her sister had moved on, and settled into this new role she'd accepted as a wife. She was soon to be a mother.

They were no longer children, lying beneath the same quilt at night whispering to one another. It had happened without Winnie even realizing it, and without giving her the proper time to mourn its passing.

Nora would always be her sister, but she'd made her choice months ago, when she'd accepted Jeb's offer of marriage. Nora had moved on.

It was time for Winnie to do the same.

Chapter Nine

The screaming started the next day.

The midwife, Widow Simmons, and her daughter, Moira, raced to the Blakes's wagon without delay.

Big John stopped the wagon train at once, and word spread quickly among the gathered families.

It seemed Mrs. Blake's baby had finally decided to make an appearance.

Hal and Hank were sent to ride ahead to scout for an appropriate camping spot. There was no water here, only a few hours into their morning, and they couldn't stay for long.

But Big John, having been present for the birth of his two daughters, didn't want Mrs. Blake to suffer doubly just to save time.

They would stop here, and they would wait.

As the hours ground on, Winnie tried to keep herself busy by playing with Elijah. She'd at last finished the cowboy doll she'd begun for him nearly three months ago, and he kept launching the doll into pretend rivers, pits of quicksand, and packs of bears, crying for Winnie to "save him!"

But the game was growing old, and Mrs. Blake's wails had not abated.

How could any woman howl for so long without going hoarse? But Winnie remembered her conversation with Mama and Nora by the river alongside Fort Kearny, and how Mama had reminisced that she thought she'd die from the pain of childbirth.

Winnie figured that if Mrs. Blake was enduring that, the least she could do was not complain about how badly the noise raked at her raw nerves.

Big John, Mae, and a cluster of men set themselves up at the wagon farthest away from the Blakes's, which happened to belong to Winnie's family. They were organizing a hunting party between some of the men, deciding who could be spared and who would stay behind.

So, when Hal and Hank returned to report what they'd found to Big John, faces grim, Winnie was right there to listen. She almost wished she hadn't been.

"The water's bad ahead." Hal jumped nimbly down from Belle's back. "The wagon party ahead of us left a warning. And there's bodies of oxen and mules everywhere."

Big John cussed, removing his hat to smack it against his pant leg. He realized quickly that Mama and Winnie were present, and cringed. "Sorry for the language, ma'am," he directed toward Mama.

Mama simply waved her hand in dismissal. "I think we're long past formalities, John."

"I suppose we are," he conceded. "But now we're in a damn hard position. Uh, begging your pardon, ma'am."

A particularly loud cry from Mrs. Blake rent the air, as though to affirm his words.

"What should we do, Pa?" Mae looked remarkably composed. "Should I ride farther ahead?"

Big John shook his head of wavy black hair, shining greasily in the sun. "I don't want to send riders any farther ahead of us. They'd be too exposed."

"Then what are we going to do?" Papa sounded almost as calm as Mae.

Winnie, on the other hand, was feeling anything but calm.

As though he sensed it with the bounty of empathy he possessed, Hal came to her side and discreetly reached for her hand.

Winnie clasped it, and hid the evidence in the folds of her skirt. Hal's fingers were close enough to brush her thigh.

The gathered neighbors waited, watching Big John as his face twisted.

He didn't like what he was about to say. Not one bit.

"We have to get moving. If the water is bad ahead, we need to press on now, while we still have full water barrels from the last crossing."

"What about Mrs. Blake?" Mama crossed her arms.

The men, most of them fathers and husbands, seemed not to know where to look. Quite a few of them cleared their throats and suddenly found their dusty boots immensely interesting.

"Pa, you can't ask her to—" Mae began.

It was the first time Winnie had ever heard Mae disagree with something her father had said.

Big John shook his head, shoulders slumping. "I know good and well what I'll be asking of that poor woman. But we can't stay here. We can't put the rest of us in danger of running out of water just to try and keep her comfortable."

Winnie's gaze found Jeb, who had moved to stand beside Hank. His thin face was pale as snow.

Nora had joined the other expectant mothers outside the Blake's wagon hours ago, intending to comfort the laboring mother any way they could.

Winnie thought rather morbidly that perhaps they should not be watching such a gruesome spectacle, when they would be experiencing it themselves soon enough.

No matter the reason, she was glad Nora wasn't there to hear the distressing news Hal and Hank had brought. As the neighbors disbanded and went back to their own wagons, preparing to move on, she kept a tight hold on Hal's hand. "Stay with me?" She knew he had to be exhausted from riding ahead. He likely hadn't even had breakfast, much less lunch.

But he only smiled and pulled her into his side, careful of her sore back. "Of course."

****

A couple of hours after the noon break, they began passing the dead livestock that littered the sides of the trail. None had been butchered since the wagon train ahead of them couldn't risk eating contaminated meat.

"Lord, protect us," Papa murmured as they continued walking. "Protect my family from such a fate."

Winnie tried not to look at the bloated carcasses, buzzing with clouds of flies, but there were so many.

Dozens had sickened and died. The bad water the poor animals had drank gurgled nearby, taunting them.

Dusk seemed to fall abruptly, perhaps because the wagons continued moving long past the time they would normally have stopped. When it was too dark to even see where Winnie was putting her feet, Mae appeared on horseback, bearing a flickering lantern that burned precious oil. "Pa says we can stop. We'll head out again at first light."

Exhausted, anxious, and thirsty, Winnie helped Elijah down from the wagon and carried him to where

Hal and Hank were clumsily erecting their tents. Once he was settled, she filled a bowl of water from their water barrel, which looked far too small now that they had no idea how long it would have to last them. Still, she snuck the bowl of water to Millie, and the cow slurped it up eagerly.

It wasn't enough, but it was all Winnie could do.

The animals were all thirsty and restless. Big John had to station men along the creek to keep them away from the bad water. The oxen grunted and moaned pitifully, not understanding that quenching their uncomfortable thirst would lead them to a painful death.

When she crawled into their tent and sat beside Elijah, he was already asleep. Nora had been changing the bandages on his leg, but Winnie did it this time, uncertain when their sister would be back. Once finished, she curled around her brother's sleeping form. Sleep found her so suddenly, she didn't even have time to marvel over the novelty that Hal slept mere feet from her, separated only by canvas.

The call to rise came early, as usual. They sat in a circle and ate a cold breakfast, bleary eyed and tense. Though they'd been desperate for sleep, poor Mrs. Blake had gotten none, and her cries had echoed across the camp all night long.

Nora had not returned, presumably having spent the night helping Widow Simmons administer to the laboring mother.

Winnie had the unkind thought that someone should just reach in and pull the babe out, if only to stop all the noise. She knew that was the broken sleep taking over her better sense, and tried to be compassionate. If it were Nora going through such pain, she'd wallop anyone who even hinted at such an idea. Mrs. Blake deserved the same care and consideration Winnie would want for her own sister.

When the bugle call came and got the wagons moving again, it seemed everyone walked a bit slower than usual. The marks of fatigue were easy to spot among the livestock and the people who trudged beside them. It would be a long, hot day without water.

And then, a mere hour into their morning trek, the Blakes's wagon went silent.

Winnie strained her ears for the cry of an infant, or for the joyful exclamations of the women who'd been tending Mrs. Blake. But there was nothing.

The hush that fell was more awful than all the agonized cries that had come before.

Slowly, Papa removed his hat and bowed his head. Hal and Jeb followed suit. Hank was already with Mae, scouting ahead for clean water.

Winnie waited a moment longer, unwilling to believe two innocent lives had just slipped away in such a simple silence.

But when Papa stopped the oxen and beckoned her, Mama, and Elijah over to pray, Winnie could doubt the outcome no longer.

"Lord, we ask that you cradle Mrs. Blake and her sweet babe in your merciful arms. Give them peace and rest, and send your angels to comfort the remaining members of the Blake family. Amen."

Mama visibly swallowed, composing herself, before echoing the end of the prayer: "Amen."

Winnie found herself unable to speak at all. It simply wasn't fair. Mrs. Blake had four other children. Why would God would allow such a thing to happen?

What kind of God would let Mrs. Blake suffer in agony for hours, only to steal her and her child away?

For the first time, Winnie felt a bitterness rise up within her, a terrible heat that was like anger but wielded the sharp edge of sorrow instead of the blunt brutality of rage.

It wasn't fair.

Nora appeared a few moments later, head bowed with exhaustion and sadness. She carried her bonnet in one hand, and seemed not to notice it was speckled with dark blood. She walked right past Winnie, who had run forward a few steps to meet her. "Not now, Winnie," she mumbled, raising a hand as though to shield herself. "Just…not now."

She climbed into the back of her wagon, not even acknowledging Jeb, who stood at the front, keeping the oxen still.

She did not emerge again.

****

Mrs. Blake and her stillborn son were laid to rest along the side of the trail. Mr. Blake had not been able to choose a spot. He was barely coherent, clutching his youngest girl to his chest and crying into her fair hair.

It was their oldest, a girl about Elijah's age, who picked the spot where her mother and brother would be buried.

The little hill was covered with bright yellow flowers, their brown centers teeming with bumblebees.

Once the grave had been dug, everyone sang a hymn—the same that they had sung at Amos McCleary's grave. This time, the Wilson brothers played a lovely accompaniment on their fiddles.

The harmony made Winnie's chest hurt. As though

the music was a tangible thing, like the breath in her lungs or the wind in her face.

The exposed dirt had barely begun to dry and lighten in color before the wagons began moving again.

Hal walked beside Winnie, holding her hand, but they didn't speak. It felt wrong to break the silence that had fallen over them all. As though their silence meant anything to the two bodies in the ground. As though their silence could change the outcome.

Chapter Ten

They traveled more than forty miles without fresh water. They took it slow, doing their best not to tire the animals out too quickly. They didn't wash. They didn't make stew or anything else that required water. They ate deer jerky and hunks of oxen meat, and washed it down with milk.

But Millie would not be producing milk much longer if they didn't find water soon.

Every bead of sweat Winnie wiped from her forehead sparked indignation. Must it be so hot, on top of everything else? Her lower back was wet beneath her petticoats, and the sweat in her stockings chafed her feet.

She had tried going to Nora and Jeb's wagon the night before, only to be gently shooed away by Jeb, who claimed her sister had finally fallen asleep. Winnie couldn't blame his protectiveness, especially considering what had just happened.

He was likely now imagining the same thing happening to his own wife, when the time came to deliver their child.

A similar fear had been plaguing Winnie's mind, and so she could only imagine how it must weigh on Nora, who had actually witnessed Mrs. Blake lose the fight for her life, and the life of her child. All the same, she wished she had been able to talk to her sister. To offer some semblance of comfort, as Nora was always able to do.

When Mae and Hank appeared on the third day, Winnie thought she might have been hallucinating. She'd been taking care to drink as little as possible, to conserve their water, and wasn't even replenishing the fluid she lost, much less adding any more.

Their grins were wide, though their faces were red and chapped.

"We found water!" Hank's joyful news danced on the wind ahead of them. "Good water!"

Cheers went up among their neighbors.

Mae rode on to finish spreading the word as Hank pulled up his horse and strode eagerly toward their wagon.

"It's the Sweetwater River," he told Papa excitedly. "We'll be there by nightfall."

Papa closed his eyes and tipped his head up, his relief palpable. "Thank you, Lord. We're halfway there."

"Halfway?" Winnie turned in surprise. "To Oregon?"

Papa nodded and gripped her shoulder. "If the Sweetwater is up ahead, then Independence Rock is, as well!"

Winnie recognized the name of that landmark.

Big John had been talking about it ever since they'd passed Chimney Rock and Scott's bluff. He claimed if they reached the rock by early July, they'd be on track to cross the mountains before the winter snows arrived.

Winnie smiled for the first time in days.

They camped along the Sweetwater that night. They filled their depleted water barrels, and happily washed their faces and hands.

The animals waded across the sandy bottom and

drank as much as they wanted of the warm, shallow water.

Independence Rock was just a humped figure looming across the north side the river. But they would spare some time to explore it tomorrow.

Big John said people had taken to carving their names in the granite, or painting on it with tar.

As they settled down for bed, Elijah complained his leg had been hurting.

Winnie had seen him running around several times that day, and scolded him.

"If you'd do just what Doc said, your leg would heal faster."

He pouted. "I want to play with my friends! Sitting is boring."

Winnie unwrapped the bandage, and he winced a little. It was hard to see much in the fading light, but the skin around the stitches felt hot and a little swollen. As Doc had warned, Winnie could feel at least one place where the wound gaped open because a stitch had broken loose.

She left the bandages off that night, hoping the swelling would be gone in the morning. They went to sleep listening to the quiet murmurs of Mama and Papa, silhouettes sitting close together in flickering firelight.

****

When Winnie woke the next morning, the side that Elijah had been pressed against was damp. She carefully unwound him from his blanket, setting it aside so he could cool down. How she longed for autumn! But she set that longing aside, knowing autumn on the trail was short, and could bring early snows. She remembered the Donner party, trapped and starving for a whole winter, and shuddered, despite the already warm morning.

Mama was still asleep, which was unusual. She and Papa must have been up late into the night. Winnie stepped over her carefully so as not to wake her, and eased out of their tent.

Papa and Hal were sitting by the cook fire, deep in conversation.

Bacon and hotcakes fried in their iron skillet, making her stomach growl.

She stood, stretching her back, and caught sight of Independence Rock in the early light. A mere shadow the night before, it now gleamed under the sun, rising above the Sweetwater like a giant turtle shell.

People walked toward it to get a closer look.

"Good morning," she said cheerfully to Hal and Papa. "The bacon smells good!"

Hal smiled. "Eat up! Your pa said we could go climb Independence Rock."

Winnie smoothed her skirt to sit down beside Hal. That must have been what they were talking about. It seemed perfectly respectable, and it looked like more than half the camp was rushing through breakfast, eager to go explore.

Winnie helped herself to some hotcakes. "Elijah busted some of his stitches yesterday," she told Papa. "We need to keep a closer eye on him."

Papa shook his head. "That boy. Asking him to sit still is like asking a mule not to be stubborn."

"Taking him to carve his name on the rock might get some of his wiggles out," Winnie suggested. "He can ride Lazy Louie."

Papa swiped a slice of bacon out of the skillet and blew on it, wincing as the heat nipped at his fingers.

"That's a fine idea. I think I'll do just that."

Hal sat patiently as Winnie finished breakfast, speaking even less than was usual. She wondered what was on his mind.

Something clearly was; he kept drumming his fingers against his pant leg, and he bore a look of almost pained concentration.

Something was bothering him.

But Winnie had no idea what it could be. She resolved to get to the bottom of it as soon as possible.

"All finished." She brushed crumbs from her lap as she stood. "Will we see you at the rock, Papa?"

He nodded, smiling a little impishly. "Soon as your mother decides to bless us all with her open eyelids." He gestured to the tent where she and Elijah still slept. "I sure won't be the one to wake her."

They stood, and Papa shook Hal's hand, leaning in a bit to whisper something into the other man's ear.

Winnie's eyes narrowed with suspicion.

Finished, Papa clapped Hal on the shoulder and leaned back. "Good luck."

Winnie hoped they wouldn't be relying on luck for a simple sightseeing venture. But she shrugged it off, reaching for Hal's hand as they turned and strode through the camp toward Independence Rock.

Doc Collins and his wife sat on a blanket outside their wagon, cradling mugs of coffee. Mrs. Collins stirred as they approached, setting her cup aside. "Winnifred! Let me take a look at your back, dear."

Winnie glanced at Hal, who once again seemed deep in thought.

It took him a moment to register that she was looking at him, waiting to see if he minded. "Of course."

He gestured toward Doc's wagon.

Winnie stepped around to the far side of their wagon, shielded from view by the canvas, and Mrs. Collins deftly undid the buttons along the back of her blue dress.

There was a moment of silence as she examined Winnie's back, which had scabbed over.

"Healing nicely," Mrs. Collins began buttoning Winnie's dress back up. "There will be some scarring, I'm afraid."

Once her buttons were fastened, Winnie turned around. "I don't mind."

After all, what were a few scars compared to her brother's life? She'd have scarred her whole body, and even her mind, for that exchange. She'd have given her life, to keep Elijah here with them, where he belonged.

Mrs. Collins smiled as they walked back around the side of the wagon, where Hal was making polite conversation with Doc. "The women in this camp have got more grit than the menfolk even know to give them credit for." She patted Winnie's shoulder. "You're no exception, my dear."

Winnie smiled, a little caught off guard by the praise. "Thank you, ma'am."

Mrs. Collins waved her off, settling beside Doc once more. "You two have fun, now!"

Hal gave Winnie his arm, and at last they made it past all their neighbors and out onto the sun-browned grass along the Sweetwater.

The herd was turned loose, roaming wherever they wished to graze and wade in the river.

It was a rare break for them, and one they needed. They had not rolled their last dying oxen to the side of the trail. Not by a long shot.

Once they were out of earshot of their neighbors, Winnie pounced. "All right, out with it. What's bothering you?"

Hal peered at her out of the corner of his eye. "What do you mean?"

Winnie tugged her arm free and flicked the brim of his hat, ever present, atop his head. "You're thinking loud enough to drown out a waterfall."

He fixed his hat and took hold of her arm again, pulling her to his body so their hips brushed as they walked. "Must you notice everything, all the time? Isn't it exhausting?" he teased.

His green eyes crinkled at the corners, and the set of his mouth was unbearably tempting, but she didn't allow herself to be distracted. "If something is bothering you, I want to help," she insisted. "Can I help?"

Hal shook his head and chuckled, though Winnie hadn't meant to be funny in the slightest. "As a matter of fact, you can. But you'll have to wait a few more minutes."

She frowned. "Why do I have to wait?"

Hal tugged on her arm, increasing their speed. They passed a few people, and the rock loomed ahead, growing taller as they approached.

"Be patient," Hal encouraged. "Good things come to those who wait, after all."

Winnie huffed. "Old age comes to those who wait."

But Hal just laughed and kept up their brisk pace. Though he'd just asked Winnie to be patient, a distinct sense of impatience radiated off him. But he seemed less tense, as though leaning further toward excitement than apprehension.

They reached the base of the rock and stopped to take it in.

She reached out to touch the granite, already able to see signatures and dates carved into it. The one nearest to her hand read: "Hanna Snow, 1844."

Who had Hanna been? Had she lived to see the fertile valleys and forests of Oregon?

Hand on the rock that was rapidly warming under the sun, Winnie felt a kinship with the faceless woman. No matter who she had been, what she had feared and endured, they had both started in the same place. They had walked the same path. Literally.

Four years had passed since Hanna Snow had carved those words. Had someone helped her to make them? Had she done it herself? Would it be strange if Winnie asked around when they got to Oregon, to see if anyone knew her?

Or perhaps this signature in the stone was all that remained. This speck of evidence, which would eventually be washed away by rain and sun. As though it had never been. Just like Mrs. Blake and her tiny baby. Like Amos McCleary, and Tom Roberts, and the girl who'd been bitten by a rattlesnake in their first week.

Winnie didn't even remember her name.

"What's the matter?" Hal stepped closer, not missing the crease in her brow or the sudden, invisible weight upon her shoulders.

"Sometimes"—Winnie began, trying to make sense of what she was feeling, and how to put it into words— "it feels like everything around us is so…temporary."

Hal watched her face, head tilted toward her. Waiting.

"Will it even matter? Everything we've gone

through to get here. Will anyone care? Will anyone remember?" She placed her hand over Hanna's name, as though she could absorb the faceless woman's essence through the stone.

After a long moment, Hal put his hand atop her own. "Even if no one else remembers," he said carefully. "We will."

"Is that enough?" Winnie whispered.

Hal laced his fingers through her own, offering what comfort he could. "I don't know."

Another somber moment passed before Winnie resolutely tugged Hal away from Hanna's name. There was nothing she could do about the past; it was fixed and could never be altered. But there were aspects of the present that were wholly within her control. And she intended to enjoy them.

They found a climbing route that wasn't too steep and began.

Hal went first, and she tried to place her feet where he did. It wasn't terribly difficult. The granite was textured, easy to grip, and they could keep their balance fairly easily just by leaning far enough forward.

Winnie wasn't even out of breath when they reached the top. She'd done far too much walking and too many chores for a little climb to bother her, even with the elevation they'd gained in recent weeks. She'd probably never been so fit, and so physically adapted to her surroundings. Even on the farm, they'd had a snug little house to return to at the end of the day. It had been easier, simpler.

But she was beginning to understand that hardship was the Lord's best method of forging. Steel was only hardened by fire.

Hal pushed his hat higher atop his forehead, letting out a low whistle. "Look at that view."

The yellowed grass of summer spread out in all directions, interrupted only by the curve of the Sweetwater River and the low Granite Mountains in the distance. The view wasn't classically beautiful, rather, it highlighted how arid and desert-like the final push before reaching the Rocky Mountains had become.

The forest encounter with the bear only two weeks ago seemed like it'd happened in another world, compared to the barren one that lay before them, as though its dense foliage and lush greenery had been a dream.

What the view lacked in beauty, it definitely made up for in size. They had likely climbed up less than 150 feet, and yet the world was changed. For once they were above the trail, rather than upon it.

This must be how a bird saw the world, and it was breathtaking. From this point, she could see the ends of the trail in both directions, vanishing into distant horizons. There was a tangible feeling of actually making progress.

For that alone, Winnie would have loved the view.

Hal cleared his throat behind her.

She turned, and saw he had removed his hat. He spun the brim between his fingers, a bit nervously, she thought. Was he afraid of heights? She didn't think the rock was tall enough to have such an effect, but maybe his perception was different than her own.

"I've been trying to figure out exactly what I want to say, but honestly, nothing I've come up with has seemed good enough." He seemed to realize he was fidgeting, and brought his hat to rest against his chest.

Winnie remembered seeing him and Papa in deep discussion before breakfast, and how lost in thought he had seemed afterward. A suspicion began to form, and she grinned. "You're doing fine so far," she encouraged. "Keep going."

Hal ran his free hand through his tawny hair and then reached into his pocket. Perhaps to touch his father's pocket watch. "When I saw you under that bear, I was more scared than I've ever been." His eyes turned somber, staring down the barrel at a memory that clearly haunted him. "I realized exactly how important you'd become to me. And since then, I've been hit with this sense of…urgency."

Winnie stepped closer. "I know what you mean."

He swallowed, composing himself. "I don't want to wait until we get to Oregon for you to be my wife. I want to experience the rest of this journey with you by my side, in every way possible." He began to bend one knee, sinking down toward the granite. "Winnie, will you—"

She really had intended to let him finish. She soaked up every word he laid upon her like a gentle rain to a drought-stricken tree. But tenderness swelled in her heart, and like a river bursting through a dam, her elation got the best of her.

She flung herself at Hal before he could finish his question, gripping him tight with giddy excitement.

Stunned, it only took him an instant to drop his hat, and then his arms were wrapped around her, even as they rocked backward from the impact of her embrace. "Well, that was easy." He gasped beneath her grip.

Winnie laughed so hard, she thought she might cry.

The neighbors nearest them had seen and heard enough to infer a new engagement had just occurred.

Cheers and applause rang out, spreading across Independence Rock and cresting like a wave toward the wagons below.

But Winnie wasn't listening. She was far too focused on the thundering of Hal's heart beneath his shirt. The feel of his hands, calloused and scratched, lifting her chin up. And then, the impossible softness of his lips pressing against hers, ever so gently.

She gasped against his mouth, not a reprimand, but a wordless supplication.

If only she had known, that night in Ash Hollow when Hal had officially asked to court her, that the affection she'd already held for him would turn into this bright, burning thing. She had been so afraid of what he was going to ask her, so afraid of exchanging her freedom for something she didn't really understand.

Now, as his lips pressed again against hers, and her hands landed in his hair, there was exhilaration, wonder, and delight. There was not a flicker of fear.

It seemed her mind had been made up before she'd ever consciously made a decision. There would be no going back from this. She was forever altered.

Together, they would chart a new course.

At last, the whoops and hollers of their neighbors reached Winnie's ears, and she became aware that she was sprawled half across Hal's lap, and they'd been ignorant of their audience for far too long.

Blushing, she scrambled backward.

Hal's expression was a bit slack, as though he struggled to reorient himself. "Wow!" He stood and extended a hand to help her to her feet. "I guess that means you find me...what was the word you used? Tolerable?"

It seemed she wasn't the only one thinking about that night in Ash Hollow. "I suppose that's what it means," Winnie chuckled as he pulled her up.

They made their way back down the rock, enduring jokes, pecks on their cheeks, and slaps on the back, the latter mostly to him.

"It's about time," Big John called, whistling through his teeth as they passed.

Papa waited for them at the bottom, a grin stretching his cheeks.

"You knew," Winnie accused, though she was far from angry.

He just opened his arms to her, laughing as she folded herself within, as she had done since before she could remember. "Of course I knew! My soon-to-be son-in-law has excellent manners."

Papa loosened his grip enough to extend his hand to Hal. "Welcome to the family. Though to be honest, you've been a part of it in my mind for some time now."

Hal took Papa's hand with a genuine smile. "Thank you, Mr. Hayes. I'm honored."

Papa waved a dismissive hand. "Enough of that 'Mr.' nonsense. You're about to marry my daughter. Call me Charles."

"Yes, sir." Hal winced. "Charles. I'll work on that."

Papa just chuckled and began to walk with them back to their wagon.

"Where's Mama? Still sleeping?" That seemed unlikely. There was enough commotion in camp to wake even the most oblivious sleeper.

"Elijah wasn't feeling well, so your mama stayed with him," Papa said.

Winnie's chest abruptly tightened. "Not feeling

well? Should we get Doc Collins?"

Papa shook his head. "Oh, it's not as bad as all that. Your mama will fix him up some camphor in his water, and he'll be up and about in no time."

Winnie had to admit they'd all been sick more times than she could count, and aside from baby Ezra, they'd all recovered. It was entirely possible Elijah had a common ailment, and not something deadly, like the names that roared up from the submerged depths of her fears—cholera, influenza, and dysentery.

She still sent up a swift prayer. Just in case.

The three of them were within sight of the family wagon when they crossed paths with Jeb and Nora, headed out to carve their names into Independence Rock.

Jeb gave Hal a timid smile. "How'd it go?"

He and Nora had known about the intended proposal as well. Had everyone in camp known, except for her? Winnie ground her teeth.

Just then, a rider caught their attention, a plume of dust elongating behind him. Winnie thought it was Hank at first glance, but as he got closer, she realized it was a stranger.

He reined his horse in among the first wagons, but his pleading voice could be heard all the way at the rear.

"For the love of God, is there a doctor among you?"

The effect on their neighbors was immediate. Even Nora shrank back behind Jeb's shoulder, as though the man's presence portended doom. Her hand dropped to her stomach and stayed there.

"There is!" One of the Wilson brothers stepped forward to hold the man's horse. The second brother took off running for Doc Collins. "How far out are your people?"

The stranger slid off his mount, which hung its head as soon as its two-legged burden stood on solid ground. He'd been riding hard. Something was wrong.

"About three hours ride," he said. "We camped here night before last. Didn't make it far before we had to stop. Too many are sick."

Winnie's mind flew to the previous night and this morning. To anything they could have been exposed to that would lead to something serious. They'd drunk the water since yesterday evening, and all of them were fine. If the water was bad, some of them would have been groaning behind the bushes by now. They hadn't foraged for any wild edibles, so there was little chance they could have been poisoned.

Doc Collins appeared among the rapidly forming crowd, pushing his way through behind the Wilson brother who'd fetched him. "I'm a doctor." He panted, hoisting his medical bag as proof.

The stranger tilted his face up briefly to the sky, as though sending a prayer of thanks. But he quickly got down to business. "Doc, we need you real bad. Can you come with me?"

To his credit, Doc Collins didn't hesitate. "Of course. I just need to hitch my oxen, and then my wife and son and I can follow you in our wagon."

The stranger looked like he wanted to argue, thinking perhaps the wagon would be too slow, but Doc stood his ground, anticipating the cause of hesitation before the stranger could even open his mouth to protest. "My family goes where I go," he said firmly. "I won't leave them behind."

The stranger sighed. "Very well. But hurry!"

Men among the crowd rushed to help Doc hitch the

oxen to his wagon, while the women helped Mrs. Collins pick up the cooking things and bedding that had been laid out for washing. Mere moments later, they had begun to follow the stranger and his horse in the direction of his camp.

"Tell Big John to wait here until I send word," Doc called. "We don't want to ride through a camp full of sickness! I need to see what it is first."

"We'll tell him," someone from the crowd replied.

"Be careful!" another called.

Winnie glimpsed Mae in her peripheral vision, sprinting from the back of the crowd toward Independence Rock, where her father presumably remained.

Mae had been napping after a night watch, and hadn't even yet had time to tie back her hair. Her long black locks streamed behind her as she ran, nimbly dodging loose rocks and cacti.

Dimly, Winnie realized Hal had taken her hand, and she looked down at their joined fingers once before watching the Collins's wagon rattle into the distance. Her stomach felt like it was full of rocks. She assessed her breathing and her pulse. Both seemed normal. She rested her free hand along her forehead. Also normal. How long would it remain so? Were they all on the doorstep of some terrible sickness? And then, a frightening thought hit her, as surely as a punch to the gut.

Elijah.

She let go of Hal, picked up her skirt, and ran.

"Winnie!" Papa called behind her. "Wait!"

She didn't stop. She heard what she assumed was Hal following her, but she didn't look back to check. She careened through the assembled tents and wagons, letting out a grateful gasp when their own appeared.

She ducked through the tent flaps as Hal skidded to a stop behind her, but he didn't follow her into the tent. She wondered if he had somehow correctly guessed where her thoughts had flown to.

She collapsed within the tent, panting, and startled her mother.

"What on earth?"

Winnie scrambled to untie her sunbonnet, feeling as though it was choking her. She scuttled to where Elijah lay, and took in his appearance. His face was a tad bit pale, but the light within the canvas was poor to start with. His lashes were golden arcs beneath his closed eyes.

She reached out a trembling hand to smooth tussled hair back from his forehead. His skin was noticeably warm, but not blazing hot, as she had feared.

Big, earthy-brown eyes popped open. "What are you staring at?" Elijah complained.

Winnie sat back on her heels and braced her hands upon her knees. She forced herself to take a deep breath, the first she'd had since Doc had ridden away. "Sorry," she told him. "I thought…never mind. Go back to sleep."

He rolled his eyes and turned onto his side, grumbling about loony sisters.

"What was that about?" Mama's steely eyes narrowed. "You gave me a fright!"

Conscious of the young ears behind her, Winnie motioned for Mama to follow her outside. When they emerged, Papa, Nora, Jeb, and Hal were all waiting for them.

The rest of the camp was visibly astir, as those

who'd been in the crowd to watch Doc Collins leave described the event to those who had been away exploring.

Seeing the family assembled, Mama braced her hands on her hips. Not even Hal was spared from her exasperated gaze. "Out with it!"

Brave as ever, Papa answered first. "Doc Collins just left. There's sickness in the wagon train ahead of us. One of their men came to fetch him."

Mama's tense frame relaxed a bit. "Is that all? It's not ideal, to be sure, but Doc will be back. There's nothing to fret about."

"Papa said Elijah was sick, and I was worried," Winnie admitted. Even now, her body still coursed with adrenaline, though the source of her fear was clearly not as serious as she had thought. "With Doc gone…"

Mama's gray eyes, so frequently akin to storm clouds, softened. Winnie had lost one brother. She was plainly terrified to lose another. Mama had no problem understanding such fears. She still harbored her own.

"It's just a bit of fever." She reached out to rub Winnie's arm. "He'll be fine." The tumult sufficiently explained, her gaze settled upon Hal. "Any other news?"

Hal opened his mouth to reply, but for once, Jeb beat everyone else to the punch. "Winnie's getting hitched!" he announced happily.

Mama smiled, even as Elijah said plainly from within the tent, "Finally, I'll have more brothers than sisters. All sisters do is fuss and nag."

Everyone laughed, even Winnie and Nora. How could they not? It was true.

Chapter Eleven

The rest of the day passed, and no word came from Doc.

No one really expected it would, but Winnie slept poorly that night, and it wasn't due to excitement about her engagement.

She was excited, of course. But she was also worried.

Others plainly were, too. There was no dancing or music to celebrate her and Hal's engagement, as there likely would have been otherwise.

Few things scared people as badly as disease. It was something that couldn't be prepared for, or avoided, and could all too easily grow beyond control. Even back home, it crept under doors, slipped between houses, and raced along well-traveled roads.

Disease was indiscriminate. It took young and old and middle-aged alike, without any care for those it left behind.

The second day dragged on, long and hot and frustrating.

Big John had ordered riders to be positioned nearly an hour's ride ahead of them, the better to carry news back to their wagon train.

Hal and Hank had taken the first shift, leaving just after breakfast.

Elijah was still asleep, tossing and turning, when

Nora and Winnie stole away to the river to do some of their washing. They had plenty of company, as idleness in times of stress often led to more worrying than was helpful.

Women and girls from nearly every family assembled in small groups along the riverbank, hauling their washtubs, handmade soap, and washboards.

Thunder rumbled threateningly in the distance, but there were few clouds overhead to reinforce it. Big John had said they likely wouldn't see rain until after they reached South Pass, which was a week's travel away. Rain fell rarely here, due to the proximity of the mountains, he claimed.

As Nora scrubbed their clothes and tried to rid them of the ever-present dust, Winnie lugged the bucket to and from the river, bringing fresh water to rinse with. Four months along now in her pregnancy, Nora said she was feeling fine, but Winnie knew heavy loads tired her sister quickly. So, she fetched the water without complaint, eager for something to occupy her hands and her mind.

"When do you think Doc will come back?" Nora asked for the third time.

Winnie tried to be patient, though her sister kept bringing up the very thing she was laboring to forget. "I'm sure he'll come as soon as he can."

"What if he doesn't?" Nora insisted. "How long do you think Big John will make us wait here?"

Ah. There it was. What she suspected was the real reason behind all the worry. She appraised her sister's stomach. It was evident Nora was with child, but she was far from huge. Unless the baby came very early, the child would be born in Oregon.

Nora likely knew that already, and yet she was still

afraid. Watching Mrs. Blake die in childbirth had affected her more than Winnie had realized.

"Widow Simmons knows as much about birthing babies as Doc does." Winnie breathed heavily as she held the heavy bucket up to pour clean water onto one of Papa's shirts. "Probably more, even."

"You're right." Nora scrubbed one of her own dresses. "I don't know why it's scaring me so."

Winnie wondered whether broaching the sensitive subject was a good idea, but decided if it helped Nora, it would be worth it in the end. "What was it like, for Mrs. Blake? It sounded...well...you know how it sounded."

Nora stopped scrubbing and looked at her, face uncharacteristically blank. "Why do you want to know?"

Winnie nudged her sister out of the way with her hip and took over the scrubbing, gesturing for Nora to sit. "I don't," she said honestly. "But I think you need to talk about it. So, I'm ready to listen."

Nora stared at her for a long moment, absently wiping her hands on her apron. At last, she sat, leaning back against one of the washtubs. "I don't want to talk about it. I just want to forget."

"You're not going to forget," Winnie said. "I wish you could, but you won't. You watched a woman die doing something that you're going to have to go through yourself, and it scared you. Of course it did! How could it not?"

"Winnie." Nora sighed and dropped her head into her hands. "I don't want to do this. Can't we just finish the washing?"

"No." Winnie dumped a soggy dress into the washtub. She marched around to where Nora sat, and knelt before her, forcing her sister to meet her eyes. "Tell me."

"I don't want to."

"It doesn't matter, this is what you need. You just can't see it clearly."

"Stop it, please."

Nora sounded so tired, and so forlorn, that Winnie nearly did stop. But then she thought about what it would feel like for her sister to continue to carry this fear with her, growing heavier with each step. If she didn't let some of it out, it would become too much to bear. And that, Winnie could not allow.

"Did she die before the babe, or after? What were her last words?" Winnie pressed. Her heart thundered beneath her ribs, like a warning about what she was prying to the surface. She forced herself to wait for a reply.

It was long in coming, but it did come. So quiet, at first, she strained to hear.

"The babe was turned the wrong way," Nora began. "Widow Simmons knew it. They tried to turn him, but he wouldn't budge. So stubborn." She smiled a mirthless smile, her lips pale. "Mrs. Blake bore down over and over, screaming like the Devil himself was ripping her insides apart."

Her eyes drilled into Winnie's, watching for any flinch, or sign of weakness. Any hint that she was less willing to listen than she claimed to be.

Winnie clenched her fists, and did not falter. "Go on."

"There was so much blood, Moira stopped trying to clean it up. Mrs. Blake bit through her own lip, and barely seemed to notice. Finally, Widow Simmons reached in to try and at least save the babe…"

Her brown-eyed gaze left Winnie's at last, drifting over her sister's shoulder to gaze at the river. "She knew she was going to die. She didn't live long enough to know that her child was dying with her."

Winnie leaned forward, pressed her forehead to Nora's, and laced her hands around the back of her sister's neck. "I'm so sorry," she whispered. She took a deep, calming breath, but the scent of lavender and line-dried cotton that Nora used to bear was long gone. The trail had buried it beneath layers of dust and sweat.

"I don't want to die like that," Nora finally whispered.

"You're not going to die," Winnie breathed. "We love you too much. Just as your baby is going to love you."

A spark returned to Nora's eyes, and she latched onto Winnie's hands, her grip strong enough to hurt. "If I die, you must take my child. Promise me!"

Winnie tried to pull back, but Nora held firm. She had forced these raging fears to the surface, and now she would have to help bear the weight of the consequences. "I promise." She let her sister hold on as tightly as she needed to. "I promise," she repeated.

The manic light left Nora's eyes, and she sagged back. "Thank you." She sighed.

Winnie moved to sit at her sister's side, and tugged Nora's head gently down to her shoulder. A few moments passed, and they watched the water, listening to the sounds of distant conversation floating along the riverbank.

Slowly, Nora's arm wound around Winnie's waist. A silent extension of forgiveness and thanks. Winnie bit her lip. The weight of tears gathered along her lower lashes.

"I'm sorry," Nora murmured, after what seemed like an hour had passed, but was likely less than a quarter of that. "We should be gossiping about Hal, and how he proposed, and how handsome you think he is. Not about death. I've had enough of death."

"Me, too." But she was fairly certain, as they were only halfway to Oregon territory, that death had not had nearly enough of them.

"I'm glad you're my sister." Nora leaned forward to kiss Winnie's cheek.

She smiled at that, realizing that for once, she had been the one to comfort Nora. For once, she'd said and done the right thing, at the right time. But she knew better than to get used to it.

****

When they returned from the washing at suppertime, Elijah had taken a turn. And not the kind they had hoped for. His fever had climbed, and he shook with chills even as sweat snaked down his temples.

Mama, who had not shown an ounce of serious concern the night before, now bore a deep furrow between her brows, and a pinched look about her face. She, Winnie, and Nora took turns feeding him broth that a neighbor had cooked from some beef bones during their day of waiting.

Even as Winnie hovered near her brother, doing her best to appear she wasn't hovering at all, she was conscious that Elijah seemed to be the only one who was ill. Out of thirty or so families, how could he be the only one?

The night was long and humid, and yet there was still no rain.

Elijah woke frequently, jerking up as though from a nightmare, mumbling and incoherent.

Winnie took a spot right next to him, leaving Mama the other side.

Nora tumbled into sleep in the corner of the tent, and Papa slept outside on the ground to give them more room.

When Elijah jolted awake, unsure where he was, Winnie or Mama would stroke his hair, sometimes getting him to take a sip of sugar water before laying him back down.

His fever grew so high, and his skin so hot, they eventually stripped him of his clothes, which were sodden and smelly anyway.

When the sun finally peeked its head over the horizon and the cattle began to call to one another, Winnie sat up with a groan.

Elijah was on his back, hands splayed out restlessly.

Mama's head lay beside his, as though she'd been whispering in his ear before she fell asleep.

His injured leg was exposed from beneath the blanket they had draped over his middle, and Winnie realized she hadn't changed the bandage the night before. She bent over his leg, unwrapping it gently, and then recoiled, her hand flying up to cover her mouth.

Oh no.

The neat stitches in Elijah's leg strained against severe swelling. It leaked fluid, especially at the bottom where the stitching had broken loose, and the taut skin around it flushed an angry red.

Nora, who'd stirred upon hearing Winnie's movements, leaned over her shoulder and gasped.

"We have to do something," Winnie insisted.

Nora looked quickly away, her face taking on a green tint. "I'll help Papa start the fire. We'll need hot water."

****

Half an hour later, Papa gently carried Elijah out of the tent and laid him as close to the fire as they dared.

Despite the warm morning, the boy shivered as though atop a bed of ice.

Hal had emerged from his tent shortly after Papa got the fire going, and he knelt beside Elijah, ready to help hold him still.

Mama hovered by his head, so he would see her face when he woke. And he surely would wake, because the pain they were about to cause him would be impossible to sleep through. "Do it." She gripped Elijah's shoulders.

With a nod from Papa, Hal laid across Elijah's torso, pinning him to the ground.

Winnie and Nora each took an ankle.

Papa dipped their ladle into the kettle over the fire, and poured the scalding water directly over Elijah's wound.

His back bowed off the ground and he howled, tearing into consciousness with the violence of a wounded predator. For one ludicrous moment, it seemed as though the bear that had wounded him had left behind an imprint of her most reactive and animalistic self.

Hal struggled to keep him still as Elijah thrashed, and Nora's face went pale as the canvas over their wagon. She lurched aside and was sick inches from his twitching feet.

Winnie held firm, carefully wiped her mind of anything attached to emotion, and only reacted to the most basic commands it sent.

Neighbors had rushed over to see what the screaming was about, and Hal leapt to his feet, aiding Jeb to turn them away.

"Unless you've got something they can use for infection," Hal announced, "They need some privacy."

Mrs. McCleary stayed when the others meandered away, and with a nod from Mama, Hal let her pass.

Mrs. McCleary knelt beside her and rested a hand upon Mama's back. "What can I do?"

Mama's lips were pressed together so tightly, they appeared like a seam in her face—a closed wound. "Can you spare any whiskey?" she whispered at last. "I gave my laudanum to Doc for…well…"

"For my boy," Mrs. McCleary finished. "I know." She fished a dark bottle from a hidden pocket in her dress. "Here." She thrust it clumsily into Mama's hands.

Mama didn't ask why Mrs. McCleary had taken to carrying a potent numbing agent in her pocket, or perhaps she didn't need to.

Winnie hadn't seen Mrs. McCleary stumbling around drunkenly in the weeks that had passed since Amos had taken his life, likely because she'd barely seen Mrs. McCleary at all.

She'd closed up after her son's death, like a perennial bloom clamped tight against the winter elements, looking for all the world as though it were dead.

Mama lifted Elijah's head into her lap and held the bottle to his lips.

He tried to turn away, not appreciating the bitter taste, but Mrs. McCleary reached out and gripped his chin. "This'll make you feel better, honey," she soothed. "Take a big drink. That's it, now."

Nora scooted back, a hand clutched at the base of her throat, and Jeb knelt beside her, offering her water from his canteen to rinse out her mouth.

Papa tossed their big spoon back into the kettle, looking as though he'd rather have hurled it into the distant grass.

He and Hal moved Elijah into the shade of the wagon, and Winnie raced to the river to soak strips of linen in the water. She ran back, avoiding the questions people called out to her, and dropped down beside her brother. She carefully laid the cool, fresh bandages across the blisters that had risen along the edges of his wound.

Finished with the gruesome task, the family watched their youngest in silence, and Mrs. McCleary took her leave. She didn't ask for the bottle of whiskey back. She knew they would be needing it.

****

The rest of the day passed without any word from Doc. Hal and Jeb cooked dinner, a surprisingly edible concoction of rice and beans, livened up with chunks of venison jerky.

When darkness settled, they moved Elijah back into the tent to pass another torturous night. His fever was still high, and whenever he woke, he complained bitterly of thirst.

Mama continued to give him whiskey, too, as it was the only thing they could do to numb his pain.

Exhausted, but restless, Winnie left Mama and Nora to care for her brother and stumbled to join Hal by the fire.

Papa slept on the other side of it, his head pillowed upon their bag of rice.

Hank and Jeb lay on bedrolls not far away, snoring softly.

Hal moved to let her have the stool he was sitting on, but Winnie waved him back down and sank to the ground beside him, leaning against his knee. "Distract me." She sighed. "Please."

He was quiet for a moment, and it wasn't until he began to run his fingers through her hair that Winnie realized she'd never braided it. It fell loose down her back, and she tilted her head toward him, willing herself to focus on the soothing sensation.

"If we were back home, I'd marry you in the winter. Just before Christmas. We'd have the ceremony between giant pines, strung with garlands of icicles, and you'd have snowflakes in your hair."

Winnie found herself snuggling a little closer. She rested her cheek against his leg.

"Elijah could pass out chunks of fudge to our family and friends, and he'd steal so much for himself that he'd ruin his appetite and miss out on the fantastic dinner."

"What would we eat?" Winnie murmured. Though her stomach was sated from dinner, her imagination was ready to dance among delicacies and dreams.

Hal continued to stroke her hair. "There'd be roasted turkey, and glazed ham. Quail in a rum sauce with mashed potatoes. Bowls full of apples and oranges. Plum pudding, lemon custard, and stacks of pies."

Winnie could barely picture it. The berries they'd collected in the forest had been abandoned, left to the birds and the orphaned bear cub. It had been so long since she'd inhaled the simple delight of a baking fruit pie. "What kind of pie?" She hoped if he just described it in more detail, she'd taste the ghost of it on her tongue.

He chuckled. "Well, pecan is my favorite. What's yours?"

"Apple." She sighed with longing. "With a dollop of fresh cream."

"I'll make sure you have a slice of apple pie on your wedding day," he promised.

"It won't be in the winter, I expect." That was a shame. His description had sounded so peaceful, she doubted she'd have minded the chill. Now in the height of summer, they were so far from snow and frost that Winnie had a hard time believing she'd ever felt them against her skin. Perhaps her midwestern winters had only been a dream.

"I was actually hoping…" Hal trailed off. "It feels wrong to be talking about this, with Elijah ill."

Winnie lifted her head from his leg and locked eyes with him. "When I'm in the tent with him, all I can do is count my brother's breaths. I need something besides numbers in my head."

He still hesitated.

"Please."

"Lord, help me," Hal murmured. "Will I ever be able to deny you anything?"

Winnie hoped not, but she didn't say so. She closed her eyes as he resumed stroking her hair, imagining if she could purr like a cat, she'd be doing so now.

"I'd like us to be wed at Fort Bridger," he said. "It's about two weeks away. We can have a real wedding there, with a preacher, and I have enough saved to buy us our own tent."

"And apple pie?" It sounded far too good to be true.

He chuckled. "Anything for you, Winnie. Even if I have to bake the pie myself."

Someone tactfully cleared their throat behind them, and they turned around.

Mae emerged from the shadows, glancing at Papa's sleeping form before coming to sit alongside them by the fire. "I heard about Elijah."

Winnie's brief distraction vanished like mist into a strong wind. "We don't know what else to do," she admitted. "With Doc gone…Mama's tried camphor, and whiskey. We even cleaned it with boiling water."

Mae raised a leather pouch from her lap, and it spun slowly from its drawstrings, casting a shadow across her face. "I brought something to help. It's from the purple coneflower. I'm going to make a salve with it and steep some into a tea."

Winnie took the small pouch, opening it to take a whiff of the dried leaves and buds within. It was pungent, as most herbs were, but not unpleasant. There was the barest hint of vanilla. A bit of sugar would make it palatable in a tea. "Have you used it before?" She handed the pouch back. "Where did you learn about it?"

Mae hesitated. "It's a Native remedy. Tatanka Pteccila taught me."

Winnie tried to keep from visibly tensing. Could she put the hope for her brother's life in the hands of a man she'd never even seen? He was dead, so she could hardly ask him how many of his people had been treated with this remedy.

He was dead, but Mae had trusted him. Mae had called him a friend, and grieved when he'd died.

She grieved still, in small ways that Winnie was just beginning to understand. "Will it save Elijah?" She studied Mae's face in the firelight.

Hal remained silent, letting her come to a decision

on her own.

"I don't know," Mae answered honestly. "The Sioux used it for pain, to bring down swelling, and to give the body a chance to heal itself."

Winnie had to admit it sounded exactly like what they needed. "What do you need to make the salve?" She focused on the logistics before she could overthink it and change her mind.

Hal released a pent-up breath behind her. He hadn't been sure she would agree.

To be honest, Winnie was a little astounded she had. But she couldn't dwell on it.

"I need some oil and some wax." Mae looked a little relieved. "And hot water for the tea."

Hal went to fetch fresh water for the kettle while Winnie went to their neighbors, asking each family if they had any oil or beeswax that could be spared for a salve.

Those in the third wagon had almond oil. Mrs. Cameron, whose family hailed from Scotland, used it on her skin at night.

The family in the seventh wagon had beeswax that Mrs. Klein, one of the other pregnant women among their party, had set aside to make candles.

Winnie returned and handed the bounty to Mae, who set about making the salve while Hal stoked the fire and boiled the water for the tea.

Winnie sat on Papa's stool and tried to keep from fidgeting.

"It's ready." Mae finally rose from her cramped position with a bowl of salve. "Are you?" She looked to Winnie, assessing.

Winnie forced herself to nod. She held a finger to

her lips as she eased a tent flap aside, urging Mae to be quiet.

They stepped carefully over Mama's and Nora's sleeping forms. Working quickly as possible in the dim light, they unwrapped Elijah's leg, smoothed the salve in a thick layer across the wound, and then re-wrapped it.

Hal waited for them just outside the tent, cup extended. "Here's the tea," he whispered. "I added some sugar."

Winnie reached through the tent flap to take it, and passed it to Mae.

She lifted Elijah's head up, and his eyes stirred behind his lids in a whiskey-induced delirium. He seemed conscious enough to swallow, so they eased sips of tea down his throat, even dipping their fingers in it to rub it across his slack lips.

When Mae motioned that he'd had enough, they slipped back outside. It was rewarding to get some breaths of fresh air.

The tent was not well ventilated and smelled of hot bodies.

"Get him to drink some of the tea every time he wakes up." Mae handed the remains of the pouch to Winnie. "With any luck, his fever will come down by morning, and he'll be able to drink without help."

She turned to go, but Winnie reached out and took hold of her friend's hand. "Thank you." She was certain she'd never meant it more than in that moment. "Even if it…doesn't work, thank you for trying."

Mae smiled at her, and Winnie felt the old admiration rise up—the hope that she might possess a fraction of Mae's confidence, from having seen and done more than most.

"It'll work. Tatanka Pteccila never let me down, not even once." Mae's dark eyes seemed to glow.

It could've just been the firelight, but Winnie felt soothed, as though an angel had drifted past overhead. "He was more than just a friend to you, wasn't he?" she whispered.

Mae blinked, obviously taken aback. But that glow, the tender memory of a bond that remained even after death, remained. "He was everything," she said simply as she turned away. "Goodnight."

Hal had finished banking the fire so the coals would be easily stoked in the morning, and smiled tiredly at Winnie from across the flames, settling once more on Papa's stool. "Try and get some sleep," he advised. "You've done all you can."

She nodded. He was right. Thanks to Mae, they had done more, perhaps, than even Doc would have known to do.

As she settled once more in the tent, filling the small space between Mama and Nora, she listened to the sound of their breathing, and Elijah's, and fell asleep so quickly, it might as well have been a brilliantly composed symphony.

Chapter Twelve

Winnie woke to the sound of someone complaining. It was one of the most beautiful things she'd ever heard.

"I'm hungry," Elijah said. "Can I have some hotcakes?"

She bolted upright, whirling toward the source of the voice. It was well past dawn, judging by the lightness within the tent, and Elijah was propped up against Nora's knees.

There were dark circles beneath his eyes, but otherwise, his coloring was better. The sweat that had beaded his face was gone.

Winnie had risen twice during the night to give him more of the tea, and she had covered the bowl of salve with a cloth to keep it from drying out and being unusable.

"I'll get some hotcakes started." Mama smoothed Elijah's hair fondly before slipping out of the tent.

Winnie picked up the bowl of salve and sat by Elijah's leg.

"What are you doing?" He eyed her warily as she unwound the careful wrappings. He clearly hadn't forgotten the incident with the scalding water the day before.

"I put some of this salve on your leg last night," Winnie explained. "And it seems to be helping. I'm going to put on some more."

Nora leaned over curiously as Winnie examined Elijah's leg. The fluid was noticeably reduced, and some of the heat had faded from the skin around the gash. Perhaps the hot water had cleaned the wound enough for the salve to do its work unhindered.

"What kind of salve?" Nora pressed as Winnie carefully spread a fresh layer over Elijah's wound.

He did his best not to squirm, but it was obvious he was still in some pain.

"It's from the purple coneflower," Winnie replied carefully. "Mae brought it last night."

Nora's eyes narrowed, and she gripped Elijah's shoulders, as though to yank him to her and shield him from an invisible foe. "Mae brought it." Her tone sharpened into an accusation.

"Yes," Winnie said calmly. "And it seems to be working, so maybe you should keep your opinions to yourself."

Nora went rigid.

Elijah noticed the change, and looked up at his oldest sister curiously.

"Does Mama know about this?" Nora demanded.

Winnie finished re-wrapping Elijah's leg and tied it with a gentle knot. "Not yet."

"She'll be furious," Nora hissed. "How could you risk our brother's life with some heathen concoction? He could have been poisoned. He could have died!"

"He was already dying," Winnie snapped. "If it hadn't been for Mae and her Sioux friends, he might not have woken up again."

Nora's cheeks flushed. She mashed her lips together and didn't reply.

Just as Winnie reached the tent flaps, the bowl of

salve in her hands, Mama opened them from the other side. How much had she overheard?

Wordlessly, Mama held her hand out.

Stomach sinking, Winnie handed her the bowl.

Mama brought it up to her nose, sniffing delicately. "This smells the same as the tea you gave him last night." She handed the bowl back.

Winnie gaped. "You knew?"

Mama smiled a bit. "You'll see when you have your own children. The slightest sound from them will wake you in the night, even when they're grown."

Nora's indignant protest came from the back corner of the tent. "Mama, you can't seriously be thinking of letting her keep giving him that...that..." She struggled to find a phrase distasteful enough. "That heathen...potion!"

"Heathen potion?" Elijah exclaimed. "Really? I can't wait to tell my friends!"

Mama folded her arms.

Winnie recognized the stubborn set of her face all too well, because it was frequently aimed at her. Fortunately, it wasn't this time.

"It's not a potion, Elijah, so don't go spreading tall tales. It's a medicinal plant, just like others we use for healing. We're just unfamiliar with this one."

Winnie felt a surge of gratitude for her mother. She should've known Mama would've backed anything that stood a chance of saving Elijah. Ignorance was not an acceptable excuse for the loss of a life.

But then Mama's stern gaze fell upon Winnie. "Next time you get a hair-brained idea to experiment with such things, at least warn me first," she admonished. "You shouldn't take such risks on your own."

Nora simmered quietly in the back corner.

It was a matter of time before she boiled over, like a kettle left too long over the fire.

Winnie hastily followed Mama out of the tent, leaving any further confrontation with her sister for another time.

Papa, who had clearly overheard the whole exchange and was well informed of the night's events, reached out to squeeze Mama's shoulder.

She leaned against him a moment, laying her forehead against the open neckline of his shirt.

"Winnie did the right thing," he reassured her. "Nora will come to see that." He held his free arm out to Winnie, offering a hug. "You did right," he repeated as she folded herself into his side.

For a moment, it was like she was a child again, crawling into their bed to escape the terror of a booming thunderstorm.

For it was nothing less than terror that had gripped her heart, upon seeing the infection gnawing away at her little brother's tenuous grip on life. Though he was far from fully recovered, she couldn't help but feel optimistic. He was improving. For now, that seemed enough. The guillotine that had been hanging over his head felt further away.

"Big John got word in the night," Papa stepped back. "Doc sent a rider. He says it was a bad bout of the summer complaint that struck the other wagon party. They must not have tended to their food properly. At any rate, it's not catching, so it's safe for us to continue."

The weight that lifted off Winnie's chest was staggering. She wouldn't have to wonder which of her family and friends would sicken and die. She wouldn't have to analyze every physical sensation, searching for symptoms of disease.

Speaking of family... "Where's Hal?" Winnie looked around.

"He and Hank escorted the rider back to the other wagon party," Papa said. "They'll wait to rejoin us there."

They spent the remainder of the morning packing their things to leave. They'd taken more out of the wagons than usual, having spent three nights at Independence Rock instead of the one they'd intended. But it seemed to have done them good. Wagon covers that had needed repairs had been sewn, axels and wheels had been tended to, and the washing finished. The livestock had also gotten a good rest, and plenty of water.

They settled Elijah as comfortably in the interior of the wagon as they could, with the promise that it would be a short trip and they'd reach the other wagon train by midday.

Nora volunteered to sit with him, completely ignoring Winnie as she climbed in, holding a canteen full of Mae's tea as far away from her body as she could manage.

Winnie just shook her head, certain her sister would eventually come around, and equally irritated by the fact that it would take longer than necessary. Nora did things in her own time, and there was just no rushing her. Pushing her sibling was like trying to push a wagon through deep mud—frustrating and futile.

They left Independence Rock, diverting a half mile south to get around Devil's Gate. The Gate was a granite gorge that allowed the Sweetwater to pass through a cleft in the rock and out the other side.

Winnie was relieved it was too narrow for wagons. She had no desire to walk through hell, regardless of which passing fur trader had named it.

She was eager to reach the other wagon party, not just to get Doc back, but to see Hal. She couldn't wait to tell him their gamble had paid off, and that Elijah had improved.

It took them nearly five hours to reach the other emigrants. Their wagons moved considerably slower than the messenger's horse had.

Hank and Hal rode out to meet them, waving their hats over their heads in excitement. They fell in with Big John first, updating him on the most recent news. Then they made their way back through the column until they reached Winnie's family.

Tired as she was, Winnie couldn't help but grin when Hal threw a leg over Belle, slid to the ground, and wrapped her in a tight hug.

"How's Elijah?" He eased her back to assess her expression.

"Come and see!" She tugged him to the back of the family wagon.

Hank, also eager to see how his adopted little brother fared, followed them.

"Howdy, Hal! Howdy, Hank!" Elijah greeted them from his seat atop their water barrel. His wounded leg was propped atop a bag of beans beside him. "Did Winnie tell you? I've been drinking a heathen potion!"

Nora rolled her eyes from her spot next to him, where she fanned herself to stir the cloistering heat within the wagon. "Mama told you not to spread falsehoods, remember?" Her tone was sharper than usual. Her mood had clearly not improved.

"Is that right?" Hank leaned in, as though Nora hadn't spoken. "Well, I bet that potion will make your hurt leg even stronger than your good one! You'll be running fast as a horse in no time."

Elijah nodded enthusiastically, even as Nora grimaced.

"Don't encourage him, Hank," she complained.

Hank rolled his hazel eyes. One of his best traits was that he never took Nora too seriously. "What shall I do, then? You and Winnie have everything else covered."

Just then, the wagons ahead of them began slowing, and then stopped. The dust that plumed around them started to settle.

The wagon train that had been only a few days ahead for the entirety of their journey was smaller than their own—fifteen wagons or so. They were spread out quite a bit farther than Winnie was used to seeing, perhaps because of the onset of the sickness that Doc claimed was only the summer complaint.

"Most of them are Scottish," Hal murmured in her ear. "There are a few German families as well. Came in on a boat across the Atlantic last season."

A bearded man wearing a fur hat and vest strode forward and extended his hand, looking relieved.

Winnie assumed he was the guide for the other families.

"Mighty glad to see some friendly faces," the guide said. "I'm Owen Bailey. Much obliged to you for the loan of Doc Collins. He's helped a lot of unsettled stomachs around here."

"John Cook," Big John replied, shaking Mr. Bailey's hand enthusiastically. "Where is Doc, anyway? I thought he'd be here to meet us."

Mr. Bailey scratched at his dark beard. "Likely sleeping. He's been up the past two nights, trying to ease the young'uns' sleep." He gestured at the collection of wagons. "We've got a whole pack of children with us."

Sure enough, Winnie saw little foreheads and eyes peeking out of wagons and tent flaps, clearly curious about the newcomers. How much did they understand of what was being said? She hoped they spoke some English. She'd love to hear stories of their homeland.

"We'll set our camp up over there." Big John pointed, indicating a spot. "And then we'll have a little get-together. If your people are feeling well enough?"

Mr. Bailey nodded. "Oh, some are, for sure. About half are still recovering. I hope you forgive the alarm we caused your party. We thought cholera had finally caught up with us."

Big John waved off the apology. "It was no trouble. We're happy to help in any way we can."

The two men walked toward a communal cooking fire being tended by three weary looking women. Dozens of cornmeal cakes cooked atop a massive griddle. Had those three ladies been cooking for their entire wagon train? What a monumental task.

Hal helped Papa get their wagon into place, and then took charge of the oxen, walking them out to join the cattle herd.

The dry grass didn't look particularly appetizing to Winnie, but at least it was plentiful.

Big John set some men to butchering one of their steers, to share with the other wagon party. Fresh meat would do everybody good, he claimed.

After peeking in on Elijah, who had fallen asleep once the wagon stopped jolting around, Winnie set to milking Millie. When she finished, she brought a cup to Nora in the wagon, extending it like an olive branch. "Truce?"

Nora took the cup, looking more tired than angry. "I suppose." She took a sip. "You got lucky last night, Winnifred. Let's hope your streak lasts until we get to Oregon."

Winnie's shoulders sagged a bit as the tension that had held them dissipated. "It's not luck," she countered. "We just have extraordinary friends."

Nora couldn't argue with that. She took another drink of the fresh milk. "Help me out of here, will you?" She kicked at the cramped barrels and trunks that threatened to entomb her. "I'm so stiff I'll fall flat on my face without help."

Winnie held a hand out to her sister. She was tempted by the thought of stepping back at just the right time to send Nora falling onto her dainty bottom, but she stood firm. If Nora's temper had cooled enough to be civil, then it wasn't worth stirring the pot again.

****

That night, the members of the other wagon train that were well enough attended the supper party that Big John hosted. There were ten Scottish families, and four from Germany. They'd decided to hire Mr. Bailey after a chance meeting in Independence. Several of the Scottish men and women spoke English, while only two of the men in the German families did. But it had been enough for them to agree on a guide, and settle on traveling together.

They made it through the dinner with a fair number of smiles and hand gestures, and the ones who spoke English translated for the rest as often as they could.

Winnie guessed it was hard to keep up, when so many people were speaking. She sat with Hal, Elijah, Nora, and Jeb.

Elijah had been warned not to eat too much. They didn't want him throwing up the healing tea they'd been filling him with all day.

Winnie noticed from across the fire that one woman seemed especially confused by all that was going on. She was jumpy, her eyes too big and her nose a bit small, reminding Winnie of a mouse. She clutched a baby to her chest, wrapped in a blanket against the evening air.

Though Winnie watched curiously, it didn't seem like a man was with them. Perhaps the baby's father had died.

After dinner, Big John gathered all the men about him for an important discussion.

Winnie, Nora, and Mama finished their chores while they waited to hear the news.

At last, Papa returned with Jeb, Hank, and Hal in tow.

"Big John is going to ask if Mr. Bailey's people want to travel the rest of the way to Oregon with us."

"It'll be good to have some new faces around here," Mama said.

"Do you think they'll agree?" Jeb reached up to massage Nora's shoulders.

"I expect they will," Hank replied. "We've got Doc with us, and Widow Simmons. A party with that many children clearly has use for a midwife. And the more wagons we have, the less likely it is that any Natives will risk attacking us."

Winnie was quite sure that the Natives they'd encountered thus far wouldn't have harmed even a single wagon traveling alone. She also hadn't forgotten what Mae had said on the fringes of Fort Kearny—that of all the tribes they'd encountered, she'd only seen one commit violence.

As small a number as it was, one was not none, so Winnie couldn't say that seeking protection among a larger wagon train was a silly idea. For all they knew, it could be what saved their lives.

But Tatanka Pteccilia's purple coneflower remedy had helped keep her brother from crossing Death's murky threshold. A Native she'd never met had saved Elijah, just by befriending Mae and passing on his knowledge to her. Would a doctor like Doc Collins take the time to teach a Native healer their ways if things had been reversed?

She wished she could say yes, but she suspected it would take a rare man to do such a thing. A rare man of any nation. That said plenty about who Tatanka Pteccilia had been. It said even more that Mae had loved him. Likely still loved him, even though death would separate them for many years to come.

Winnie could not call Mae a friend and then fear those who had befriended a younger Mae, and given her the tools she needed to survive. No, her time spent blindly fearing the Natives was over. She could not stomach being as foolish as her sister. She could not travel such a great distance as they were trekking and allow herself to be unchanged.

Because of the kindness of a Sioux man, Elijah would live.

And that, Winnie would never forget.

****

Another week's travel brought them to the ascent

through South Pass. The incline was so gradual, Winnie found it hard to believe they were gaining much elevation.

Ridges and hills carpeted with sage filled the horizon on both sides of the plateau, and Big John told them they were crossing the Continental Divide.

From this point on, all the rivers emptied into the Pacific Ocean instead of the Atlantic.

She had never seen an ocean before, but had heard a fair bit about the crossing the German and Scottish emigrants had made.

They'd befriended one of the German families, Mr. and Mrs. Vogelsang, and their five children. Mr. Vogelsang spoke English, and was patiently teaching his wife, who seemed kind, if easily frustrated.

Winnie suspected having five children under the age of eight might've had something to do with that.

In fits and starts, over the course of chores and shared meals, the Vogelsang family's odyssey had been revealed. They'd departed Germany from the port of Hamburg last spring, fleeing a burgeoning revolution. It had taken nearly six weeks to cross the Atlantic in an overcrowded passenger hold, with poor conditions, repulsive food, and little sleep.

It was a relief, Mrs. Vogelsang conveyed, to escape the ship and its throngs of unwashed bodies and crying children. From New York, they'd gone south in various stage coaches. Eventually, they secured passage on a steamboat, and traveled by river the rest of the way to Independence.

The enormity of their journey astounded Winnie, who had been born and raised in central Missouri. The Vogelsangs had already seen more of the country than she ever would. It was hard to imagine traveling for months just to get to the start of the overland trails in Independence, and then choosing to go on for six more.

The Vogelsangs had four daughters and one son.

Only three years old, Andreas was doted on by his sisters.

Adda, the eldest, had taken to following Nora like a shadow.

Winnie could tell that Nora didn't mind, in fact, she seemed a bit relieved to have someone new to talk to.

It would be good for Nora to have another friend. She hadn't taken to Mae the way that Winnie had. She suspected that Nora viewed Mae as reckless and ill-mannered, not someone to emulate in any way. It didn't bother Winnie that Nora took Adda under her wing, but she wished Nora could see what she valued so much in Mae. She wished her sister could be grateful for the Native medicine, rather than resentful of its origin.

There wasn't good drinking water along the plateau, so they pressed on, relying on their water barrels, until they reached Pacific Springs. They made camp early, eager to celebrate.

At last, they were beginning to get into the mountains.

Pacific Springs was a marshland —shallow water that supported a network of floating sedges.

Their departure the next day would be sure to be slow and muddy. But for now, they turned the livestock loose to drink their fill, and attempted to find a semi-dry place to set up campsites.

After pitching their tents alongside the family wagons, Hal and Hank each took a shovel and began digging into the spongy earth.

"What are you doing?" Winnie wandered over to watch.

"Big John said there's ice here sometimes," Hal explained. "Buried beneath all this peat. We're trying to find some."

"Ice?" Winnie scoffed. "Here?" She gestured around the marshlands. "I think you'd have more luck panning for gold."

"Don't tempt me," Hank chuckled. "There's talk of men finding gold in California. Can you imagine? Digging up a nugget and never having to work again?"

"The trail divides not too far ahead," Hal mused. "One path crosses the Sierra Nevada mountains into California. Any of us could choose to go there."

Winnie suppressed a shudder at the mention of the mountains that had trapped the poor Donner party last year. "You're not considering going to California, instead?" The possibility made her heart race, and not with excitement over gold.

Hal stopped digging, assessing her reaction. "I go where you go." He wiped his brow with a sleeve. "And your Pa wants to settle in Oregon."

She tried not to appear too relieved. But no prospect of gold and a life of leisure would convince her to go to California. She'd rather be poor the rest of her life than suffer from exposure in the mountains as her friends and family withered and froze around her.

"Fort Bridger is only a week or so away." Hank changed the subject, and they began digging again. "Will we be hearing wedding bells there?" He winked at Winnie.

"That's the idea," she said. "Hal wants to get us a tent, and we don't want to wait until we reach Fort Hall."

"It's about time you show him some mercy," Hank teased. "He's been waiting for months!"

"She's worth it," Hal replied.

"I'm happy you think so." Winnie leaned over to kiss him on the cheek.

At that moment, Hank's shovel hit something solid.

Winnie lifted her brows incredulously.

They dropped to their knees and began peeling the peat back excitedly. Moisture seeped into her dress, but she hardly noticed.

The ice stung Winnie's hand when she laid her palm against it. She laughed aloud, drawing back and resting her chilled hand against her hot cheek. "Oh!" She gasped. "I just realized! We have ice, and salt, and with the cream from Millie's milk…"

The grin that spread across Hal's face was glorious. "Ice cream!" He said it as reverently as a sailor who'd been stranded on a tropical island.

Winnie could nearly taste it on her tongue, drawing away the heat that had hounded them every step for the past two months.

The three of them raced among their neighbors, hoping someone had cared enough to bring (and not throw out) a hand-cranked churner. Of course, no one had. It was a ludicrous thing to haul across the prairie.

So, they improvised.

Hal and Hank gathered some men and set them to digging up more ice.

Winnie grabbed Nora, Adda, and Mae, and they returned to the wagons, asking people to bring a bit of their sugar and salt, and cream if they had a cow.

Together, the whole wagon train made ice cream.

They placed the mixture into barrels full of ice and

salt and let the children kick them around, churning the contents so that when they opened the lids…the mixture had frozen into ice cream.

Winnie hadn't tasted anything so delicious since the lemonade that Hal had bought at Fort Laramie. She would be hard-pressed to have to choose between the two, if such an opportunity were ever presented to her.

Hal lounged beside her, smiling around his spoon, eyes rolling comically back with each bite.

Now she knew what treat to fix him if she ever needed to smooth things over after an argument. Grinning at the thought, she leaned over and plopped a dollop of ice cream onto his nose.

Hal blinked, trying to focus on the white blob that now adorned his face. "I'm under attack!" He ducked behind his spoon, raised like a puny shield.

Winnie took a final bite and relaxed back onto her elbows. "Don't worry, I ate the last of my ammunition."

"I wish we could have ice cream every day." Elijah sighed longingly. He was sprawled out beside their fire, his healing leg left unwrapped to air out.

"It's a good thing we don't," Mama said. "Or else we'd have to turn sideways to fit through doors."

Papa chuckled. "That'll be Lenora, soon enough."

"You'll have to measure me before you build the doorways, then." Nora took a deliberate bite of her considerable amount of ice cream.

Everyone laughed, and for a moment, Winnie felt like they were sitting in their little farmhouse, relaxing in wooden chairs before the hearth. Were it not for the additions of Jeb, Hank, and Hal, it could have been any July night. The feeling of peace and familiarity was the same.

It seemed contrary that adding more people could've made their family feel more tight-knit. She knew they had the trail to thank for at least part of that. They had come to rely on one another in ways they'd never had to before. It was comforting, the feeling of never being alone.

Perhaps seeking that feeling was why people got married in the first place.

Winnie glanced at Hal, who'd wiped the ice cream from his nose.

His attention was fixed on Hank, who'd begun telling Elijah a story about Daniel Boone. As if he noticed the weight of her gaze, Hal turned to smile at her.

Her heart swelled. She wished Fort Bridger was only a day away, even though they still had plenty of preparations to make. She didn't have a wedding dress, for one thing, though Mama had assured her that she'd be able to acquire something "suitable."

Winnie had tried to press Nora on the issue, asking if she should alter one of the three dresses she'd packed, but Nora had refused to tell her anything.

It would be Papa's task to find a preacher at the fort to marry them, and Mama would find a suitable place to hold the ceremony. The members of their wagon party would never fit into a tiny frontier church. And they would all want to be there, to celebrate the fact that life went on, despite hardship, thirst, dust, and pain.

Life went on.

Chapter Thirteen

"We've got a choice to make," Big John announced. He stood beside Mae at a fork in the trail, shielding his eyes from the sun as he addressed everyone who had gathered. "If we take this cutoff, it'll save us more than two days of travel. But there's no water 'til we reach the Green River. And there's not much grass, either."

Worried murmurs rose among the crowd.

"The cutoff bypasses Fort Bridger," Mae clarified. "If we take it, there won't be a chance of a re-supply until we reach Fort Hall."

The murmurs rose in volume, and Big John raised his hands, asking for quiet. "It's not worth it, in my opinion. But I wanted you to know your options, just the same."

Winnie looked to Papa and was relieved he didn't look tempted by the thought of the cutoff. They'd had enough of baking in the sun without fresh water, in her opinion. Why re-create the experience if they didn't have to?

Ultimately, seven families decided to take the cutoff. Four of them were Scottish families from Mr. Bailey's group. They planned to use the extra days they gained to stop for a good rest while they waited for the rest of the wagons to catch up from Fort Bridger.

Winnie supposed that to someone who'd already been traveling for more than half a year, two days was a bigger relief than it currently felt to her.

Mae would lead the families along the cutoff, fording the Big Sandy River with them before crossing over forty miles of desert and joining the rest of their wagon train northwest of Fort Bridger, in the Bear River Valley. They'd all have to cross the Green River, but Big John said there was a ferry near the fort, run by mountain men and fur trappers.

It remained to be seen if they'd even be able to afford to use the ferry, so Winnie tried not to get her hopes up. She made her way to Mae as the families who'd decided to take the cutoff said brief goodbyes to those continuing to Fort Bridger. "Over forty miles without water. Why risk it?"

Mae slapped her hat against her pant leg, dislodging some dust, before settling it firmly atop her head of dark hair. "It's doable, don't worry."

"Have you taken this cutoff before?"

Mae shrugged. "Not personally, but I've read all the guidebooks. And I've studied the maps." She reached out and pulled Winnie into a hug. "We'll be fine."

Winnie sighed. She didn't like the idea one bit. But it wasn't her decision. Mae would always make her own way; follow her own path. That was partly what Winnie loved about her. It wasn't fair to pressure her friend into acting otherwise.

She stepped back and flicked the brim of Mae's hat, as Hank so often did. "Be careful. I plan on eating a lot more ice cream with you once we reach Oregon. Don't make me indulge alone."

Mae laughed. "Don't worry, I'd never turn down ice cream." She led her horse to the start of the cutoff route, and began checking her gear.

Winnie turned to walk back, and saw Hank approaching, leading his horse. "Going somewhere?"

He slowed, looking abashed. "I know it means I'll miss your wedding, and I'm really sorry, but I just…I can't let her go alone." He glanced at Mae, who'd bent to examine her horse's hooves.

Winnie stepped forward to squeeze his arm. "Of course, you can't," she murmured. "I understand."

Hank's eyes softened, and he smiled a little. "Thanks, Winnie."

She bit her lip, but decided to press on before she lost her nerve. "Why haven't you told her?" She glanced in Mae's direction. "Why hide your feelings?"

Hank gently pulled his arm from her grip. "I can't change her." He eerily echoed what she had thought only moments before. "She is who she is."

Had Mae confided in Hank about Tatanka Ptecilia? It wasn't her place to ask. As much as she wanted to see them happy, whatever was between them deserved to stay between them. She wasn't going to stick her nose in the middle of it.

She watched as Hank reached Mae, and the woman's face lit up. She was clearly happy to have a friend with her along the cutoff. And who knew? Time and distance often made way for big changes. Maybe Hank would become something more.

****

The chaos began before they even reached the Green River.

First, they woke to screaming. Mr. Vogelsang had been up most of the night taking his turn at guard duty, and nodded off next to the fire. He woke with his hands blistering in the coals.

The Vogelsang wagon was parked next to Nora and Jeb's, so they were the first there to help.

The flesh had peeled back, exposing glimpses of muscle and tendon.

Doc Collins slathered some axel grease on it to keep the wound from sticking to the wrappings he applied.

Then, as they approached the river, a rifle misfired and killed a mule pulling the wagon next to it. The mule dropped like a stone, blocking the path. They had to unbuckle it from the harness and drag it to the edge of the trail before they could continue.

"What if this bad luck is a sign meant to deter us?" Nora mused to Winnie and Adda as they walked. "Maybe we should wait to cross another day."

Adda trembled, gripping her elbows. Her blonde braid swayed against her back in the breeze as she beheld the river, which Winnie had diligently avoided looking at, until now. "The water is too fast." Her accent was thicker than usual, betraying her nerves. "Not good for us."

Winnie was feeling more than a little trepidation herself as Papa and the other men went to settle the ferry costs with the mountain men who operated them.

The water level was near its peak, swelled with snowmelt off the mountains. The river was 400 feet wide, and too deep to ford with the wagons. The only choice was to pay for the ferry, or risk floating the wagons across and making the livestock swim.

When Papa returned with Jeb and Hal, he threw his hat down into the dust with a grunt. "They want ten dollars a wagon. Ten dollars! It's robbery."

Mama came and put her hand on his arm. "And what are the lives of our children worth?"

Papa sighed heavily. "Much more." He bent to retrieve his hat. "Much more than that."

"I can't afford to use the ferry," Jeb said into the tense silence. "I'd appreciate if you'd take Lenora with you, and let me float the wagon without worrying over her and the baby's safety."

Nora started to protest, but Jeb held his hand up, uncharacteristically firm. "No." He shook his head. "It's settled. You'll ride the ferry with your parents."

Nora fumed as he began tying down their belongings so their shifting weight wouldn't throw the wagon off-balance.

Hal moved to stand with Winnie. "I'm going to swim across with Ol' Belle. She'll spook if anyone else tries to take her."

She wanted to protest. The thought of Hal swimming in the river alone was nearly too much for her to bear. But like Jeb, Hal had already made up his mind. He gave her a swift kiss on the cheek before leaning in to murmur in her ear, "Can you swim?"

She nodded, her mind flitting back to summers she and Nora had spent cooling off in ponds and flowing streams.

"Good." He hesitated, as though he wanted to say more, then strode abruptly away.

Adda joined her father, who was unable to do any of the work to ready their wagon, thanks to the burns on his hands. It would likely be over a month before he could even stand to grip a rope.

Big John wove among them, organizing their party into two lines: those that would wait their turn for the ferry, and those that would float their wagons across.

It was tedious work. First, the contents had to be tied

down, as Jeb had done. Then the teams were unhitched, the wheels of the wagons removed, and the wagon box caulked to make it water tight.

But one benefit was that the ones crossing in their wagons didn't have to wait in line.

The Vogelsang family, having spent so much already on their journey, didn't have any money to spare. They decided to cross with Jeb and Hal.

Winnie's family was third in line for the ferry when Jeb got his wagon into the water, and Hal helped Mr. and Mrs. Vogelsang.

Adda waved to Nora, who waved back weakly with a tight expression.

Winnie imagined her face looked the same. She felt as though she were made of glass, perfectly poised to shatter.

The five Vogelsang children had been instructed to sit still in the center of the wagon. Mr. Vogelsang was unable to hold the livestock ropes with his burned hands, so his wife took them. The children vanished from view behind their canvas roof as the wagon lurched and bobbed its way across the current.

Jeb sat stiffly at the front of his wagon, holding the ropes of his own oxen, which swam ahead.

Hal was the last into the river, and he didn't look back as he led Belle into the water. The blanket Winnie had given him was tied neatly to his saddle.

Winnie gripped Nora's hand tightly, and Nora didn't complain, though she was certain she was pinching her sister.

Nora kept a hand to her rounded stomach, breathing uneven.

Hal began to swim alongside Belle, leading her

toward the opposite shore. The horse strained her neck, keeping her muzzle out of the water.

They overtook the Vogelsang wagon, weighed down with the family within. Then they passed Jeb's wagon, as well.

Winnie was relieved to see Hal appeared to be a strong swimmer. Perhaps he'd spent a lot of time in ponds as a child, as well.

The wagon in front of them was loaded onto the ferry, and she took a fortifying breath. It would be their turn in moments. And then they could put this wretched, swollen monster of a river behind them.

She didn't see it happen. Sudden shouts signaled that something had gone wrong.

Winnie pushed away from Nora, racing for the river's edge, flanked by concerned neighbors. Her sister followed, a few precious steps slower.

The current was swift, and at first it was hard to tell what the cause of the alarm was. But then she saw a dark head in the water, little arms flailing.

Andreas Vogelsang had fallen out of his family's wagon. His sisters shrieked his name.

Andreas was drowning.

Adda rushed to the side of their wagon and braced a foot, pulling herself up so that she could jump in. The wagon tipped precariously, in danger of taking on water. Mr. Vogelsang grabbed for Adda, pulling her back from the edge.

"Jeb, no!" Nora shouted, as though her husband could hear.

Winnie looked over just in time to see Jeb dive into the water, aiming for Andreas, who was bobbing up and down like a tiny, swamped boat.

Mrs. Vogelsang screamed, rising from her position at the ropes. Mr. Vogelsang shouted something to her, and leaped over the side, disappearing with a splash.

"Jeb can't swim," Nora gasped. A trembling hand rose to clutch at the base of her throat. "He can't swim!"

Winnie grabbed her sister, afraid she'd run for the river. "Protect them, Lord!"

She wanted Nora to pray with her, but her sister was beyond prayers. Her unblinking eyes never left Jeb, flailing in the water.

He was hardly doing any better than the boy he'd finally reached and managed to wrap an arm around.

Mr. Vogelsang struggled to get to them, but was being pushed by a strong current. The power and speed of his strokes made no difference, and he cried out in agonized frustration as he was swept farther away from his son.

Nora made a choked sound, and Winnie feared the worst.

Hal had turned back, sending Belle on with a slap to the rump. He swam swiftly for Jeb and Andreas, who struggled to keep their heads above water.

Jeb was doing his best, trying to sidestroke with Andreas splayed atop his ribs, but the boy fought him, panicked. He seemed to be sucking in near as much river water as he was air.

Winnie had not been this afraid since the bear attack, and the visceral clench fear held her body in was painful. She couldn't get a full breath. She couldn't focus on anything except the glimpses of Hal's determined expression, rising and falling with each stroke.

If her heart had stopped beating, she wouldn't have noticed.

Cries raked over her ears as Andreas slipped out of Jeb's grip, his slick head disappearing beneath the water.

But Jeb didn't hesitate.

He plunged beneath the surface, reaching....

Hal got to the spot where they had gone under, took a deep breath, and vanished.

Time slowed to a crawl.

It limped along Winnie's senses like a hunted animal.

The distressed cries along the riverbank faded into an awful, all-consuming silence. Not unlike the silence that had fallen after Mrs. Blake had stopped screaming, and they'd waited to hear the cries of an infant that never came.

No, Winnie thought. *No, no, no.*

Please, no.

Nora's nails dug into Winnie's knuckles. The pain made her take a deep breath. Time righted itself, as though the wounded animal it resembled had eluded a hunter's second shot.

Hal emerged first, tawny hair plastered to his head, mouth gaping as he choked. He clutched Andreas against his chest, and had an elbow linked through Jeb's. There was a collective cheer from their neighbors gathered along the bank.

"Oh!" Nora released Winnie to stagger a few steps into the water, as though to reel Jeb into her arms.

Mama reached her first.

Nora ducked her head against their mother's shoulder and sobbed, her back heaving with the strength of it.

"Hal has got them." Mama wrapped her arms around Nora. "They're going to make it."

Winnie watched every inch of Hal and Jeb's progress as they struggled against the current, slowly hauling Andreas to land.

When Jeb and Nora's wagon pitched over, the canvas top slamming into the current and flooding with water, it took a moment for her to register the sight.

The wagon box had partially fallen on Jeb's lead ox, pinning the poor beast beneath the surface. The rest of the oxen got tangled up in the rope, and all four collided, becoming further enmeshed. They cried out as they fought for breath, bellowing in fear.

The animals would all be drowned. There was no saving them.

Hal saw the wagon go over, and the oxen go under, and Winnie almost felt the adrenaline flood through his muscles. She could see it, written as plain as a sunrise on his face.

If they didn't get out of the way, the wagon and the struggling oxen would smash into them.

They'd all be swept downstream together.

He shouted something, and Jeb redoubled his efforts, swimming alongside Hal with all his strength.

"Come on," Winnie ground through her teeth. She'd done her praying. Now it was up to them. "Come on!"

The Vogelsang wagon had nearly reached the far bank, though the sisters still screamed for Andreas and their father, who was out of sight. By some miracle, they'd kept still enough to avoid tipping over themselves.

Nora's dress was soaked up to her thighs from standing in the river, but neither she nor Mama moved to step out of the water. They were like statues as Nora hid her eyes against their mother's shoulder. Her free hand clutched her stomach, as though to shield her unborn child from what was happening.

Hal and Jeb swam, towing Andreas, the oxen sank, and the people on the river bank held their breath.

The overturned wagon and the tangled oxen missed them by a few feet. If they'd stopped to rest, even for one moment, they'd have been overtaken.

The men of the families already on the other side of the river plunged into the water, linking arms to safely extend farther into the current. Moving as one, they gripped Hal, Jeb, and Andreas, and hauled them out of the water.

Cheers rang out downstream as Mr. Vogelsang clambered, exhausted, onto the far bank.

Men grabbed the Vogelsang wagon and hauled it aground. Mrs. Vogelsang threw the ropes at them, and then was out and running, skirt clutched in one hand.

Winnie knew she was breathing, because she was standing and not flat on her back, but she couldn't feel it. All she could feel was her heartbeat, racing as though it had been trying to outpace the river itself.

Mama reached for Papa, and together they dragged Nora out of the water.

She shook so badly she nearly fell to her knees.

Papa picked her up and carried her the rest of the way.

Mama hurried behind, arm extended to usher Winnie with them.

She blinked a few times, trying to see Hal through the throng of neighbors who had surrounded him, Jeb, and Andreas on the opposite bank.

"Winnie!" Papa's voice broke through the babble of conversation around them. "We have to go. It's our turn now."

She stumbled toward the ferry, struggling to focus on the rocky ground beneath her feet. She tried counting her breaths. She reached thirty-four, lost count, and had to start again.

Crossing on the ferry was a blur. She didn't notice the money Papa passed to the operator, or the way the oxen shifted their feet nervously. She stared at the wet hem of Nora's dress, dripping onto the wooden planks.

Nora wouldn't have any dry clothes to change into, she realized dimly. All her things had disappeared down the river. It seemed so much worse than having to leave wedding gifts and furniture along the side of the trail those weeks ago. So much more pointless.

When they reached the opposite shore, Winnie and Nora pelted for the crowd that had gathered. Hal, Jeb, and Andreas had been safe for a few minutes now, but Winnie felt the need to feel Hal's skin beneath her hands, to feel his chest rising and falling.

Upon reaching them, Nora slammed into Jeb so hard that he rocked back, gasping for breath.

Andreas was surrounded by his older sisters, cooing to him in German.

Mrs. Vogelsang wept beside them, supported by her husband, who was drenched and shaking. His burned hands stuck out somewhat awkwardly behind her back.

Winnie stopped a mere foot from where Hal crouched, assessing him. She watched his chest swell with air, watched color bloom back into his deathly pale cheeks. His white shirt was plastered to his form, showing glimpses of skin beneath.

When she crossed the final distance between them, he lurched upright, swaying a little. "Winnie," he rasped.

Water still dripped from his chin.

She reached out a trembling hand and rested it against his cheek. He hadn't shaved since yesterday morning, so stubble pricked at her palm. A tear beaded on her lower lashes, and she struggled not to blink, even as it grew heavier and spilled over.

"You fool." Her voice cracked. "Will you ever stop saving people?" First, he'd saved her and Elijah from the bear, and now he was jumping into rivers as well.

He reached up to grip her wrist. "Would you love me if I did?"

Winnie bit her lip, but the words came out anyway. "I do love you, you reckless man."

Hal grinned. Then he was kissing her, lips slick against her own, and tasting of the river.

She only pulled him closer. She didn't care that their neighbors were assembled around them, tossing relieved cheers into the air.

Hal was alive. Jeb was alive, and they had saved Andreas from the river's grasp. Nothing had ever been worth celebrating more.

****

It took nearly two days to get all the wagons across the Green River. Many of those stubbornly holding out against paying the ferry fees had a change of heart after witnessing what happened to Jeb and Nora's wagon.

If he had been in it when it tipped over, it was entirely possible he'd have been trapped inside. Leaping out to save Andreas had probably saved Jeb's life, as well.

When Nora demanded to know what Jeb had been thinking, jumping into the river when he knew full well that he couldn't swim, Jeb had ducked his head, embarrassed. "I suppose I forgot," he'd answered.

"You forgot you couldn't swim?" Nora had screeched incredulously.

A fear-driven argument had ensued, but Winnie knew Nora wasn't really angry at Jeb. She was actually very proud of him. But her sister had been more frightened than she'd been in her life, and now she sought a way to shed some of the weight of what that fear had broken inside of her.

She would no longer have to wonder what it would feel like to lose her husband. She had come close enough to it to have glimpsed the path that wound into that unforgiving darkness.

Though the river had not managed to take any lives dear to Winnie's family, the wagon train had still suffered losses in the crossing.

A cowhand named Gabe had been swept away, and so had one of the Wilson brothers, who had played a hymn so sweetly on his fiddle at Mrs. Blake's funeral.

But the loss that hit Winnie the hardest was that of Mrs. McCleary.

A few witnesses whispered she had been drunk, and didn't even fight when the current began to drag her under, but that didn't really matter. She was gone now, drifting with the river, which neither cared nor had mercy for the heartbroken mother who had lost a son.

Winnie knew it was a sin for someone to take their own life, but she still found herself hoping that God would allow Amos and his mother to be reunited in Heaven. It was the only end for them she could bear to consider.

In addition to the three deaths, four wagons and their teams had gone under, including Nora and Jeb's.

They held a brief funeral at the river's edge at the end of the second day, though there were no bodies to bury. If they were ever found, it would be by someone far downstream, who would have no idea where they'd come from, or what their stories had been.

The surviving Wilson brother played a different hymn this time, perhaps unwilling to evoke cherished memories of playing alongside his brother. Head bowed, he said goodbye wordlessly, letting the music speak for him.

Those gathered finished singing together, allowing the lone fiddle to fade into the hush that lingered, unbroken by birdsong or calling insects.

Winnie clutched Hal's hand throughout, as she imagined Nora was doing with Jeb and Mrs. Vogelsang was doing with her husband and Andreas.

She watched the river with dry, unfocused eyes, even as people tossed wildflowers into its current, following the spots of color as they swirled and danced out of sight.

Chapter Fourteen

Fort Bridger had begun as an outpost for fur traders and trappers, and it still bore the rough charm of its origin. There were two long log structures, and a large paddock for horses. There was a blacksmith shop, and an array of livestock for sale: sheep, chickens, mules, and oxen.

There wasn't a physical church that Winnie could see, but as long as they had a travelling preacher, it wouldn't matter.

Winnie and Hal learned they weren't the only ones hoping to get married. Mr. Blake had arranged to marry the Scottish widow with the baby that Winnie had thought resembled a mouse.

It wasn't a match based on love, or even affection. With his wife gone, Mr. Blake had four children who needed a mother to look after them. And the widow, soon to be the new Mrs. Blake, had her baby to consider.

As Mama had said: "Feelings can come, but only if you're still alive." A bit callous, but true, none the less. As long as one still had life and breath, there was still possibility.

After they found good grazing for the animals and got their wagons settled, a man approached from the fort, riding a black mule. He wore a fringed deerskin jacket and a black felt hat. An unkempt beard covered half of his face. "John Cook!" The man bellowed, slinging a leg over his mule to dismount. "I thought I saw you stomping about!"

"Quit your hollering, Jim!" Big John yelled, equally as loud. "You've caused enough stampedes in your day!"

They two men resembled clumsy bears as they embraced each other, presumably squeezing hard enough to pop joints.

"How are ya, John? And where's the little miss?" The man glanced around the gathering faces, brows lowering. "She all right?"

"Mae's taking some other families along the Sublette Cutoff. We'll meet up with them later."

The man scratched at his beard, looking relieved. "That's good. How're your people doing?"

"We lost a few when we crossed the Green," Big John admitted. "And more lost their wagons and will need to re-supply." He turned, so the rest of the wagon party could better hear. "Folks, this is my friend, Jim Bridger, and he'll make sure you get whatever you need."

Mr. Bridger tipped his hat. "Welcome to my neck of the woods. Any friends of John are sure to be friends of mine. Just let me know how I can help."

Winnie was surprised when Papa stepped forward. "Have you a preacher, Mr. Bridger?"

The mountain man chuckled. "I'm beginning to think I should commission a chapel. So many folks are getting hitched on the trail these days! Yes sir, we have a preacher. Mr. Campbell wintered with us last season. He started work out on his own spread this spring, but I can have him here by morning."

Papa nodded. "That'll do. Thank you, Mr. Bridger."

Tipping his hat once more, Bridger turned back to

Big John. "Join us by the fire and tell us all the news."

The two men walked toward the fort, leaving the rest of them to get their campsites established.

Hal saddled Belle, preparing to take his turn standing watch over the herd overnight.

Winnie stroked Belle's long face, watching as he deftly tightened the cinch and checked to make sure it wasn't pinching her.

"Well—" He straightened and winked. "—I suppose I'll see you at the wedding."

Winnie laughed. "It sounds strange when you say it like that."

"It does, doesn't it?"

She took his hand. "There's still time for you to ride away and escape," she teased. "You could take up trapping."

Hal smiled and shook his head. "My time was up the day I heard you talking to Millie like she could understand you."

"See you at the altar, then?"

Hal raised her hand and kissed the back of it. "I'll do my best not to smell like horse."

"Only God can work miracles," she joked. But she'd happily smell horse for the rest of her days if it meant she and Hal were safe and together.

"I've already experienced a miracle," Hal murmured, lowering her hand. "Being led to you."

Winnie grinned. The man certainly had a way with words. "Go on." She shooed him toward the saddle. "Before you sweet talk me into something else."

Laughing, Hal mounted up, clicking to Belle with his tongue. "Enjoy your last night as a Hayes," he called over his shoulder. "You'll officially be a Clark tomorrow!"

"I'm ready," Winnie replied, too softly for him to hear.

A moment later, Nora appeared, just as Winnie was settling to milk Millie for the evening. "I've come to steal you for a dress fitting."

"But, the milking…" Winnie protested.

Nora waved a dismissive hand. "Elijah can do it. He's perfectly capable."

Sure enough, their brother raced over, barely impeded by his healing leg. He'd been slowly allowed to walk on it, and took any chance of activity he was offered, even when it was in the form of chores. "I can milk her," he said excitedly. "Papa showed me how!"

Winnie reached out to muss his golden hair. "All right then, I'll leave her in your care. Try not to spill!"

"Who, me?" Elijah widened his eyes innocently.

Nora patted Millie on the rump as she tugged Winnie toward the family wagon. It had been tight since the tragic river crossing, since Nora and Jeb no longer had a wagon of their own.

Papa and Jeb had been sleeping under the wagon, leaving the tent for the women to use at night, but that wasn't sustainable. And it certainly didn't offer any privacy.

Jeb likely wouldn't be able to afford a new wagon here at Fort Bridger, much less the new team of oxen or mules needed to pull it. He didn't want to borrow money from Papa to purchase them, either. But he had said he'd be able to furnish them a decent sized tent, which he would be at the fort to see about in the morning.

Nora hadn't complained about losing the small wagon full of the supplies and belongings deemed essential or sentimental enough to remain after the purges required to lighten it.

But Winnie knew Nora had only the dress on her back, and an old spare sweater that remained in the trunk they'd shared at the start of their journey. It probably wouldn't even fit her, now that she was really beginning to show.

It seemed wrong to be re-making one of her dresses for a wedding when Nora needed it much more.

"Winnie, there you are." Mama hustled around the corner of the wagon. She ushered the sisters into a makeshift fitting room, nothing more than two quilts strung between their wagon and the Vogelsang's to offer a place to change.

"Which dress did you make over?" It could only be one of the two spares she had, since she'd been wearing her current one for weeks.

Nora grinned mischievously. "We didn't."

"You didn't?" Winnie echoed. "Should I just wear this one, then? I'm sure it'll be fine, if we just beat some of the dust out…"

"Hush." Nora came up behind her and clasped her hands over Winnie's eyes. "You're not wearing that old thing on your wedding day."

Winnie began to tingle with anticipation. If they'd done what she was beginning to suspect, then they'd been putting in a lot of work when they should have been sleeping.

"You didn't just get cloth for your new dress at the clothiers in Fort Laramie, did you?" She could sense Nora's smile, even though she couldn't see it.

"No, we didn't." Nora drew her hands back, and Winnie saw her wedding dress for the first time, as

Mama held it up for display.

Her sister and mother had indeed been busy. It was a miracle they'd been able to make such a beautiful dress, much less after finishing their never-ending chores.

Winnie had never worn finer.

The cream-colored calico bodice was accented by a high collar trimmed with lace, and sleeves that cuffed at the wrist.

Pale-blue ribbon adorned the edges of the bodice.

Somehow, Nora had remembered Hal joking about liking blue ribbon, nearly two months ago.

The skirt was the same color blue as the ribbon, though perhaps a shade or two darker.

Winnie nearly burst into tears. "It's so wonderful," she managed, blinking furiously. "I can't believe you did this for me."

Mama brought the dress over as Nora helped Winnie out of her dusty old one. "You deserve every bit of happiness we can give you on your wedding day. And that includes a new dress."

They slipped it over Winnie's head, twisting and pulling at the fabric to place pins for the final alterations. Luckily, there didn't seem to be many needed. It already fit well, and they'd made the skirt just the right length. They'd surely measured her other dresses before even beginning.

"Go on, do a little spin." Nora twirled her finger in encouragement.

Winnie obliged, and the skirt swung out around her legs like a blooming flower. It hardly mattered they were camped alongside an old fur-trading outpost in the middle of nowhere. Or that it was dry, dusty, and surrounded by unbroken wilderness.

In that moment, spinning in a new dress, Winnie felt like she was exactly where she was supposed to be.

****

The following morning, the whole camp rose early to begin preparations for the wedding, which would take place just before sundown.

Mama had selected the spot for the ceremony, but refused to tell Winnie anything about it. "You'll see it when you see your new husband, and not before."

Nora went with Winnie to bathe in the Blacks Fork, a tributary off the Green River that ran near the fort.

The water was calm and the sandbars wide.

No one was doing laundry today, since the wedding was mere hours away. Most were bent over cook fires, baking bread, buying needed supplies at the fort, or making repairs.

But Winnie had no doubt that after lunch there'd be a crowd of people washing in the river before dressing in their best for the ceremony.

Their best might be the only shirt or dress they owned, or perhaps one they'd saved to wear to church in Oregon. It might be a necklace, a pair of earrings that only came out on special occasions, or even just a ribbon in freshly brushed hair. No matter how frugal their current circumstances, this was still a wedding, and weddings were big celebrations among family, friends, and neighbors.

There would be feasting and dancing well into the night, and everyone would want to look their best for it. Or as good as they were able in their current circumstances.

With that in mind, Winnie scrubbed down quickly,

rubbing handfuls of sand along her skin until she was pink and clean all over. Then she used a precious bit of their homemade soap, even in her hair.

When she was finished, Nora combed her hair out and began to braid it while it was still wet. Rather than the plain braid Winnie usually favored to keep her hair out of her face, Nora twisted several smaller braids together into a bun, even weaving spare ribbon between the strands of dark hair.

"There." She stepped back. "Perfect."

Winnie took her word for it, since she couldn't see it for herself.

They made their way back to camp and went with Papa into Fort Bridger to see a bit of the sights to help pass the time until evening.

The blacksmith shop was interesting, though far too hot for Winnie. She wasn't keen to sweat through her clothes so soon after a bath.

They stopped to examine the livestock next, and Papa eyed the chickens with interest. "It sure would be nice to have eggs for breakfast," he said wistfully. "But I suppose we can wait a little while longer."

Fort Bridger was smaller than Fort Laramie had been, and quite a bit rougher around the edges. Men dressed in furs and leathers were a common sight, and so were Native women that seemed to be the men's wives.

Winnie saw several children of such unions, and tried not to stare. She knew lonely men would want the company of women – especially strong women who were adept at frontier life. But she hadn't expected the Native women would have felt any pull to stay. They didn't appear to be there against their will, rather the opposite. She witnessed them laughing with the men and cooking a meal to share with them.

Their children looked happy and well cared for. Surely, if they were here against their will, their families would have already rescued them?

She knew what high society back east would say of such unconventional unions. But she thought of Mae and the faceless Tatanka Pteccilia, and felt a surge of disdain toward the snobbish, closed-minded opinions of those who would have denied her friend any chance at happiness with the man she loved.

She hoped that Mae and Hank were all right.

They wouldn't know how the shortcut crossing had gone until days after leaving Fort Bridger. She wished they'd been able to be with her today. Taking a firm hold of the worry that threatened to overtake her, Winnie refocused on her father and sister.

When they ran out of things to explore, they went back to camp.

Haunches of venison already roasted on spits, and the smell made her stomach rumble. She'd have to eat something at the wagon, or else she wouldn't be able to stand long enough at the altar to be properly married before diving for the delicious supper that awaited them.

"There you are! Hurry, the lot of you! We need to get dressed." Mama ushered Nora and Winnie into their makeshift changing room, leaving Papa and Jeb to get Elijah ready.

Once she was dressed, a circle of neighbors, most of them mothers and grandmothers, surrounded her, exclaiming over how fine she looked with her new dress and fancy hair.

Winnie wondered what Mrs. McCleary would have said if she were here, before solemnly easing the thought aside. Mrs. McCleary would have been kind, and there was no point to imagining it further.

Her thoughts wandered to the soon-to-be new Mrs. Blake, who was still learning English and had only been with their party for about three weeks. Were her wedding preparations as exciting as Winnie's? Or was she alone right now, feeling as though she'd lost the reins to a horse bolting beneath her?

Winnie supposed that it didn't matter, really. They'd both chosen this, albeit for different reasons. She could only hope the young mother would eventually find in her new marriage what she had lost in her previous one. Was that naive? Maybe.

But Winnie had learned something important about hope these past few months. Hope was more than a candle in the darkness, or an ember on a cold night. It was a rope to cling to in a raging current, a trail to follow through unfamiliar lands.

Hope was what led to all great destinations. Knowing this, Winnie could never set it aside.

Nor would she ever want to.

Chapter Fifteen

Mama had chosen the place well. The Blacks Fork was just out of sight, but Winnie could hear the water going by.

Lanterns lit the grove of trees, and bundles of flowers hung from their branches. Brilliant oranges and pinks stained the western sky.

Their neighbors had already assembled in their best dress, and Hal and Mr. Blake stood on opposite sides of the preacher, Mr. Campbell.

Hal stood with hands clasped, likely to keep from fidgeting. He had forgone his hat for the occasion, and his tawny hair was neatly combed out of his eyes.

He wore a clean white shirt and a buckskin vest Winnie had never seen. The chain of his father's pocket watch glinted. He looked both excited and nervous, which perfectly described how she was feeling.

Mr. Blake had cleaned up as well. His everyday overalls were freshly washed. His children stood next to Mama, Nora, Jeb, and Elijah in the front row of guests.

Nora cradled the widow's young baby.

At last, the preacher motioned to Papa, who leaned down, extending his arm to her. "Are you ready?" He looked splendid in his gray church coat and trousers, and he smiled encouragingly.

Winnie managed a nod. She hadn't expected to be nervous to stand in front of the same people she saw day in and day out.

On Papa's other side, the widow was escorted by Mr. Bailey, since she had no family among them. Her gray dress was plain, but she wore a beautiful tartan sash over it, a tribute to her Scottish heritage.

They began to walk, and it was a moment before Winnie could take her eyes off her bouquet, comprised of sagebrush and pink Indian paintbrush. But then she looked up, and Hal grinned. Her nerves began to melt like sun-warmed snow into spring grass.

When they reached the makeshift altar and Mr. Campbell, Papa unwound her arm from his and placed her hand into Hal's.

"Who stands here today to give these women to these men before the eyes of God?"

Mr. Bailey and Papa answered that they did, and merged back into the expectant crowd.

Hal gave her hand a squeeze, and Winnie lifted her head to meet his gaze.

"You look wonderful," he murmured, even as Mr. Campbell said something about the Lord's love and bounty.

"So do you." She had a hard time looking away from his face; she so rarely saw him without a hat covering his forehead and shading his eyes. She supposed he rarely saw her without her sunbonnet, so at least they were on even footing in that respect.

Mr. Campbell cleared his throat meaningfully.

"I'm sorry, what?" Winnie blushed and looked down at her bouquet again.

"Winnifred Hayes, do you take this man as your wedded husband, to have and to hold from this day forward, for better or worse, for richer or poorer, in sickness and in health, to love and to cherish…"

He continued, and she had the sudden and ridiculous urge to laugh. She'd spent the past few weeks thinking about this day, and now that it was here, all she wanted was for it to be over so she could dance with Hal, and steal a kiss from him without worrying about who might see.

She realized Mr. Campbell's droning had stopped. "I do, of course," she said hastily.

Hal grinned, as though he realized she was having a hard time concentrating, and reveled in it. The same vows were repeated for Hal, and he held her gaze as he said, "I do."

Mr. Campbell moved on to address Mr. Blake and his new bride, and Hal reached for her hands, smoothing his thumbs over the back of them.

When all the vows had been finished, they were given the opportunity to exchange rings.

Mr. Blake had been wearing his first wife's wedding ring around his neck, and he looked physically pained as he removed it from its chain and slipped it onto the new Mrs. Blake's thin finger. Of course, he wouldn't have had any opportunity to seek out a new ring. Perhaps he would be able to when they reached Oregon.

Did the young mother beside them have any qualms about wearing a dead woman's wedding band?

She didn't expect a ring from Hal, so she was mightily surprised when he pulled one from his pocket and eased it onto the fourth finger of her left hand.

"With this ring, I thee wed," he murmured.

Winnie gaped at it. It was the first jewelry she had ever been given that wasn't from a family member. A pair of her grandmother's pearl earrings were hidden away in her trunk, and her mother had given Winnie one of her own necklaces on her twelfth birthday, but this ring was something altogether different.

It was wrought like three tiny silver branches intertwined. She had never seen anything like it. It evoked the depth and power of a tree's roots while simultaneously reaching among its branches for the stars. "How?"

Mr. Campbell was busy orating his closing verse.

"The blacksmith at Fort Laramie," Hal whispered. "I had it made from one of my mother's silver spoons. She never had any daughters, so she gave one each to me and my brothers, for our future wives."

"Will she mind it's been used for a ring?" Surely, if his mother came to Oregon to join then in the future as Hal wanted, she'd notice that the heirloom was missing.

Hal shook his head. "A happy bride is more important than a spoon. And technically, the blacksmith only used the handle."

Hoots and hollers swept across the gathered crowd, nearly drowning out Hal's words.

Winnie glanced bewilderedly over her shoulder, just in time to see Mr. Blake give his new wife a chaste peck on the lips. Oh, they'd reached that part of the ceremony.

She beckoned Hal closer, curling one finger.

He complied, taking his time, mouth quirking into a crooked smile. He paused just long enough to breathe "You are quite charming, Mrs. Clark," onto her lips, and then, he kissed her.

His hands cupped the nape of her neck, and she found herself reaching to grip his vest, tugging him closer.

The mountain men of the fort bellowed their

approval from the rear of the crowd when the newlyweds finally pulled apart.

"That's my daughter," Papa complained, but he was smiling when she turned and caught his eye. He winked at her before turning and kissing Mama soundly.

She'd been busy clapping, and bore a dazed look of surprise when he released her.

Officially man and wife, Winnie and Hal turned themselves over to their neighbors, accepting hugs, thumps on the back, and compliments.

The crowd made their way back to camp, where food had been roasting, simmering, and spreading its decadent aroma since before lunch. More bunches of flowers had been hung from the wagons, and sweet-smelling sage smoldered in the fires, keeping the mosquitos at bay.

Mr. Bridger and his men had provided a motley assortment of tables and chairs, hewn from local timber. Those who still had stools or chairs brought them, and others spread quilts atop the grass, making for a festive reception that was part banquet, part picnic.

Mrs. Klein, who had given Winnie the beeswax she and Mae had used to make the salve for Elijah's leg, had clearly been busy fashioning candles.

They flickered wherever there was a spare candlestick, and where no candlestick was available, someone had poured hot wax down and then firmly set the candle upright in it, keeping it from toppling over.

The tables of food were spread with an assortment of borrowed tablecloths—some of carefully crafted lace, others of sturdy linen. Haunches of roasted venison sat atop beds of gathered greens. Ears of corn, blackened by the fire, were piled in neat triangles. Platters of biscuits and cornbread sat among precious jars of honey. There were even bowls of ripe berries, ready to stain fingers and lips.

A smaller table bore desert, and Winnie squealed with excitement when she beheld the numerous pies that rested there.

"I promised you an apple pie on your wedding day," Hal said. "Remember?"

She bent over a pie, greedily inhaling the scent of spiced apples, melted butter, and sugar. The smell was so comforting; it transported her mind back to cheerful Thanksgivings and Christmases, and church weddings in town.

"It's all so wonderful!" She clutched Hal's hand. "Thank you."

"You deserve all of it, and more. Shall we eat first, or dance?"

"Eat, of course!" She could barely wait to enjoy all the delicious food. It seemed to border on excessive, but she suspected being on the trail these past months had radically changed the way she viewed food.

It would be a welcome respite to enjoy the spread before them as a hard-earned luxury of tastes and textures. They had grown so accustomed to shoveling simple, quick meals into their mouths, solely for the fuel and energy they provided during long hours of travel. Savoring flavors again would be remarkable, and Winnie intended to try at least one bite of everything before coming back to fill her plate.

They joined her family on a blanket and eagerly dug into their food.

Nora wore her only surviving dress, but she'd woven flowers into her hair. She still held the new Mrs.

Blake's baby, allowing the bride a bit of time to enjoy the party and get to know her new husband. She'd just become a mother of five, by taking on Mr. Blake's children, and it would likely be a long while before she had any time to herself.

Cute as the baby was, nestled in the crook of Nora's arm, Winnie didn't envy Mrs. Blake's position. It would likely be a rough transition for her.

Papa, Jeb, and Elijah rose from the blanket, excusing themselves and slipping into the falling darkness with a suspiciously covert air.

"They'll be right back." Mama reached out to trace one of the ribbons in her hair. "We have a surprise for you."

She looked to Hal, to see if he knew anything. His knowing smirk told her that he most certainly did.

"You'll see in a moment." He chuckled. "I'm not saying a word."

She narrowed her eyes at him, then busied herself with a generous slice of pie while they waited. It tasted even better than it smelled; a remarkable feat. At this rate, she'd be popping the seams of her dress before bedtime.

At last, she caught sight of Papa and Jeb, carefully making their way along the edge of the crowd. They led two oxen, and something even more surprising.

"A wagon?" She hastily set her plate aside and ran to meet them. Hal, Mama, and Nora followed close behind her.

"Surprise!" Elijah yelled from his perch atop the narrow front seat.

"How did you get this?" Winnie stepped forward to run her hands over the wooden planks. "And the team to pull it?"

"The wagon is from Hal." Papa patted an ox fondly. "The animals are from your Mama and me."

She whirled to Hal, half a dozen questions on her face. He joined her at the back of the wagon, and pulled the hinged back down so she could peer inside.

"A couple sold it to Mr. Bridger a few weeks ago. They decided to settle here near the fort for the rest of the season."

She'd expected they would get their own tent, but she'd never dreamed of having their own wagon. Granted, it was small; only half the size of her family's. But Hal didn't have much, since he'd been hired on by Big John. His only personal belongings were Ol' Belle, her tack, and his clothes.

She only had the one small trunk she'd shared with Nora. The rest of the things they'd been using along the way, like the cookware, food, and tools, all belonged to her parents.

An empty water barrel sat inside the wagon, and the canvas and poles for a small tent. A line had been fastened across both the front and back of the wagon, each bearing a curtain that was currently pushed aside, but could be closed for privacy or in case of rain. There were hooks hammered along the top edge of the wagon box for hanging things. And that was it. The rest of it was a blank canvas, ready for them to make into their own.

"Thank you!" She flung her arms around Hal and squeezed tight. Their wedding day had been so much more than she'd expected, and it wasn't even over yet.

"You're welcome." He brushed her cheek with his lips.

They went to examine the oxen and to thank her

parents, who waved off their gratitude with ease.

Elijah begged to be able to ride in the wagon with them when they left the fort. He was nearly as excited as Winnie.

Papa led the pair of oxen out to join the others in the field, and the rest of them returned to their blanket to finish their meal.

She helped herself to another piece of pie.

Hal just laughed, pushing the remains of his slice onto her plate. "I don't think I can eat another bite," he confided. "I'm so stuffed I may not be able to dance."

Neighbors began making their way over to offer their own small wedding gifts, as though the wagon and oxen had been the signal to the rest of the camp. The gifts were nothing like the heirlooms and home furnishings like Jeb and Nora had received, but they'd been married before starting the journey to Oregon.

Winnie didn't mind simple gifts. They were gifts of time as well as thought, items handmade or sacrificed, rather than purchased in a store.

Mrs. Klein gave them beeswax candles, wrapped with a bit of ribbon. Big John had a new saddle blanket for Hal, and a bag full of penny candies for Winnie. Doc Collins and his wife presented them with a tiny medical kit, complete with a bottle of camphor, essence of peppermint, and castor oil. Mrs. Vogelsang and Adda gave them several bars of homemade soap, scented with sage.

Mr. McCleary brought them his wife's favorite mixing bowl.

Winnie took it gently, turning it in her hands to admire how smooth it was. "Thank you," she told him. "But I'd hate to take something of hers you might miss."

His mouth twitched, as though he'd attempted a reassuring smile. "That's all right, Winnifred. I've got memories enough to last a lifetime." He patted her hand and walked away.

Others brought them bundles of wildflowers, to hang upside down in the wagon. Some gave small cooking utensils, including a hand-carved set of spoons. There was even an embroidered pillow, like the kind Nora had been saving feathers to make.

Their last gift was presented by a whole group of women who'd come together to make them a wedding quilt. It was embroidered with plants and animals they had seen along the trail, including buffalo, deer, and even a bear.

It was so large that Winnie couldn't hold it up by herself. Mama had to help her.

"It's beautiful!" Winnie gave each woman a kiss on the cheek. "Thank you."

Hal carried the new things over to their wagon, carefully laying them inside to be sorted through later. When he returned, he held a hand out to Winnie, the picture of gentility. "May I have this dance, Mrs. Clark?" He winked, and his grin betrayed how long he'd been waiting to be able to say that out loud.

"You may, Mr. Clark." Though she rather liked her new name, it would still take some time to get used to.

There was not yet any music, and the camp musicians scrambled to assemble themselves as Hal spun Winnie round and round, clearing them a space safely away from the tables laden with food.

Big John started blowing his harmonica, and the surviving Wilson brother, Samuel, began sawing on his fiddle.

Mr. McCleary did not reappear with his banjo, but she wasn't surprised. It would be a miracle if he could ever stand to make music again. The trail had been cruel to his family, taking both his oldest son and his wife within a few short months of each other.

Mr. Vogelsang produced a guitar, but he couldn't play with his burned hands, still encumbered by bandages. Adda took up her father's strings, deftly strumming and dancing her fingers along the neck with ease.

Hal spun Winnie around and around, twirling them in and out of their clapping neighbors. Then she was spun from hand to hand, passed all through the party, and slung back to her new husband, breathless and a bit dizzy.

She danced with Papa, Jeb, and even Elijah, though Mama grumbled a bit about straining his leg. She even danced with Big John, who stepped on her feet more than once, and Mr. Bridger, who was surprisingly nimble.

She and Hal danced and sang and laughed well into the night. The stars came out, and their sweat cooled in the brisk night air. Winnie had never seen such stars— she was usually asleep before they made their appearance. It became clear to her why Mr. Bridger and his mountain men had never moved on to an established town, or gone back to the big cities of the east coast.

How could anyone ever live away from stars like these, once they had glimpsed them?

Eventually, things began to calm down. People started falling asleep atop their blankets. Some indulged in a bit too much whiskey. Families with young children retired to their tents for the night.

Winnie did her best to ignore Nora's shameless

giggling as she and Hal made their way to their new wagon. She knew well enough what was to come, and she didn't need her sister making her more nervous about it.

Hal helped her into the back of the wagon, and then climbed in himself, drawing the curtain behind him. Though the noise had diminished somewhat, there was still music playing, and people laughed and talked with one another.

She was grateful for that. It made the sudden aloneness with Hal seem a bit less awkward.

"Here, sit down." Hal moved their wedding gifts to the front seat so there was more room. He'd already laid down their new quilt, and he carefully took his boots off and set them aside, so as not to get it dirty.

Winnie sat, and the reality of the sudden change her life had taken began to make itself clear.

Never again would she share a wagon with her family. Or lie beside Nora in the tent, whispering of the men they adored. Her mother and father wouldn't be the last people she'd bid goodnight, or the first ones she greeted in the morning.

In the span of a day, everything had changed.

"What are you thinking?" Hal removed his vest so he could lounge more comfortably. He sat at the opposite wall of the wagon, somehow guessing she might be needing the bit of space he could offer.

"I'm thinking that everything will be different," Winnie admitted. "And I'm a little afraid."

Hal leaned forward earnestly. "If you're worried about sharing a bed with me—" He stopped to clear his throat. "—we don't have to. I mean, we can just go to sleep."

Winnie tried to make out his expression in the darkness within the wagon. Though fires still burned nearby, they threw things into shifting shadow, and Hal's face was shrouded. She found herself reaching across the space between them and lacing their fingers together.

She'd come to know his hands well, in these past weeks. They'd touched her, held her, and even saved her. She knew these hands, and she knew Hal. A ring on her finger didn't make him a different person. His body wasn't wrapped in some cloak of mystery. He was just a man.

But there were parts of him she had yet to explore, and that was where the nervousness pressed in.

"I'm not afraid of you," she clarified. She scooted a little bit closer.

"Please don't be." He raised their joined hands and rested her palm against his chest. "Feel my heart? How fast it's beating?"

It was indeed racing, thudding along at a noticeably more erratic pace. "What are you thinking?"

He hesitated. "Are you sure you want to know?"

"Always."

He pulled her hand up from his chest and kissed it. "I'm so happy you're my wife. There's so much for us to do, and see. But right now, all I want to see is you."

She blushed, grateful the darkness hid her from his observant gaze. "Well…" she said at last. "I suppose you should help me with my dress, regardless." She turned, offering her back to him, so he could undo the laces that held the back of it closed.

"I've never actually helped someone out of a dress before."

"It's easy," Winnie encouraged. "Just undo the top

knot and then loosen the others."

She felt his fingers at her nape, and focused on breathing as they traveled lower and began to untie the laces. When he reached her lower back, she turned around and slid the dress down her legs, feeling as though each movement was exaggerated.

She fought the urge to wrap her arms around herself. Hal was her husband now, and there was nothing for her to be embarrassed about. She told herself that as sternly as she was able.

He eased back to pull his shirt over his head, and the rustling of clothing filled the small space. Then he settled down upon their quilt, leaving the pillow for her to use.

She could barely see his arms as he extended them to her.

"Get comfortable," he said. "I'll keep my hands to myself, I promise."

Winnie took a fortifying breath. She lay beside him, trying not to shiver as his body heat soothed her chilled skin. His bare chest and arms were familiar, and yet brand new.

Carefully, he wrapped an arm around her, and kissed her on the shoulder. "Goodnight, Winnie." He tilted his forehead to rest against her own.

She struggled to label her rushing emotions. She was nervous about the unknown. Embarrassed about how exactly to go about it. Undeniably excited, despite it all. And yet, she had a hard time making her hands move.

It was tempting to try and stay in the world she was familiar with for a little longer. In the world where she was a daughter, and a friend, but not a wife. Where she'd never held a man in the dark before, or lain beside one. The one where she only answered to her parents and her own conscious.

But if she stayed in that world, she would never know the happiness of what beckoned from beyond it. She loved Hal, and he deserved the best of her. As their children would, someday.

She reached through the darkness and grazed his face with her fingers. Then she traveled downward, exploring his bare skin, and testing the resolve of her nerve. Rather than send her running to the other side of the quilt, she grew bolder the longer she touched him. His breathing hitched, and a strange kind of awe overcame her.

He felt for her all the things she felt for him. He wanted her, but didn't ask out of respect for her own comfort. He put her first, as he had always done.

With that realization, the uncertainty vanished like smoke into the night sky. She'd been blessed, in so many ways. She'd married for love, when others around her were forced to marry for convenience and safety, like the Blakes, or had loved ones taken from them, like Mr. McCleary and Mae.

She wouldn't waste such a precious gift. It could be snatched back at any moment, as they had all come to learn too well.

She rolled toward Hal, splaying her hand against his shoulder blade, and tugged him to her. She kissed him, gently at first, and then with more demand, more intent.

He gripped her shoulders, and their legs twined together.

She had to remind herself to breathe.

Breaking away, Hal tilted her chin up, gaining access to the sensitive skin along her collarbone.

She threaded a hand through his hair, marveling at

the way his scent seemed to sink into her, simultaneously soothing and sweeping away.

A twig snapped outside their wagon, and they jolted in surprise. It was the only warning before chaos stomped all over their peaceful interlude.

Their neighbors surrounded the wagon and made as much noise as they could. They banged on pots and pans, fired shots into the air, and sang bawdy songs that made Winnie's ears heat.

"You didn't think you could escape without a good ol' shivaree, did ya?" Mr. Bridger yelled. "Let 'em have it, folks!"

They endured the cacophony for several minutes before Hal finally moved the curtain aside and thrust his head out of the wagon. "All right, that's enough," he shouted. "Leave us be."

Mr. Bridger waved him off. "Aw, it's all in good fun." He turned back to the crowd. "Let's give 'em one last serenade to put them to sleep!"

The crowd cheered and burst into song about a prostitute and the man who loved her because of her…assets.

Winnie started laughing, despite herself. She'd attended shivarees after weddings back home, but it was certainly different being on this side of it. A little more embarrassing, for one thing.

Hal seemed relieved to hear her laughing rather than being upset. "I'm sorry." He rubbed at the back of his neck. "They're almost gone."

Sure enough, the lyrics of their song faded into the distance, and the gunshots stopped. A pack of coyotes yipped from across the hills.

Winnie rubbed briskly at her bare arms. "Come back

to bed. It's getting cold."

Hal sank down beside her, blowing out a sigh. "Their timing was uncanny."

"Nora was with them." She looped her arm through his. "I'd bet money on it."

They settled back against the quilt, and she pillowed her head on his shoulder.

"Are you tired?" He murmured against her hair. "I could go to sleep just like this."

"Yes. But I don't want to sleep."

He lifted his head to look at her, but she was already rising to kiss him. Would it always be like this? This feeling of charting new waters, to find that they already led the way home?

His hands slid down to grip her waist, and she lost track of time. Sleep had never obliterated her the way his reverent touches did. Sleep had never gifted her with such a bubble of peace and sensation.

She became his wife, in every sense of the word, and he became hers even more completely. If there had ever been another route for them to take, Winnie no longer wanted to remember it. This was her home now…because her home had become a heart, beating inside a kind man.

Chapter Sixteen

More than a week later, the wagon train stopped for a few hours at what Big John called Soda Springs.

Naturally carbonated water bubbled up, and there was even a geyser there, the first Winnie had ever seen. When it erupted, it whistled like a steamboat chugging down the river.

Big John had warned them not to drink too much of the water, as it was too alkaline, but almost everyone had a cup or two.

Hal added sugar to theirs, and they pretended it was lemonade.

Local tribes believed the water had healing properties, and it would have been a convenient place to do laundry. But they elected to move on before setting camp for the night, as the springs smelled unpleasantly like rotten eggs.

They had not yet caught up with Mae and Hank and the rest of the cutoff wagons. Big John had expected to rendezvous with them when they emerged into Bear River Valley several days ago. They speculated the cutoff wagons had been forced ahead, possibly by Natives, as they were within the territory of the Shoshone tribe.

Winnie was worried. It was also possible something had happened to delay them, and they were lagging behind rather than being forced ahead. There was simply no way to know.

The valley itself was beautiful, ringed on both sides by mountains and carpeted with good grass for the livestock. They followed the Bear River northward toward Fort Hall. It was possible, Big John said, the cutoff wagons had been driven to Fort Hall for safety. A much-smaller company, they were more vulnerable to attack from bandits or Natives.

The anxious weight on her chest grew with each day that passed.

Mae had seemed so confident about the cutoff. Was it even possible they had gotten lost? Had their oxen died in the waterless crossing, stranding them? Each possible option seemed worse than the one before.

"She'll be all right," Hal repeatedly soothed. "Hank won't let anything happen to her."

But Winnie knew, as well as he did, that many things were simply out of their friends' control.

Her worry grew as the days passed, like an insatiable predator that hounded her steps and her thoughts.

Big John was uncharacteristically quiet and stony. He took to riding ahead for hours at a time, leaving others to lead his oxen.

The one positive that she clung to was the fact that they had not come across any signs of disaster in the valley. They hadn't found any corpses, dead livestock, or abandoned wagons. Whatever had happened had either happened on the actual cutoff, or their friends were still ahead of them, for a reason they couldn't comprehend at the moment.

Fort Hall was only two days ride away when Hal came racing back from the front of their column, Big John galloping close behind.

It was beginning to rain, big, fat drops that made pleasant background music as it strummed against the canvas wagon covers. They usually stopped to take shelter when a storm rolled in, so Nora left Winnie with her pair of oxen and went to help Jeb and Papa.

Big John leapt off his horse, stumbling in his haste, and left the reins to drag in the dust, which was rapidly darkening into mud. "They're alive!" he shouted, startling livestock and children alike. "They made it through!"

Hal reached Winnie a moment later.

"What did you find?" She was so impatient that she nearly dragged him off Belle's back. "Where's Mae? And Hank?

He walked Belle to the back of their wagon to tie up her lead. "They painted a message in tar on a boulder at the side of the trail. They were stalked by Natives all the way across the valley, and they intend to wait for us at Fort Hall."

"Natives?" Winnie pressed. "But Mae said…"

He began removing Belle's saddle that was already slick with rain. "Now you know as much as I do. I wish I could tell you more."

Winnie realized her worry for her friends was driving her to be inconsiderate, and she reached out to Hal, wordlessly asking for forgiveness. He rested his cheek on the top of her head, and she could tell by the way he leaned on her that he was exhausted. "Come on, let's get you dry," she encouraged. "You need rest."

"I need you more," he countered, but ruined the intended effect by yawning in her ear.

"Maybe later, when you can stay awake throughout the whole experience." She gently pushed him toward the wagon. "I can handle the oxen for a few more hours."

"Big John wants to get to Fort Hall straightaway." Hal yanked his boots off and turned them upside down on two dowels he'd fashioned to dry them out. "He'll likely push well into the evening."

Winnie didn't doubt it, nor did she blame him. They'd been worrying for long enough. "I can handle it," she repeated. "Sleep."

"You're very demanding, Mrs. Clark." He shucked his wet shirt off and flopped back onto their quilt. "Have I told you how much I love it?"

"Not quite enough." Winnie grinned.

Resigning herself to a wet afternoon, she donned Hal's hat and affixed the grain bag to Belle's halter. The horse nickered with what she took as appreciation. And then they were off again, trudging through the slow, steady rain.

Her thoughts kept straying to the cutoff wagons, to Mae and Hank, and what their tale would be when they were finally reunited.

Why would Natives have followed such a small party? Had they been waiting for an opportunity to steal the livestock? Papa had told her mules were nearly as desirable as horses, though they could be far more difficult. But oxen were too slow to be of much use to the Natives.

Surely if they'd had desires more sinister than theft, the Natives would have acted on them. There were only five families in the cutoff party, and their defense would have been minimal. Much as she tried, Winnie couldn't solve the puzzle without the missing pieces from Mae and Hank.

So, she kept walking alongside the oxen, keeping

them moving in the right direction at their plodding pace through the mud.

****

They arrived at the fort exhausted, having pushed much later into the evening than they were used to and rising again before dawn. Though Fort Hall was owned by the Hudson Bay Company, it had the same trapper-and-mountain-man feel as Fort Bridger, which made sense, considering the trading posts were only about two hundred miles apart.

Hal had told her that many trappers in the region had begun to work under contract with the HBC, as it held a complete monopoly on the local fur trade, and ruthlessly targeted its free American competitors.

Jeb and Big John rode ahead, and Nora walked with Winnie and Elijah behind the family wagon, a hand resting fondly on her rounded stomach. She was five months along now, and her last remaining dress had been let out as much as possible. She said she was nearly finished with the new dress she'd made from the cloth from Fort Laramie, and Winnie hoped it would be big enough to last.

They spotted the wagons from the cutoff party camped on the banks of the Snake River, and set up alongside them, a distance from the wooden fence that branched around the fort and connected smoothly to the one large adobe gatehouse.

The open gate was flanked by two British soldiers in bright-red coats, each holding a rifle to their shoulder.

The new Mrs. Blake was immediately surrounded by the other Scottish families that had taken the cutoff.

Her baby was passed around for kisses, and the pleasant lilt of their native tongue made Winnie's lips turn up.

She looked for Mae and Hank, but didn't see them. They couldn't be far; Big John and Jeb had not returned, and they'd never have left the safety of the fort if Natives had been following them.

As soon as they turned their oxen and Belle out to graze, Winnie and Hal strode purposefully through the open gate.

The inner workings of the fort weren't complicated. There were a few log barracks for the British soldiers, a blacksmith, and a well-appointed townhouse she assumed was for officers. The smaller livestock, like goats, sheep, and poultry, were neatly penned, making use of every bit of space within the walls.

In the back corner, Winnie spotted a figure with a long braid that she recognized, in a black hat and dusty woolen pants.

Mae spoke with a Native man of imposing height who was wearing buckskin breeches and a shirt decorated with porcupine quills.

Hank and a British officer stood with them, and the exchange seemed to be a calm one. Friendly, even.

"What on earth?" She wondered aloud. "I thought Natives were what drove them here."

"The Hudson Bay Company has trade agreements with most of the tribes in this area," Hal mused. "Maybe he represents one of them."

At that moment, Hank noticed them, and waved them over with a relieved expression.

Mae turned to see who he had gestured to, and her face lit up.

Winnie grinned and quickened her steps.

The British officer excused himself as they

approached, but the Native man remained.

"You're here!" Mae threw her arms around Winnie. "Thank goodness."

"We were so worried!" Winnie replied. "What happened?" She assessed the Native man over her friend's shoulder.

His height was imposing, as were his muscular shoulders and legs, noticeable even beneath his buckskin clothing. But his face was well lined around the eyes and mouth, giving the impression he smiled often.

Hank noticed where her attention had settled, and turned from eagerly shaking Hal's hand. "Winnie, Hal, this is Sahale. He and his men are the reason we got here safely."

Winnie sensed a complicated story behind the brief explanation. "Did they scare off another tribe stalking you?"

It was Sahale that answered, in well-practiced English. "Thieves have grown common in this valley. We were coming to trade at the fort when we saw your friends, and then we found bandits waiting to ambush them."

She tried to keep from gaping, but was just as sure she failed. "So, you..."

Sahale looked mildly affronted. "We stopped them, of course. They were cowards, stealing from women and little children."

Hal appeared as enthralled as she felt, and Winnie glanced at Mae, not the slightest bit surprised to see the smug set of her friend's face.

"We didn't know what their intentions were, at first," Hank admitted sheepishly, rubbing the back of his neck. "Sahale and his men stayed within sight of our wagons, but never approached. We didn't know what they'd done for us until we got to the fort and Sahale came to explain."

Sahale shrugged, as though what he and his men had done was barely of note. "Sometimes it does not go well when my people approach yours without invitation." There was no need for him to elaborate further.

Winnie knew many travelers along the westward trails would rather scare Natives away with a show of force than allow them close enough to see what they intended. And most would not readily believe that they came to help.

She was beyond grateful she was no longer counted among those people. And Hal never had been. Inspired by a sudden idea, she held her hand out to Sahale. She wasn't certain he was familiar with the custom of a handshake, but he clasped her hand firmly and gave it a single pump. "Thank you for helping our friends. We'd love for you and your men to join us for supper, if you're able."

There were a few heartbeats of silence.

Mae and Hank exchanged a glance.

Had she somehow overstepped?

"Absolutely." Hal stepped smoothly into the pocket of awkwardness and through to the other side. Offering solidarity, as he always did. "Join us."

Sahale seemed taken aback, but recovered quickly. "That's kind. Are you sure we will be welcome?" He gestured over their shoulders with a jut of his chin, and they turned to look.

A huddle of their neighbors had stalled near the gate of the fort, obviously surprised to see them conversing with Sahale.

Nora and Adda were among them. Her sister narrowed her eyes meaningfully before turning away.

Resolutely, Winnie spun back to the tall man. "I'm sure. It will be our pleasure."

****

Sahale and his companions arrived nearly half an hour before sunset, and they didn't come empty-handed. The oldest among them, whom Winnie could easily have called her grandfather, carried a basket of filleted fish, covered with broad leaves to keep the bugs away.

News had spread rapidly through the camp that the newlyweds had invited the Natives to dine with them, and their neighbors firmly divided into halves. Those who disapproved stayed away, some going as far as to move their wagons, as though distancing themselves from disease.

But there were many among them who were curious about the Natives, nerves soothed by the fact that the soldiers at the fort were within earshot should anything unexpected occur. The Vogelsang family kept their wagon alongside Winnie's parents' wagon. Adda and her sisters prepared a seemingly endless number of biscuits.

Mama was less than thrilled about the invitation Winnie had extended, but Papa soothed her with ease. "If it weren't for those men, Lord only knows what would have happened to Hank," he reminded her, thumbs stuffed beneath his suspender straps. "They protected our family, same as Mae has done, and we owe them for it."

Mama nodded, the steel in her eyes like a tangible thing, and said no more.

Nora, on the other hand, made her complaints known to any within earshot of the wagon. It was Jeb who finally stood up to her, with uncharacteristic firmness. "They saved my brother. I plan to shake each and every one of their hands for it."

Nora huffed, unused to such resolution from her husband.

Winnie gave him a not-so subtle clap on the back.

When all was said and done, they had a larger party gathered than she'd expected. Alongside her family, and the Vogelsangs, all the cutoff families had come, along with the Blakes, the Kleins, and Doc Collins and his wife.

Widow Simmons and her daughter Moira also came, though Winnie was unsurprised. She'd seen Moira talking to Natives before, after all.

Mr. McCleary brought his children, and Mae and Big John were among the first to arrive.

Winnie knew Mae wouldn't have missed it. If anything, she'd probably have preferred if fewer of the neighbors attended, so she could have more uninterrupted time among the people she admired so much.

When they came, the oldest among them presented his basket of filleted fish to Mama, who took it with a sincere smile.

That seemed to set the tone for the evening. Even those who'd seemed a bit hesitant at first grew noticeably more relaxed.

Sahale spoke the best English of his friends, but another, introduced as his brother-in-law, was decipherable about half the time. He seemed to understand more than he was able to speak. He spent a good portion of the evening pointing at objects and naming them to Jeb and Hank, who sat on his right. A pattern quickly emerged.

"Fish," he said, using the English term or what he thought the English word was.

Jeb and Hank nodded enthusiastically when he got it right, and helped when needed.

Then he'd say the same word in his native tongue, and Jeb and Hank would repeat it, much to the delight of the other Natives. They laughed good-naturedly when the brothers butchered their lyrical language, though it truly wasn't for lack of trying.

Mae also enjoyed their game, and she was far better at it than the others, which didn't surprise anyone.

Nora, stubbornly seated on the other side of Jeb, seemed more interested than Winnie had expected. More than once, she caught her sister studying the Native men, a thoughtful crease between her golden brows. But if anyone looked her way, she dropped her gaze to her plate.

Elijah sat between Hank and Papa, more enraptured than Winnie had seen him in weeks.

Hank had regaled the Natives with a re-telling of their encounter with the bear, and Elijah puffed up at the murmurs and looks of approval the Natives gave him.

"Bears are fierce creatures," Sahale said. "You must have earned your name after that encounter."

"My name? I've already got a name."

Sahale waved a dismissive hand. "Children in our tribe are named after something occurs to set them apart—something that marks their spirit."

"You mean you've got kids running around that don't have names yet?" Elijah demanded.

Winnie couldn't help but chuckle at his incredulous tone.

Luckily, it seemed Sahale wasn't the type to take

offense. He simply shrugged and said, "Of course," before continuing his methodical chewing.

Late into the evening, the eldest man set his plate aside and stood. The other Natives quickly followed. Dipping his head briefly, the old man spoke, a flurry of syllables that drifted like snow.

"He thanks you for sharing your fire and your meal," Sahale translated. "He hopes your people will remember this night, when the time comes."

"What time is that?" Papa stood, as well.

Sahale turned to clarify, and shrugged at the old man's brittle reply before translating again. "He says you will know. And it will be sooner than anyone would like."

With that, the Natives left, striding purposefully away from the firelight and into the rapidly chilling darkness.

Winnie assumed they had set up their trading camp on the other side of the fort.

Their neighbors dispersed and went to their own fires, and Hal extended a hand to pull her off the ground.

She shivered a bit as they turned away from the dwindling fire. "How can August feel so cold?"

He wrapped an arm around her waist, tugging her close to his side as they walked. "It will only get worse." He sounded almost cheerful about that fact. "Good thing you've got me to keep you warm."

She rolled her eyes, then planted a surprise kiss on his cheek. "Thank you, most handsome of blankets," she said drily. "What would I do without you?"

"Freeze to the bone."

"You're in a suspiciously good mood."

He smiled down at her. "Why shouldn't I be? Our

friends are safe, and we just had hours of interesting conversation. I've got a full belly and a tent waiting for me and my lovely wife."

Her mouth twitched. He was so grateful for the smallest things. She suspected it was why he so seldom complained. "Sounds like you're a lucky man."

Hal's teasing smile vanished beneath a suddenly earnest expression. "I definitely am."

As they approached their wagon and tent, pale ghosts out of reach of the firelight, Winnie tugged him to a stop. She was barely able to find the shadows of his eyes beneath the brightness of the stars appearing overhead. "Thank you, for being so supportive about Sahale. You didn't flinch when I invited them, even though you knew it would stir up mixed feelings."

Hal looked mildly affronted, as though she had stated the obvious. "You're my family now. I'll always support you."

She thought back to Nora's initial disapproval, and the other negative reactions that had come before, all the way back to when they'd met the first trio of Pawnee outside of Fort Kearny. She thought of her sister's fear, mistrust, and the anxiety that hounded her. "You might support me," she said a bit bitterly. "But not everyone will. Not everyone can."

"Nora is a complicated person." Hal speared toward the heart of Winnie's thoughts with uncanny accuracy. "She's stubborn, but she loves you. And she's brave, in her own way."

"Nora, brave?" Winnie scoffed, though that wasn't entirely fair. Until their time on the trail had challenged them so differently, her sister had been her best and most faithful friend. Had that really changed?

She was afraid to look at where they stood too closely, for fear she might see the cracks and shifting of unstable ground.

"Yes, brave." Hal gently tugged on her braid until it draped over one shoulder. "She trusted Jeb to become the type of man he didn't seem to be on the surface—bold and resolute. And now she's carrying their first child across the wilderness, where everything frightens her."

Her face grew warm with embarrassment and guilt. Her sister deserved her love and support, not to be buttressed by Winnie's own husband against the judgement of her secret thoughts.

Hal chucked her gently under the chin, tilting her face up toward his. "You're not afraid of wild things and places the way your sister is," he finished. "But she's still here. And I'd bet my best horse she'd follow you into far worse than this."

He pressed a light, tender kiss to her chilled lips, and it eased some of the guilt. He was far too good for her, she decided as he dotted her cheekbones and forehead with teasing pecks and nuzzles. He was far too good for anyone.

But she'd gotten lucky somehow, and as she grabbed the back of his neck to turn his teasing mouth to more serious matters, she vowed she would do whatever it took to be worthy of him.

Chapter Seventeen

In the days that followed, Big John and Mae led their wagon train along the south side of the Snake River. They parted ways with some of their neighbors along a split in the trail that led southwest across the Sierra Nevada into California. Nearly ten families said their goodbyes to the friends they'd made over the past four months, and tears were shed.

Winnie's family was fortunate not to lose anyone they had grown especially close with, but there was still a lump in her throat as she watched the other wagons split away and move down the new trail on their own.

Big John had given them extensive directions, and Mae had drawn them several maps. It was no doubt more reliable than some of the pamphlets that other groups were following.

When the rest of them made camp that evening, it was a little more somber than usual, and there were noticeably fewer cook fires.

"I hope they make it all right." Nora helped Mama stir the stew with some venison Hank had brought down the day before. "I keep thinking about...the Donners."

Mama and Winnie shared a taut look, both aware that this kind of talk led could lead to dangerous places.

"I'm sure they'll be just fine." Mama added some wild parsnips to the stew. "Mr. Bailey is with them. And I doubt they'll see even a dusting of snow for weeks, yet."

Born and raised in central Missouri, they were no strangers to snow. But they'd never seen it in the amounts that the stories described, reaching the eves of barns and completely obscuring roads and trails, as though they'd never existed.

"Mrs. Klein went with them," Nora said a bit hesitantly, as though even she knew this kind of worry was poisonous. "She's due to deliver any day. I can't imagine…" She wrapped a protective hand over her rounded stomach. "I can't imagine watching my baby starve and freeze. It would be so unfair."

"You've another three months to go, at least," Mama said firmly. "My grandchild will be born next to a roaring fire, beneath a good roof. And Mrs. Klein will be just fine. They'll be well out of the mountains before any real snow falls."

Winnie remembered telling her sister something similar, months ago.

Nora nodded and went back to stirring, though her brown eyes kept their distant look. "Of course," she murmured. "I'm sure you're right."

Winnie knew as well as anyone the surprise snow that had trapped the Donner party had fallen in early November. In just over two months' time, it was entirely possible their friends would encounter significant snowfall if they were still in high altitudes. But it did no good to say so, and she kept her mouth shut.

It was out of their hands, and only God had any say in the matter. If He even cared.

The senseless deaths of Mrs. Blake and her baby had planted a seed of doubt in Winnie's mind, and the drownings during their crossing of the Green River had worsened it. She was no longer certain God cared about their progress, or about how many of them would live to see Oregon.

A few more days went by as they followed the Snake River, which thundered on their right with an ominous tumult. Though they heard the water day and night, Big John had advised there were only a few places where they would be able to get down to it. Most of the river had carved itself deep into a gorge, which it now twisted and burrowed through like the snake for which it was named.

It was usually an intimidating drop off, and when they stopped in the evening, many people walked toward its edge and peered down, taking in the sight that was slightly different each night and yet still managed to seem the same. Were it not for the shifting mountain scenery in the distance, they could have been standing still again, as they had so often seemed to do on the Plains.

Sometimes there were waterfalls, which Winnie had a particular fondness for.

When the light hit the spray just right, it created tiny rainbows, fractures of bouncing light and color.

One morning, as Hal was hitching their team, Winnie found Mae at the cliff's edge, bent intently over a sketchbook in her lap. The nub of a pencil she was using was barely longer than her bent knuckles, and Winnie resolved to get her friend a new one when they reached Fort Boise.

Peering over Mae's shoulder, Winnie looked curiously at the drawing. The river came to life on the page. Otters fished along a sandbar that slowed the current, and Natives waded knee-deep into the water, fishing with pronged spears. It was so lifelike, she looked at the real river again, nearly surprised to find it empty, with no fishermen or otters in sight.

"That's wonderful. I wish I could draw like that."

Mae shrugged off the compliment. "It's not much use out here, but I like to look through the pictures during our winters in town. It…helps."

"Can I see more?" she dared to ask, not at all certain that Mae would comply.

But Mae did, flipping to the beginning of the small leather-bound book. "I start a new one each year." She sounded a bit nervous as Winnie turned the pages.

At first the pictures were mostly of buffalo and the tall, billowing grasses of the Plains. A few were of their wagon train, winding into a never-ending cloud of dust. Close profiles of wildflowers and edible plants also dotted the pages, labeled with narrow, cramped handwriting.

And then, Winnie caught sight of herself, walking alongside Hal and Ol' Belle. He was turned toward her, saying something, and the faint smile on her lips betrayed her growing fondness for him.

If she'd ever thought she'd kept her feelings discreet, Mae's drawing proved just how badly she'd failed.

"I hope you don't mind," Mae said a bit sheepishly.

"Of course not! Show me more."

There were pictures of Hank and Elijah, and of Big John whittling by the fireside and roaring with laughter.

Winnie felt herself being drawn back through time. Glimpses of Chimney Rock, the expanse of South Pass, and the bubbling waters of Soda Springs flipped by.

Mae had drawn the bear cub, feasting on berries in

the brief moments before it had been left an orphan. She had even sketched Nora and Mama, bent secretively over Winnie's unfinished wedding dress, needles and thread in hand.

"They're wonderful," Winnie murmured. "These would make anyone want to make the trip to Oregon."

At that, Mae grinned, snapping the sketchbook shut and knotting the thin leather wrapping closed. "Then I should toss it into the river, because I want us to keep it all to ourselves."

Winnie knew her friend was joking, but she still felt a flash of relief when Mae tucked the book protectively into an inner pocket of her worn coat. It would be a shame for such irreplaceable moments to be lost to something as feral as the river that churned below.

The rest of the day passed by without much incident.

Elijah and a pack of his friends got into trouble for chucking clods of mud at one another, as their aim was less than ideal and innocent victims found their only remaining jackets and aprons smeared.

Mae rode ahead with Hank, though they stayed in sight most of the time, likely unwilling to get too far ahead after the separation the cutoff route had caused.

When the bugle call echoed down the line and signaled them to make camp for the night, Winnie sighed and arched her back to stretch some of the soreness out. She had spent a portion of the afternoon hidden in her and Hal's wagon, adding to the shawl she and Mama had been piecing together for Nora. It was intended to be a surprise, so she couldn't just pull it out around the family fire. The wagon box jolted mercilessly, and she knew she'd have trouble sleeping on the ground tonight.

Dinner was a less-than-exciting combination of rice,

bacon, and beans. The sun was setting earlier these days, so they often now found themselves eating in near darkness.

Usually, they were able to finish their dishes by firelight, but Winnie found herself thinking rather fondly of the days when they'd been in bed, chores finished, before the sun had even set.

As much as she missed the summer sunshine, she didn't miss the oppressive heat. It was so nice to not be chafed by wet layers of linen and wool all the time.

She was just setting aside her empty plate when yelling burst from the darkness around their camp.

Loud yips and shrieks encircled them, like some devilish pack of coyotes.

Elijah darted to his feet, eyes huge. Multiple gunshots cracked nearby, splintering wood, and Mama tackled him, driving her youngest down into the dirt.

Jeb grabbed Nora, scuttling to pull her behind the closest wagon wheel.

"How many are there?" Winnie heard Hal shout, but she was already scrambling toward their wagon. His rifle, ammunition, and powder were there, and he needed them. Head down low, she couldn't see anything but the dirt and mangled grass beneath her hands.

"I can't tell!" Jeb called back from beneath the wagon. He'd had his own rifle as well, an heirloom of his father's, but it was lost to the river with the rest of his and Nora's belongings. The knife Mama had used to cut the bacon had been left out next to the skillet, and Jeb rushed to snatch it before falling back behind the wagon wheel.

Nora gripped his leg, as though to physically prevent him from leaving her a second time.

Winnie reached their wagon, choked down a breath, and leapt over the back. Her shoulders hit the wagon box with a painful thud.

Screams and shouts of alarm scattered through the camp, and gunshots ripped through unprotected space.

She could hear them thudding into wood and ricocheting off the dirt.

The distressed cries of their remaining livestock sounded farther and farther away. The animals must have scattered at all the noise.

She gripped Hal's rifle, heaving it over the edge of the front seat. Sheltering behind the seatback, she sighted down the barrel, praying Hal kept the powder pan filled. She clicked the cock into firing position and peered out into the darkness. Waiting.

The shrieks and hollers continued. It sounded like a poor imitation of a Native attack, as though they wanted to scare the wagon train into a frenzy before even encountering anyone. It didn't seem likely that Natives would give up the element of surprise, especially after intentionally waiting for nightfall. It didn't make sense.

Winnie tried to block out Hal's voice, shouting for her over the din. She had no idea if he'd seen her get into their wagon, but she couldn't give up her position. Mae and Hal might be the better shots, but she was the one with the rifle now. She couldn't waste it.

She had no idea if Papa had been able to reach his gun. For all she knew, she was her family's only defense.

With her back to their cook fire, her eyes finally adjusted to the darkness. Shadows that had seemed insubstantial began to solidify. Pale shapes sat astride darker ones—men on horseback. They were shirtless, imitating Native warriors…. But Winnie could now see they were not Natives at all.

They were white men, trying to scare the wagon party into thinking they were going to be the next tragic emigrant massacre, whispered about fearfully around next year's fires.

"Bandits!" Winnie shouted, struggling to be heard over the noise. "Bandits!"

She prayed her family heard, and others would soon be able to see for themselves. The doubts she had come to feel about God were forgotten amid such tangible danger. It seemed she still instinctively spoke to Him in times of need, whether she knew He was listening or not.

It was hard to keep a solitary attacker in her sights. Their horses were fast, and their riders retreated to reload. Some of them seemed to have split away, chasing after the livestock. They'd likely round them up and keep them for themselves, which would mean hunger and hard times for the wagon train. Without the remaining animals in their herd, they'd need to rely on wild game to provide their meat over the next month and a half.

A growing determination took root, solidifying like the rifle in Winnie's grip. Nobody stole food from the mouths of her family and friends. She simply would not allow it.

This deep in the wilderness, food was life. They hadn't struggled for so long and come so far just to starve at the hands of greedy men.

At last, one of the attackers slowed his horse, pausing to take aim at something to Winnie's right. The Vogelsang family's wagon was there, but she couldn't see any of them. She allowed herself a brief assessment of the bandit.

A cloth was tied over his nose and mouth, and his

rear elbow jutted into the air as he readied for the shot.

His face was shrouded in shadow, and Winnie was grateful for that as she clutched the trigger, adjusted her aim, and fired.

When the bear charged her and Elijah, she'd hardly had time to consider what her body was doing. She'd been lucky her shot had hit the bear at all. Panic and adrenaline had overtaken her senses, and she'd cared more for the brother cowering behind her than contemplating if the bear deserved to die.

The mother bear had been a wild animal, a creature that operated outside of the morals of humanity. She hadn't attacked them out of animosity, or greed. She'd been protecting her cub from what she saw as a threat.

Winnie had cried for the mother they'd left lying lifeless in the woods. It had been an unfair end for such a beautiful animal.

But when the recoil of the rifle jolted her shoulder and the outlaw tumbled off his horse, Winnie felt no remorse.

The stench of burnt powder stung her nose, and a wisp of smoke trailed from the rifle barrel. The thud of the man's body hitting the ground was obscured by the pandemonium: screams of her neighbors, shouts of the bandits calling to one another, and the neighs of frenzied horses.

She measured more powder and poured it into the powder pan with a surprisingly steady hand. After she reloaded with the ramrod and was ready to fire again, she peered over the back of the seat, searching for a new target.

A sudden thud in the wagon behind her was her only warning before a hand came down on her shoulder. She whirled, determined not to be dragged off without a fight.

"What did you plan to do when the rest of them found your hiding spot?" Hal demanded, gesturing toward the fallen man. "Dammit, Winnie! You can't reload as fast as they can shoot."

She abandoned the rifle just long enough to grip her husband around the neck, pulling him to her. His skin was slick with sweat, the chill of the night overridden by adrenaline. She swept a tangle of tawny hair off his forehead as she drew back, sparing a second to admire the tight clench of his jaw. He looked as though he meant to take the outlaws apart with his bare hands.

She wanted to help him do it. But she knew Hal would tell her to go hide with Mama, Elijah, and Nora. The surprise of the attack had worn thin, and the men would be getting themselves organized to defend the camp.

"I need your help," Hal said instead, taking her by surprise. "I can pick some of them off, if I can get up on a horse."

Barely a breath passed before Winnie made her decision and passed the rifle to him.

His smile was tight, hardly more than a twitch. "Let's go."

He jumped down from the wagon first, but Winnie was right behind him, skirt tangling around her ankles. He clasped her hand, and they darted from their wagon toward her family's camp, where Lazy Louie was still miraculously tied, thanks to Elijah insisting on braiding his tail before supper.

"Watch my back." Hal tossed the rifle over the horse's rump.

She caught it, though the weight of it drove the iron parts into her palms. She kept an anxious lookout, certain he'd be struck in the back by a bullet any second, but luck was with them.

Louie had tightened the knot by jerking on the rope, but Hal was able to work through it, showcasing an efficiency earned only through repetition. A moment later, he jumped onto Louie's bare back.

Winnie lifted the rifle up to him.

He hefted it, grabbing her extended palm and tugging it up to his lips for a hasty kiss.

Before she could think of what to say, he was gone, spurring Louie into a gallop with a slap of the rope.

Her heart raced, as though trying to keep time with Louie's rapidly disappearing hooves. As Hal's white shirt vanished into the darkness, she desperately tried to avoid acknowledging the fear he'd never return. Her vision blurred, and she wiped clumsily at her eyes.

"Winnie!" Nora cried, drawing Winnie's attention away from her husband and back to her vulnerable family.

A bullet bit the dirt mere inches from Winnie's boot, and she lunged for the wagon.

Nora and Elijah lay between the wheels, keeping as low as possible. Nora had her hands clamped over his ears, covering much of his body with her own.

Winnie was grateful the oxen had already been unhitched; otherwise, they might have spooked and hauled the wagon away. They'd all have been completely exposed without it.

Mama, Papa, and Jeb had taken up defensive positions along three corners of the wagon, and she took the fourth, straining to see what she could.

With Hal out of sight, she felt as though she could finally take in some of the details around her, rather than be distracted by his presence.

Papa had been able to reach his gun, and he fired round after round, pausing only long enough to reload.

Jeb still clutched the knife he'd taken from beside the cook fire, and for once, the fierce look on his face made him seem capable of actually using it.

A wagon across the circle was in flames, the canvas burning so brightly, it stung her eyes. Some of the bandits had dismounted and were rummaging through wagons, taking what they could carry and lashing it to their saddles. They seemed to be keeping to organized pairs; one would hold the family at gunpoint, and the other would make the short work of robbing them.

The outlaws had had the foresight to bring two empty wagons with them, and were loading those up as well. Their wagons were well guarded, each boasting at least three men.

Winnie glimpsed some of the hoard they'd collected. It was the last of the precious heirlooms her neighbors had clung to, when everything else that could be spared had been left on the side of the trail.

These cowards wouldn't just leave her people starving, they'd leave them without any trace of wealth. They'd arrive in Oregon penniless, if they even arrived at all.

It was easy to see why their attackers still held the upper hand. They'd caused so much commotion at the start of the raid that most families had taken shelter in or under their wagons, isolating themselves unintentionally. It had been easy for the bandits to start pillaging.

There were pockets of resistance, mostly families with older sons who were able to help their fathers and uncles. Those with younger children, like Mr. McCleary and a few others, had been forced to choose between protecting their youngest and standing guard over their food and other belongings.

Winnie watched, feeling helpless, as wagons were emptied of their most essential and valuable items. Worst of all was the sight of several bodies sprawled in the grass, victims either to the trampling hooves of livestock, or bullets that had found their mark.

Her gaze was drawn back to the man she'd shot. He'd been even closer to the Vogelsang wagon than she'd thought. She now had an unobstructed view of him, and if Mama and Papa hadn't been distracted elsewhere, they'd probably seen her shoot him.

She was trying to force her gaze elsewhere when she noticed something that made her breath hitch. Bent over his horse, most of the man's torso had been a blur in the dark. But now, lying flat and immobile, it became obvious he was wearing a gun belt.

She'd flung herself to her knees at her father's side before her idea had even fully formed.

He was flat on his stomach, elbows braced to support the rifle. His finger was steady on the trigger, waiting for a clear shot.

"I need you to cover me." She pointed toward the fallen outlaw. "So I can get his pistol."

Papa spared a glance for her, face streaked with sweat, dust, and gunpowder. Whatever his initial reaction was, he quickly overpowered it. They were not in the position to turn down a second method of defense. Worse, he couldn't leave Mama, Nora, and Elijah exposed by going with her.

His reply was terse, at odds with his eyes, which were filled with concern. "Go, now!"

Winnie bolted, diving the last few paces and landing near the man's boots. She scurried closer, fingers scrambling around the belt to find the holster. His rifle had to be somewhere in the grass, but she didn't have the spare seconds to search for it.

She purposefully avoided looking at his face as she pulled the revolver free. She didn't want to know how old he looked, or what color his hair was. She didn't want to know anything about him other than what she already knew. He'd attacked them, unprovoked and under the cover of darkness.

She gathered her skirt in one fist, envious of every single man who got to wear pants, and clutched the pistol in the other. She bolted back toward the safety of the wagon, which had seemed so close only a moment ago.

At first the way had been clear, but a horse and rider careened out of the darkness while she was still out in the open, taking her by surprise. There was little to do but drop to a crouch and cover her head. She didn't even have time to raise the gun she'd just taken from the dead man.

A loud crack split the air, and the bandit tumbled off the horse's back mere feet away, groaning. The horse kept going, spooked by the noise and loss of its rider. With the way clear once more, Winnie sprinted the last of the distance to the wagon, skinning her knees as she skidded to a stop next to Papa.

"Thank you," She gasped.

Papa was busy reloading, but managed a grim smile. She didn't have much experience with pistols, but she knew how to check if it was loaded. They'd gotten lucky; it held five of its six shots. Winnie moved to hand it over to Mama, crouched at the rear wheel, but Mama shook her head.

"Best that you hold onto it," she said. "I'm a terrible shot."

Winnie didn't argue. It made her feel better to hold the pistol, even though she'd only fired one a handful of times. Papa had kept an old, heavy one at the farmhouse, but his rifle had been far more reliable.

She could only hope if she had to use this one, she was close enough not to miss.

It was hard to focus on all that was going on outside of their little bubble under the wagon. Elijah was barely holding himself together, even with Nora's soothing presence. Though the six-year-old had been on hunts with Papa and even shot his own game, he had no experience with anything on this scale.

Neither did Winnie or Nora, for that matter. Jeb had stretched out to keep a reassuring hand on Nora's ankle, and the sight of it made Winnie's chest hurt. She desperately wished Hal was with them, too.

"Do you hear that?" Papa asked.

She strained her ears. Any livestock not tied up had fled, so some of the tumult had died down. She could hear the outlaws shouting to one another, and screams of people pulled from their wagons. But there was something else. A booming voice, hollering expletives that would have made Mama box her ears if Winnie had ever been foolhardy enough to say them.

"Is that Big John?" She could hardly bear to hope for it. If Big John was nearby, then Mae wasn't far behind.

"He's rallying everyone!" The relief in Mama's voice was an almost tangible thing.

From the sounds of it, Big John was calling as many men to him as he could, gathering the strength and numbers to push the outlaws out of camp.

"I see him!" Jeb announced. Everyone scuttled to his corner of the wagon to look.

Winnie saw a cluster of neighbors gathered half a dozen wagons away, armed with whatever they could grab. Quite a few had managed to hold onto their rifles, but more were holding shovels, butchering tools, hammers, and even lumber saws. A bit of the panic within her began to ebb at the sight.

A big hand closed on her shoulder, and Winnie turned.

"I'm proud of you," Papa told her. He reached out with his other arm, and Nora and Elijah scooted closer to him. "All of you."

She started to smile, but then she noticed Mama close her eyes with a pained expression. Her brow creased as though withstanding a deep, familiar ache.

Then, Winnie understood.

"Go." Mama sighed, resigned.

Winnie caught sight of the slightest tremble of her lips before Mama flattened them into a thin, uncompromising line.

Nodding, Papa transferred the rifle to the crook of his elbow as he eased past Mama and out from under the wagon.

Elijah tried to protest, but Papa shushed him. "I'll see you all real soon. Stay low, and stay quiet." His piercing gaze shifted to Jeb. "Take care of them, son."

Jeb flushed, but with pride rather than

embarrassment, Winnie thought. He'd become a stronger man since leaping into the river to save Andreas. He no longer bent and swayed with the wind, as she'd imagined of him when they'd first met.

"I will," Jeb replied.

And then Papa was gone, darting out toward the crowd Big John was summoning with surprising swiftness.

"Will Papa come back for us?" Elijah broke through the silence that had fallen upon them like a blanket of thick snow.

It was Nora that answered him. "Always." She drew Elijah close again, tucking his head under her chin.

Winnie was reluctant to give up her line of sight toward where Papa had gone, especially when she realized Hal would likely wind up there, as well. But she forced herself to retreat to the corner Papa had vacated, propping her shoulder up against the wagon wheel.

She peered into the darkness with renewed determination. With everyone rallying, it was a matter of time before the bandits decided the risk was no longer worth the reward. It would all be over soon, she was sure of it.

She pushed aside the nagging fear that hinted at all the terrible things that could happen to Hal and the others. She cast her gaze out, focusing on every figure that passed by, putting names to faces she knew. None of the names matched the faces she feared for the most.

Until at last, Winnie saw Mae.

She was helping Mr. McCleary move his three young children to the safety of Doc Collins's wagon. His youngest dangled from Mae's neck, and Mr. McCleary carried the other two in his arms. Their own wagon had been flipped on its side, and Winnie's thoughts flashed back to when Amos had lain helplessly within it, suffering from his broken back.

Once the McCleary family was hidden in Doc's wagon, Mae whistled, calling her horse to her. Even among all the commotion, he came, tossing his head as though impatient to join the fight. She used the spoke of a wheel to boost herself up, and then they were off. She drew her rifle as she went, pulling it from the saddle scabbard and cradling the butt of it under her arm.

Mae seemed to be headed toward Big John's group, on the opposite side of where Winnie was crouched. She wished she could get the other woman's attention, but she knew better than to distract her friend when so much was at stake.

A sudden gunshot at painfully close range made her drop the pistol and clap her hands over her ears. The ringing in her head was so loud, someone might have been screaming.

Mae's horse went down, as though the earth had vanished beneath him. Mae went flying, and slammed to the ground on her back. The rifle vanished into the dark. Her horse rolled, whinnying in pain and terror, and though he kicked, he did not rise again. Blood gushed from his belly.

Mae shifted her legs weakly, but didn't get up. She turned her head and cried out at the sight of her struggling horse.

A tall, lanky man stepped out from behind the McClearys' overturned wagon, swiftly withdrawing the ramrod from the barrel of his rifle as he reloaded. He stalked toward Mae, aiming his rifle with precision. The sneer that twisted his shadowed face made him seem deformed.

This was it, Winnie realized slowly, as though her mind struggled through axel-deep mud. She fumbled for the fallen pistol and slid out from her hiding place. Only the small wagon she shared with Hal separated her from Mae and the outlaw, and she eased around the wagon tongue with predatory silence, counting each step and praying for time.

Up ahead, the outlaw had reached Mae. He pointed the rifle straight into her face, which was blanched with pain. "You killed my brother tonight," he snarled down at her.

Winnie was close enough to hear Mae's reply, defiant even in her compromised position. "He was ugly as a snake and twice as mean. You're better off."

The man ground his teeth, reaching for the trigger as he loomed over Mae.

Winnie raised the pistol, sighting down the short barrel as best she could. She paused, pulling in a deep breath. It eased a bit of the shaking in her fingers. Then she pulled the trigger, bracing for the recoil into her palm.

There was an echoing click, and nothing more.

The outlaw whirled at the sound, and grinned when he saw her standing there, gun still extended. But it was no good to her jammed.

"I'll be with you in a moment, sweetheart," he taunted, turning back to Mae. "I'm nearly finished with this one."

Winnie could barely breathe, much less think. This wasn't right; it wasn't fair. What would Hal do? What would Mae do? What would even Nora do, if she were backed into a corner?

They had come too far and fought too hard to be cut down by a coward in the night.

Each footprint in the dust, every broken blister and itching mosquito bite they had suffered…it had all been a part of getting to this point, together. Every cross that had been hammered into the dirt, every laugh that had been silenced forever…it couldn't all have been for nothing.

She would not allow it to be for nothing.

She charged the outlaw with a yell. She raised the pistol, trying to bash him across the head. But he spun just in time and hurled her aside, slamming the butt of his rifle against her ribs. Pain blasted through her, and she collapsed to the dirt. She couldn't catch her breath. Her empty lungs spasmed.

He turned back to Mae, who'd risen onto her elbows, staring the rifle dead center down the barrel with her bottom lip gripped between her teeth.

"No," Winnie gasped, struggling to get her feet under her.

A shadowed figure sprinted toward them, and she caught the reflection of moonlight off the blade of a knife. There was a bellow, and for a fleeting instant, Winnie was reminded of the mother bear, protecting her cub. She blinked, pressing a hand against her throbbing ribs.

The shadow solidified into a familiar face at the last second, as Big John slammed into the outlaw with elemental force. A shot rang out, and the pair of them tumbled sideways.

They landed in a tangle of limbs.

Mae cried out, scrambling toward her father. As she rolled Big John over, Winnie caught sight of the hunting knife he'd buried deep in the limp outlaw's neck.

Someone grabbed her from behind, and Nora's breathless voice filled her ears. "Winnie, are you hurt?"

She couldn't bring herself to answer. Nora had never seemed to be the strong one. She'd allowed herself to be viewed as the timid sister, the one most easily shaken. But Winnie sagged back against her, and Nora held her up, strong and solid as a tree trunk.

A pocket of stillness and terrible inevitability enveloped them as they overheard Big John's last words to his daughter.

"I gave the pistol to Amos McCleary," he wheezed. The wet shine of blood spread across his lips. It seemed impossible something as small as a bullet could bring down such a large, animated man. But it was happening before their eyes.

Mae clutched his hand, leaning closer. There was no judgement in her expression, only earnest concentration, as though she was committing his face to her artist's memory. "I understand why you did it."

He shook his head, and a broken sigh escaped him. "He was just a boy...I shouldn't have..."

"You were trying to help," Mae said more firmly. "He was suffering. You didn't make the choice for him."

Big John's voice turned imploring, as though he knew his time was drawing to a close. "His pa...needs to know."

"You can tell him yourself, when you're well again." The thickness of unshed tears in her voice exposed the hopeful lie.

His eyelids fluttered. Every breath seemed more strained than the last. "You have to get them the rest of the way," he pleaded. "They need you, Mae."

Her lower lip trembled. "No, I-I don't think I can."

"You're ready." The words were more air than sound. "It's your turn, now."

A sob erupted from Mae as she bent and rested her forehead against her father's burly chest.

Nora and Winnie waited in silence, clutching each other…but he didn't speak again.

Big John was dead.

****

When the men of the camp drove the outlaws away mere moments later, the resulting silence felt like an inhalation. Slowly, people began to assemble around their fallen trail guide. A few laid consoling hands atop Mae's back, but she didn't acknowledge being touched.

Hal rode up and rushed to dismount, almost tripping in his haste. Breathing hard, he dropped to his knees at Winnie's side. His bewildered gaze absorbed Nora, the grip Winnie maintained on her aching ribs, and the stillness of Big John.

"Are you all right?" He reached for her. Before she could summon a reply, he whirled to Nora. "Is she all right?"

Nora laid a hand on his arm and spoke to him in her most soothing voice, recounting what she'd seen.

Winnie focused on breathing past the slowly receding tightness in her chest, and gripped Hal's hand. He seemed to be fine; there wasn't any blood on his clothes. It felt selfish to be grateful for his safe return when Mae mourned only feet away.

As he absorbed Nora's every word, Winnie ducked her head against his shoulder and squeezed her eyes shut against rising tears. She wished that she'd been faster, smarter, that she'd grabbed a different gun…. She wished for any outcome other than the one that stood in stark reality before her. "I'm so sorry, Mae," she whispered at last.

But Mae made no reply, and only the reassuring squeeze of Hal's hand confirmed that Winnie had actually spoken.

"We should find Papa." Nora reached down to help pull Winnie to her feet. "Jeb will be worried sick, and we've got to find Hank, as well. There's lots of work to be done."

Braced between her husband and her sister, Winnie took a last look back at Big John, and the bowed heads of the neighbors who still stood around him.

A true frontiersman had fallen tonight, and the sense of competency the wagon train had struggled to earn was shattered.

Would anywhere feel safe again, when they knew what it felt liked to be raided without warning? In that moment, even the mountains that formed nearly impenetrable walls along the horizon didn't seem like enough protection.

Once again, they'd been dealt the painful reminder that safety was a well-crafted illusion.

Safety didn't exist on the trail.

Chapter Eighteen

Mae didn't speak to anyone for nearly two days.

The wagon train had moved on at first light, unwilling to spend another day in the same place where the bandits had found them. Most hadn't had any sleep, but they had no way of knowing if they would be attacked again, and anxieties were high. So, they loaded their dead into one of the wagons, intending to stop and bury them at least a day's travel ahead. They left a warning for following travelers about the bandits, and set off.

The trail was clear, the sky bleak and overcast, and the Snake River still twisted along to the north.

That whole day, Mae walked alongside the wagon that bore her father's body, as though standing guard.

As devastating as the loss of Big John was, they hadn't only lost their trail guide. One of the German men, the father of three boys, had also been killed while defending his family.

Several others had been injured and were being tended to by Doc Collins and his wife.

Hank was one of them; he'd been shot in the calf while riding his horse alongside Hal, picking off bandit riders.

Winnie, Hal, Nora, and Jeb took turns checking in on him, though Winnie knew that it was Mae's face he most wanted to see. But she had already told an unresponsive Mae about Hank's injury, and she didn't have the heart to push her friend any further by asking why she hadn't yet gone to see him.

"She just needs some time," Hal told her as they all made camp and divided up the labor to get the graves dug and the chores finished before nightfall.

She knew he was right. "That's what worries me. She doesn't have time. We need her. She's the only one who's actually been to Oregon."

Hal looked troubled. "How can we ask Mae to do more than should ever be expected of her? It feels like whipping a horse that's already broken."

Winnie put a hand on his shoulder. There were dark circles beneath his eyes, and she wished she could just tell him to rest.

He'd been out riding until dawn, searching for the scattered remains of their herd. With Hank injured and Mae a ghost, he'd been forced to go with only one other cowhand. They'd brought back fewer than two dozen cattle. The oxen, luckily, had been much easier to round up that morning. They'd been too slow for the outlaws to bother with, and hadn't wandered far.

"If Mae can't do it"—she conceded—"then we'll just have to do it for her."

Hal nodded resolutely, kissing the top of her braided hair.

Winnie found Papa and Mama together at the cook fire, preparing a simple but blissfully hot meal of johnnycakes.

Elijah dozed nearby with his head propped on a bag of rice. Bandit, the ragged horse Big John had made for him at the start of their journey, was tucked in the crook of his elbow.

She paused, taking in her little brother's sleeping form. She could only imagine how lost he would feel, if their parents succumbed to the dangers of the trail they followed. At least he could count on his sisters to take care of him. Mae's only sibling was dead.

All day, Winnie had been plagued with the thought of what Mae would face when they reached Oregon. Their wagon train would break apart as families found places they wanted to settle; some would not want to cross the Cascades to go all the way to the famed Willamette Valley.

When Mae's task was complete, where would she go? How would she make a living? Big John's position and reputation had sheltered her from the pressures of society thus far…but an unmarried woman without family faced a harsh reality. It wouldn't be easy for Mae to work as a guide on her own. Most men beginning the journey from Independence would be unwilling to trust a woman with the safety of their wives and children.

Mae hadn't merely lost her father; she'd also lost the freedom of the life she loved so dearly.

Winnie was determined to change that, in any way she could. She was fairly confident her parents would agree, but she still felt the flutter of nerves in her stomach as she approached them. "Will you hire Mae on for the winter?"

Papa looked up, raising his brows, but she rushed on before he could object. "She could help us clear land, and we could build her a lean-to on the side of the cabin. I know she'd be a big help to Hal with the hunting and skinning, and she'd be a real asset in trading with any local Natives—"

Papa held a hand up, silencing the rehearsed petition

that had somehow collapsed into a nervous ramble. "Honestly, Winnie," he reprimanded, shaking his head. "Do you think we'd let Mae be passed from family to family like some sort of gypsy? After all she and Big John have done for us?"

Winnie sagged a bit with relief as Mama approached, holding out a plate stacked high with johnnycakes.

"Mae can stay with us for as long as she wants. She's earned that, far as I'm concerned."

Winnie accepted the plate, savoring the warmth of its bottom against her fingers. "You don't think people will talk? About Mae not being married?"

Mama scoffed and plucked a johnnycake from the top of the stack. "People always talk, Winnifred. But there isn't a soul in this wagon train who wouldn't defend Mae against people aiming to smear her reputation."

Papa nodded his agreement, and she noticed the admiration in his eyes as he took in the stubborn set of Mama's jaw. She'd long suspected Papa not only endured Mama's outspoken nature, but that he rather enjoyed it.

"Mae has more gumption in one finger than some men have in their whole bodies," Mama added. "I doubt the judgement of a few strangers will matter much to her."

"Or to any of us," Papa finished. "But you never know what changes time can bring. She might decide to go off on her own, come spring."

"That won't happen," Winnie said confidently. "She'll want to stay."

Papa hesitated, as though he wanted to say more but

decided against it. "We'll see."
****

They held a twilight vigil on the cliffs above the Snake River, where a dramatic waterfall cascaded into the depths of the canyon. The water was invisible so late. The only proof of its continued existence was the steady roar that threatened to drown out the prayers of the people who'd gathered there.

Mr. Bauer, the German father who'd been killed defending his family, had been broad and quick to smile, but somewhat slower learning English. Most of the families who were close with his were also German. Several had even traveled across the Atlantic on the same boat.

Mrs. Bauer leaned heavily on her brother-in-law, and her face was hidden against his shoulder. Her trio of boys sat by her feet, staring dismally into the grass.

Winnie found herself tuning out a fair bit of the spoken German that she couldn't understand. She'd picked some up from the Vogelsang family, but even the few phrases and words they'd taught her felt like they'd been drummed out of her head, pummeled by the unforgiving roar of the river.

Then Papa and a few other volunteers stepped forward to deliver Big John's eulogy.

"John Cook was a mountain man down to his bones," Papa began. "The land he led us through was the love of his life, matched only by the love he bore his family…"

Winnie could just make out Mae's stiff silhouette, standing alone before the mound of disturbed dirt that obscured her father's body from view.

Word had spread of Big John's involvement in

Amos McCleary's death, and it was plain that many didn't know how to feel about it. Most clearly wanted to support Mae in her grief, but the revelation of her father's choice had complicated things.

Mr. McCleary was notably absent from those assembled along the cliffs.

Easing out from under Hal's arm, Winnie silently made her way to her friend's side.

"I'm grateful that we got to have John as our guide, and as our friend. He was always ready to eat a hot meal and tell a good story. He looked you in the eye when you spoke…"

As she got closer, she was surprised to see someone had beaten her there, and was already reaching out to tug on Mae's left hand.

Elijah.

Winnie reached them just as Mae glanced down at Elijah with surprise. She didn't say a word, and for a moment, she thought Mae might ignore him.

But then Mae reached out and tentatively wrapped an arm across his shoulders, tucking him against her side.

Winnie offered her own hand to Mae, almost like a question.

"John was a good father, and a good friend. I think he'd like this spot, just like I think he'd be proud of the way the Lord decided to call him home…"

When Mae's chilled hand slid into her own, Winnie exhaled in relief. An image came to mind of a map, sketched out of the scratches and callouses that marred their joined palms.

Mae didn't say anything, and even young Elijah remained uncharacteristically silent as the solemn vigil wound on to its end. But in that moment, Winnie knew

Mae was going to get them to Oregon. All of them.

Despite all that had happened, Mae would find a way to lead them home.

Chapter Nineteen

They finally crossed the Snake River at a place called Three Island Crossing. It was one of the few spots where the river wasn't penned in by high cliffs, and though the water wasn't deep, the current was swift, with the full might of all those raging waterfalls behind it.

They reached the crossing at midday, and Winnie, Nora, and Mama spent the rest of the afternoon packing things away as best they could, so as not to lose them to the rushing waters.

Though Big John was buried along the cliffs behind them, his previous advice about crossing the Snake had not fallen on deaf ears. They knew they'd be able to ford the wagons and ride the horses across, but the wagon beds would still likely get wet in some deep spots. Since the raid, it was even more important that everyone protected the food they still had, and not allow moisture to spoil it.

Winnie was the best at knots, thanks to Hal's teaching, so she rigged harness after harness for them to hang their precious remaining supplies from the wagon bows overhead, where they swayed like mangled hammocks.

Nora, being the tallest, got the job of moving their depleted bags of cornmeal, rice, and other dried goods up into the ropes.

Mama stood in the wagon box beside her, braced in

case Nora lost her balance atop any of the barrels and crates.

Nora seemed to be growing rounder by the day and, to her mortification, was becoming clumsy.

Hal tended their livestock while Papa and Jeb tried their hand at fishing for trout along the banks of the river.

When milking time came, Winnie glanced sadly at the back of Mama and Papa's wagon, where Millie had been tied for so much of the journey.

But Millie was gone now, lost to the bandits and their thievery. Her milk and butter would be sorely missed in the days ahead, as would the steady comfort of her company.

Hank had just been released from Doc Collin's care, who'd declared Hank's leg "most likely wouldn't turn septic," and returned to his remaining patients.

Mama and Papa's wagon was already crowded these days, since the loss of Nora and Jeb's wagon, so Hal brought Hank over to his and Winnie's wagon instead, helping him up into the small sleep space.

"I'm about as much use as a blind horse," Hank complained, leaning heavily on Hal's shoulder. His lower leg was wrapped in linen, and he carefully elevated it, resting his heel on the edge of the wagon box.

Winnie leaned against the wagon wheel and gave him a wink. "You eat as much as a horse, too."

Elijah bounded over, excited to see Hank up and about. He eyed Hank's leg, as though he could see beneath the linen to examine the wound.

"My leg was worse." He sounded proud, as though he'd won a contest.

Hank pretended to look miffed. "Your story is better, I'll give you that. A bear mauling is tough to beat.

But not everyone can say they were shot by bandits!"

A playful argument ensued between the pair, and Winnie was delighted to see a bit of sparkle appear back in Hank's hazel eyes. It had been difficult to see them clouded with pain.

Someone cleared their throat behind them.

They realized it was Mae, and the group stilled, as though a timid deer had stepped into their midst.

She looked exhausted. Her eyes were like bleak caves, and her hair was knotted and unkempt. Her pants were dusty, and for the first time since Winnie had known her, she seemed uncertain.

"Sorry to interrupt," Mae said. "I went to Doc's wagon, and he told me Hank was here."

Hank perked up at that, leaning sideways to catch her attention from his perch behind Hal. "I'm here, all right. How are you?"

Mae shrugged, looking down at her feet, and an awkward silence settled between the friends who had laughed so easily only a few days before.

"Well." Hal plopped his hat atop his head with finality, "We're off to see if the fish are biting. C'mon, Elijah."

He tugged on Elijah's elbow and gave Winnie a meaningful look as they passed, as though urging her to follow them.

She didn't need much prodding. She had no business being in the conversation that was about to take place. She snatched the sewing basket and Nora's nearly finished shawl from the wagon, and followed her husband and brother to the river.

****

It took three days to get everyone across the Snake

River at Three Island crossing.

When they'd first started out from Independence, Winnie had been afraid of rivers. Now, they mostly made her tired. She'd long lost count of the rivers they'd crossed—big, small, and barely flowing.

She'd never forget the sight of Hal swimming to a struggling Jeb and little Andreas, nor could she forget the lives lost while crossing the Green. But enough time had passed to dull some of that trepidation. Most crossings were simply tedious, with no loss of life or livestock.

She, Hal, and Hank crossed on the second day, along with Nora.

Jeb stayed with Mama, Papa, and Elijah, riding Lazy Louie across while Papa kept the oxen steady.

Mae rode her new horse back and forth between the islands that bridged the river like a crossing of well-placed stones, and only the dull look in Hank's eyes betrayed his disappointment.

Whatever they had discussed prior to the crossing had not gone as he'd hoped.

To her credit, Mae kept everyone organized and moving. No teams were lost to tangled harnesses, and they managed to stay together, helping each other against the pull of the current.

Their own wagon box emerged from the river holding several inches of water because they'd splashed into a rut along the river bottom. Their belongings would certainly have gotten wet had they not been tied up.

In that way, Winnie supposed the work had been worth it. A wet hem in September wouldn't kill her, but starvation would.

Once on the other side, they made camp and waited for the remaining wagons to make their way across.

Hal was noticeably anxious, admitting that if the bandits had tracked them, the wagons on the other side of the river would be tremendously vulnerable to another attack.

Winnie supposed such fears would plague them for a long time, but they were lucky.

On the fourth day, they were able to move on, without any injuries or losses. It was a welcome reprieve.

She finally was able to speak to Mae that day, to extend her family's offer of a place to stay when they arrived in Oregon.

To her surprise, Mae accepted without any hesitation. She was relieved to know Mae would be with them for the winter. When her friend had time to grieve and got her feet back under her, Mae would be a force to be reckoned with once again.

That night, Hal pitched their tent near the trees to give them some much-needed privacy.

Winnie was no stranger to keeping their interludes quiet, but she still wondered if she'd eventually bite her lip as Hal made love to her, gripping her tight as though to keep her from slipping away.

What would it be like, to have a roof over their heads, and a bed beneath them? The idea was so foreign, she could barely picture it. It felt as though she'd never slept in a bed, or eaten off a table. When they stilled and drew close again for warmth, Winnie rested her head on Hal's shoulder, more of a pillow than any she'd had before. "I love you," she murmured onto his skin.

"I know," Hal said drowsily. "You've grown excellent at showing me."

She pinched him, and he chuckled.

"Scoundrel."

"I have to be, occasionally." He yawned. "I don't want my wife to grow bored."

"We won't have time to be bored. Not for a long while, yet."

For a moment, she considered all they would have to do when they finally chose a place to settle. It would be backbreaking work, cutting timber to build a cabin and barn, acquiring new livestock, building fences, and then plowing the ground when it thawed in the spring. Their challenges would not end when their wagon wheels left the westward trail behind. Far from it.

Hal's hands, which had been tracing the scars on her bare back, began to slow. "Don't worry" he whispered, sinking into sleep—"we can handle anything, as long as we're together."

Winnie smiled wistfully at that, and snuggled closer, soaking in his warmth beneath their quilt.

Chapter Twenty

When Mae abruptly stopped her wagon only a week later, people craned their necks, trying to locate the source of the hold-up. Now that September had shown its face, the winter that had seemed so far away in April and May now seemed positioned to pounce on them without warning.

Winnie shaded her eyes, watching as Mae mounted her horse and rode down the column, stopping every few wagons to spread whatever news was deemed worth stopping for. Maybe a broken wheel or an axel, and a need to make repairs.

When she reached their wagon, Winnie was prepared for a civil but brief exchange.

Mae had stepped into her new role with a blunt and tired proficiency, preferring to lead from the head of the column and let her orders trickle through the wagons like a chilled rain.

So she was surprised when Mae dismounted, striding toward them with a shadow of the confident swagger she'd once possessed so easily.

"What is it?" Hal called. "Did we lose the trail?"

Mae shook her head and pushed her hat off her head to fall against her back. "I wanted everyone to know that it's official."

Hank watched Mae from his seat on the back of the wagon, but he didn't ask the obvious question.

Winnie didn't know what had been said between them, but it was plain that he wasn't ready to speak to her yet.

It seemed up to her to ask, "What's official?"

Mae gestured to the front of their wagon train, and Winnie realized the people there were racing from wagon to wagon, hugging, and even dancing. Squeals of delight pierced the air like they had stumbled upon a carnival.

She whirled to her friend, breath catching as she finally understood.

The corner of Mae's mouth twitched upward as she nodded, and she reached out to squeeze Winnie's shoulder. "Those are the blue mountains. We've still got a few weeks to go—but we're in Oregon territory now."

Hal came to stand beside his wife, wrapping an arm around her waist. "So, this is Oregon." He looked pointedly around. "There really ought to be a sign."

A smile flickered across Mae's face, so fast that Winnie might have imagined it. Then she was gone, making her way to the end of the column to finish spreading the news.

Without warning, Hal bent to kiss her, pressing his lips to hers with the kind of fervor he usually reserved for the rare nights there wasn't an audience.

But she didn't mind. She clutched the sides of his face when he tried to pull away.

Mae's words had brightened everything.

"We made it!" she said past a rapidly tightening throat.

"We did."

"There were times when I wasn't sure…"

Hal kissed her again, smoothing tears from her

cheeks. "I know. Me, too."

"Winnie!"

She turned to see Nora racing for her, the rest of their family close behind. Though Nora had slowed significantly in recent weeks, Winnie still staggered when her sister slammed into her, somehow managing not to let go.

"Can you believe it?" her sister exclaimed.

Jeb reached them, chuckling as he helped untangle Nora's deceptively strong grip. "She needs to breathe, Lenora."

Nora leaned back and wiped her eyes, laughing.

Elijah whooped and hollered at the top of his lungs.

Mama and Papa gave up trying to shush him, and stood close together, as though holding each other up.

During the days they'd waited on the edge of Independence for the grass to grow green enough for their journey to start, Winnie had wondered what this moment would feel like. In her mind, it had been some kind of culmination, an ending to the chapter of a particularly perilous story.

But now she understood it wasn't a culmination at all.

It felt like they'd spent a long time climbing a mountain, and instead of finding themselves at the pinnacle as they'd expected, realized that they'd been traversing a foothill, part of a much larger range.

Oregon. They'd made it to Oregon.

And there was still so much to do.

She watched her sister and Jeb, and Elijah as he ran to celebrate with Hank. She grinned when Papa spun Mama around and kissed her before she could protest. And then Winnie's gaze came to rest on Hal, the part of the adventure she'd never expected, and hadn't even been sure she wanted.

Life with him would turn out to be the biggest journey of all.

He smiled at her, and the few feet that separated them seemed to shrink to inches. The intimacy of his expression took her breath away, as though he'd touched her with phantom fingers.

Holding her gaze, he tipped the brim of his hat with one finger.

"If he keeps looking at you like that, you'll soon look like me," Nora joked in her ear. "I'd better set Jeb to building a second crib!"

Winnie reached back to swat at her, laughing. "I don't think so! You're the motherly one."

Nora just smiled that knowing smile of hers, the one she'd acquired after marrying Jeb, that showed itself with increasing frequency.

Married women seemed to carry the keys to a lot of secrets. Winnie was just beginning to unlock some of them, herself.

As the excitement began to die down and everyone split off to ready their teams and continue to their campsite for the night, she let her mind drift. Once, she'd imagined curling up in Hal's lap in a chair before the fire while snow swirled outside. But now, she allowed herself to picture a slightly different scene. The fire remained, but tawny-haired children played on a blanket before it, squealing with laughter as Hal chased after them on all fours, growling ferociously.

It was the most wonderful thing she'd ever dreamed.

As she took in the wagons around them, she realized her family was much larger now than it had been a mere six months ago. Jeb had joined them, bringing Hank along. Hal had ridden in on Ol' Belle and changed everything. Mae had blazed ahead, dodging expectations and limitations. And Nora's baby, soon to make an appearance, would be doted on by them all.

Each wagon, ahead and behind, bore a similar story. Every family had grown larger, or merged with another.

She wouldn't be surprised if the Vogelsang family settled in the same area as her parents.

Adda would want her home to be near Nora's, so they could share the garden they spoke of so frequently.

Mr. McCleary and the remaining Wilson brother, the only survivors of the train's musical quartet, would likely play together at many more weddings next spring.

Moira and her mother, Widow Simmons, would birth the babies.

It was like they'd created their own corner of the world.

Winnie knew there would also be new faces. There'd be an established town somewhere they'd use for trade, to post the mail, and shop for supplies. They'd have to find a teacher to start up a school, and…

"Stop thinking so hard," Hal teased. "So many projects are glazing your eyes over that I already want to take a nap."

She grinned. "If only you knew."

He got the oxen moving, pulling them into position just ahead of her parents' wagon, and Winnie fell into step beside him.

There wasn't a single blister on her feet at the moment, and the peaks of the Blue Mountains beckoned them closer with each step.

Winter was on its way, along with all its hardships.

But after all the ways they'd been tested, and all the ways they'd managed to pull together and to pull through, it didn't seem quite so frightening anymore.

With determination, and a bit of stubbornness, any distance could be traveled. Any mountain could be climbed. Their journey had begun with a single step into the unknown, crossing the invisible line between civilization and wilderness.

That journey was nearing its end. They were so close. All they had to do was to keep moving forward, one step at a time.

Winnie smiled at the irony. It was exactly how they had begun.

A note from the Author

The daunting journey along the Westward trails covered more than 2,100 miles, and an estimated one in ten emigrants died during the crossing. Writing accurately about their journey required a lot of research, which I took seriously. I did my best to portray the wilderness they traversed as one of rugged beauty, but there were very real dangers, and many routes to choose from.

I did a lot of research regarding the Native American tribes who were most frequently encountered along the way, and did my best to portray them fairly—but I must admit to a bit of bias. When I was young, my grandpa told me of his great-great grandmother, a Cherokee woman. I have no tribal affiliations, but I hope that my admiration for Indigenous People and their culture shines through, especially in Mae's character.

Any mistakes in languages, tribal names, etc., are made without ill-intent.

Some terminology is used purely for historical accuracy. "Sioux" is one such example, which was used by emigrants to collectively include the Lakota, Dakota, and Nakota people. Today, we place value on using preferred terminology, but the emigrants of the 1840s would not have known those terms, and so would not have used them.

For more details about my research and recommended reading, please see my website.

www.facebook.com/KCurtisWriter

A word about the author...

Kaci Curtis was raised in Missouri, only minutes away from the town of Independence, where the Westward Trails began. She is a military spouse and mom.

She loves reading, hiking, writing with hot coffee, camping, thunderstorms, rescuing animals, and traveling.

www.facebook.com/KCurtisWriter